THE AVENGERS

THE TIMES THEY ARE A-CHANGIN'

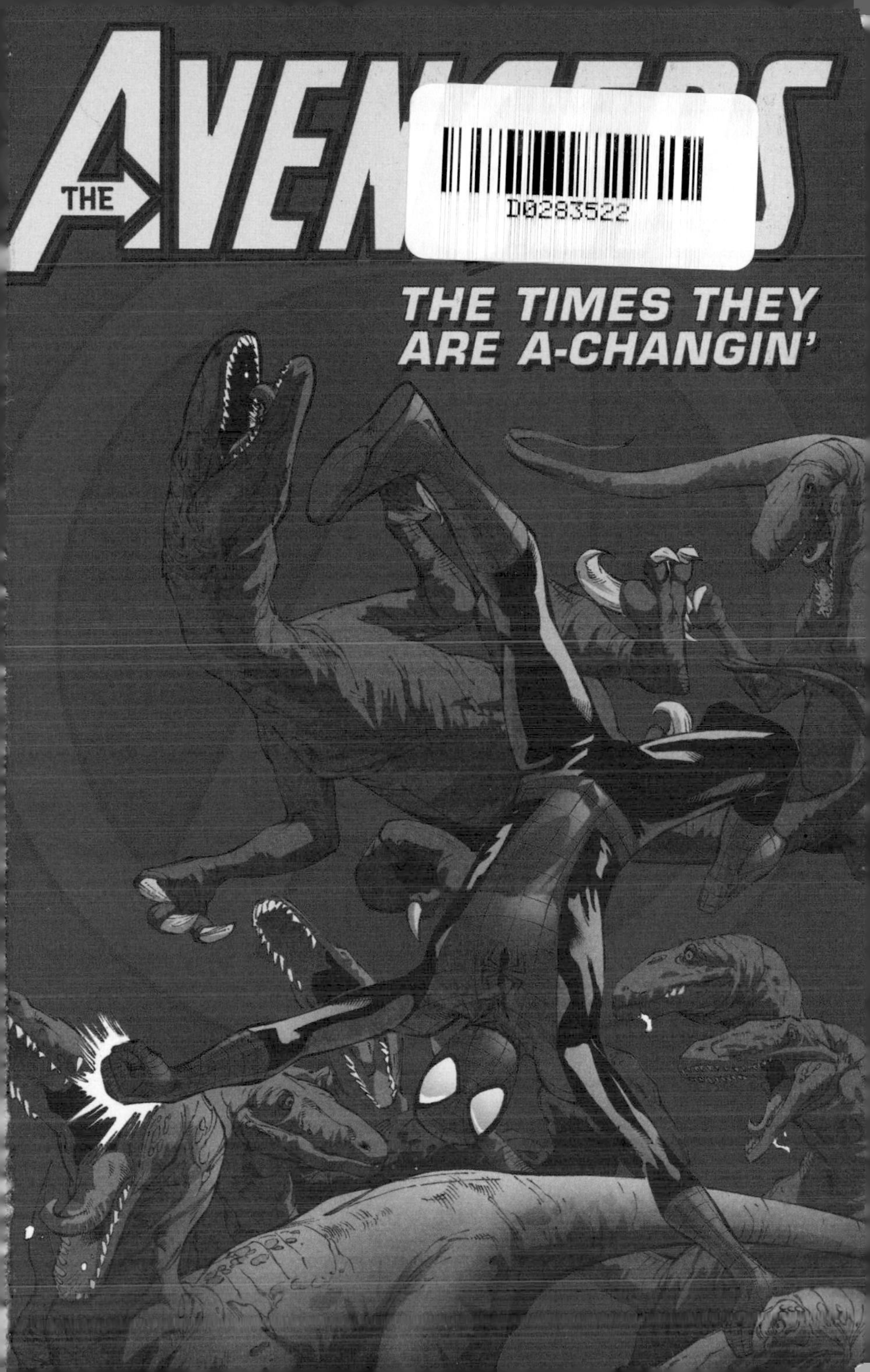

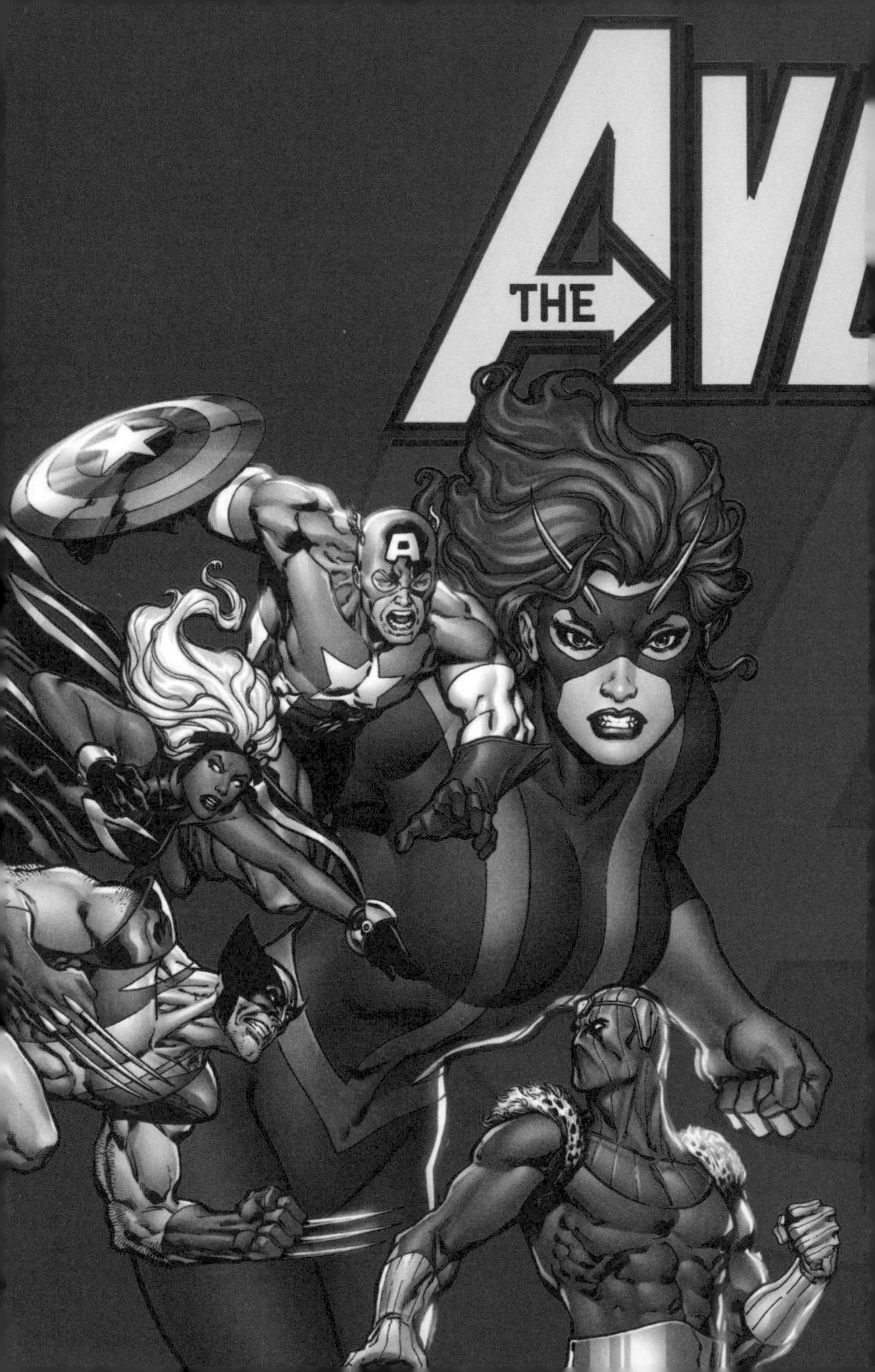
THE

THE TIMES THEY ARE A-CHANGIN'

Writer: **Paul Tobin**
Pencils: **Matteo Lolli, Ig Guara & Casey Jones**
Inks: **Christian Vecchia, Sandro Ribeiro
& Casey Jones**

Colors: **Sotocolor**
Letters: **Dave Sharpe**
Cover Art: **Salva Espin & Wil Quintana; Roger Cruz &
Val Staples; and David Williams & Chris Sotomayor**
Consulting Editors: **Mark Paniccia & Ralph Macchio**
Editor: **Nathan Cosby**

Captain America created by Joe Simon & Jack Kirby

Collection Editor: **Jennifer Grünwald**
Editorial Assistant: **Alex Starbuck**
Assistant Editors: **Cory Levine & John Denning**
Editor, Special Projects: **Mark D. Beazley**
Senior Editor, Special Projects: **Jeff Youngquist**
Senior Vice President of Sales: **David Gabriel**
Vice President of Creative: **Tom Marvelli**

Editor in Chief: **Joe Quesada**
Publisher: **Dan Buckley**
Executive Producer: **Alan Fine**

#32

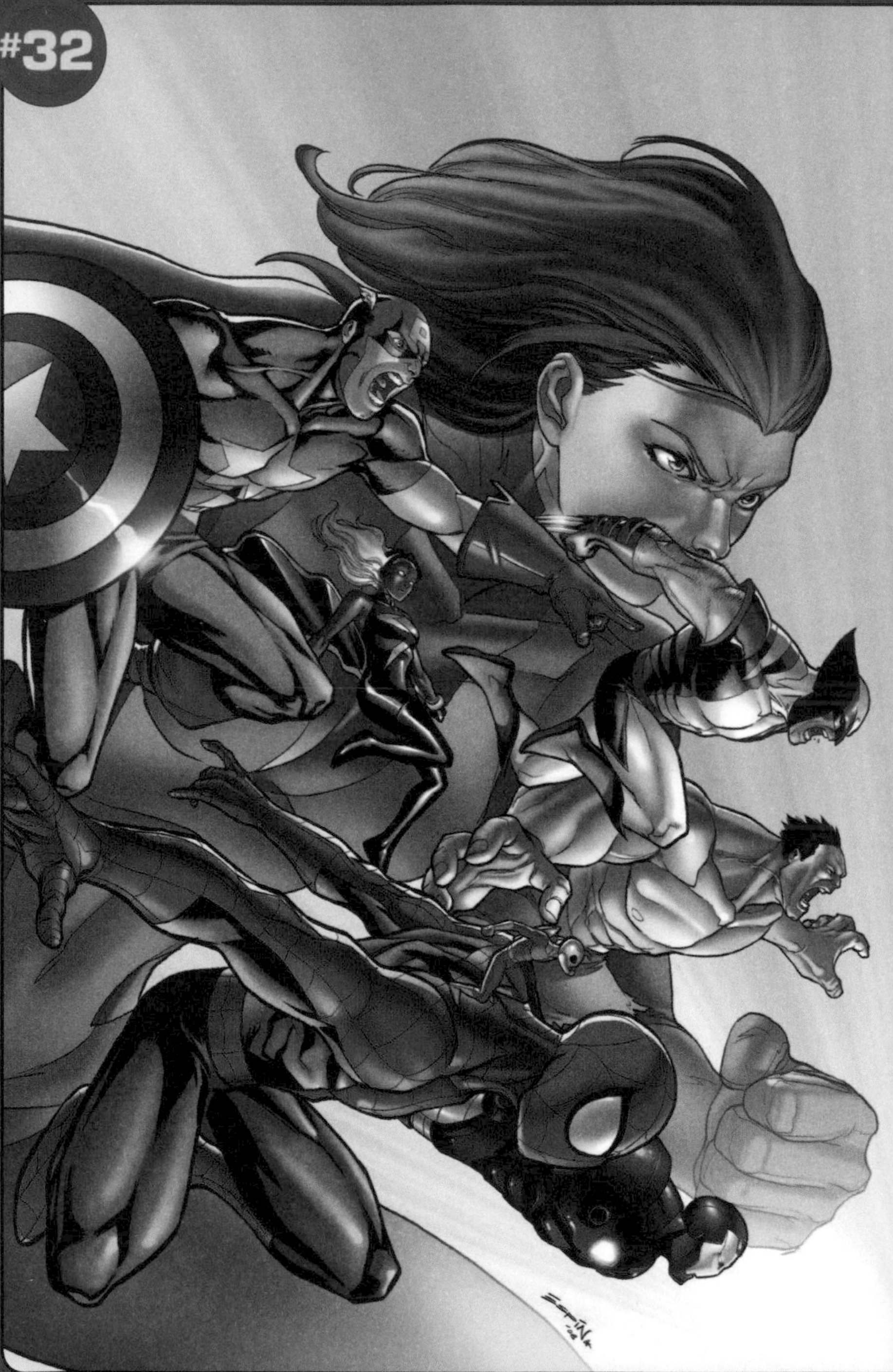

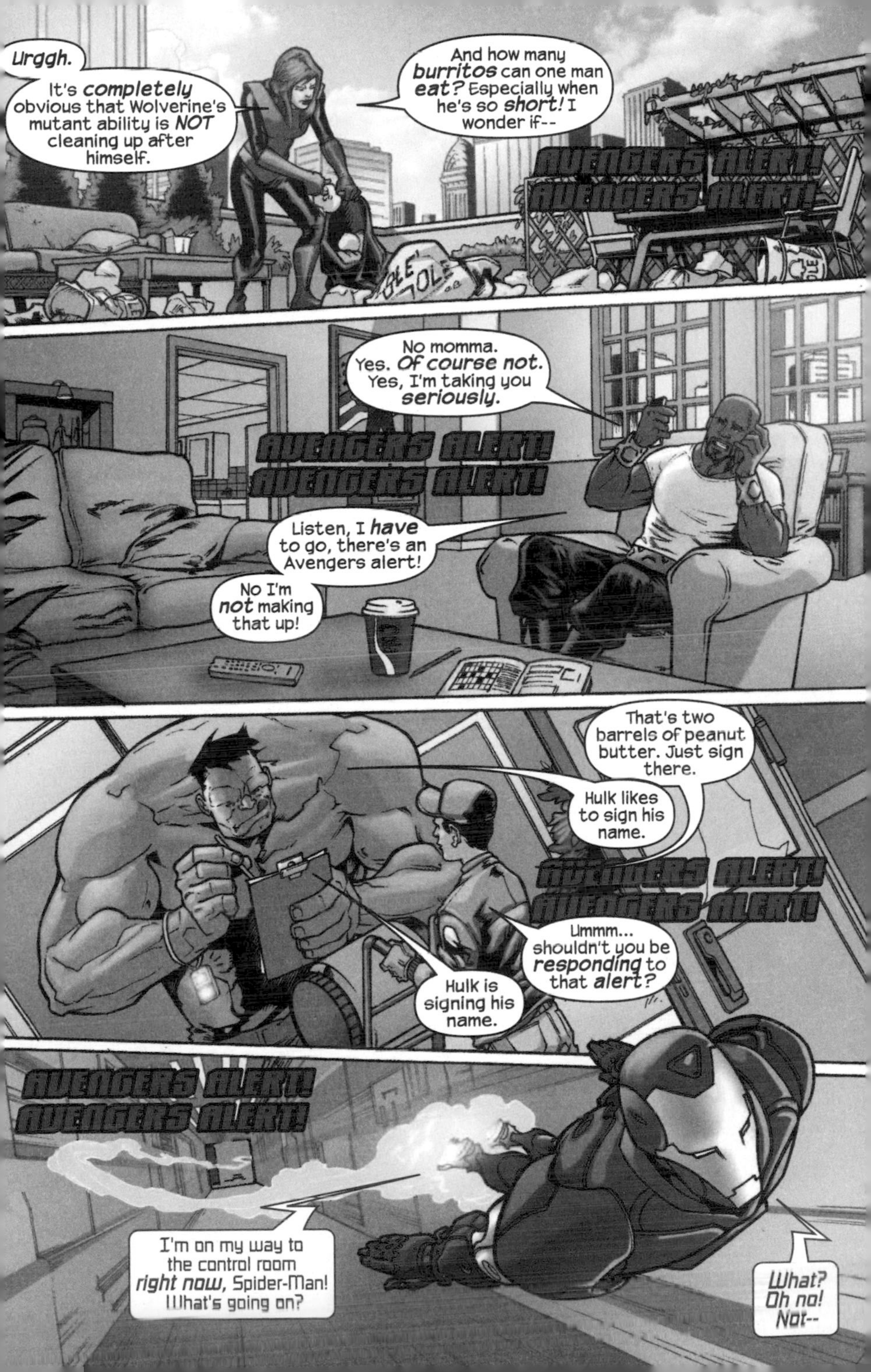
Urggh.
It's completely obvious that Wolverine's mutant ability is NOT cleaning up after himself.
And how many burritos can one man eat? Especially when he's so short! I wonder if--
AVENGERS ALERT! AVENGERS ALERT!
No momma. Yes. Of course not. Yes, I'm taking you seriously.
AVENGERS ALERT! AVENGERS ALERT!
Listen, I have to go, there's an Avengers alert!
No I'm not making that up!
That's two barrels of peanut butter. Just sign there.
Hulk likes to sign his name.
AVENGERS ALERT! AVENGERS ALERT!
Ummm... shouldn't you be responding to that alert?
Hulk is signing his name.
AVENGERS ALERT! AVENGERS ALERT!
I'm on my way to the control room right now, Spider-Man! What's going on?
What? Oh no! Not--

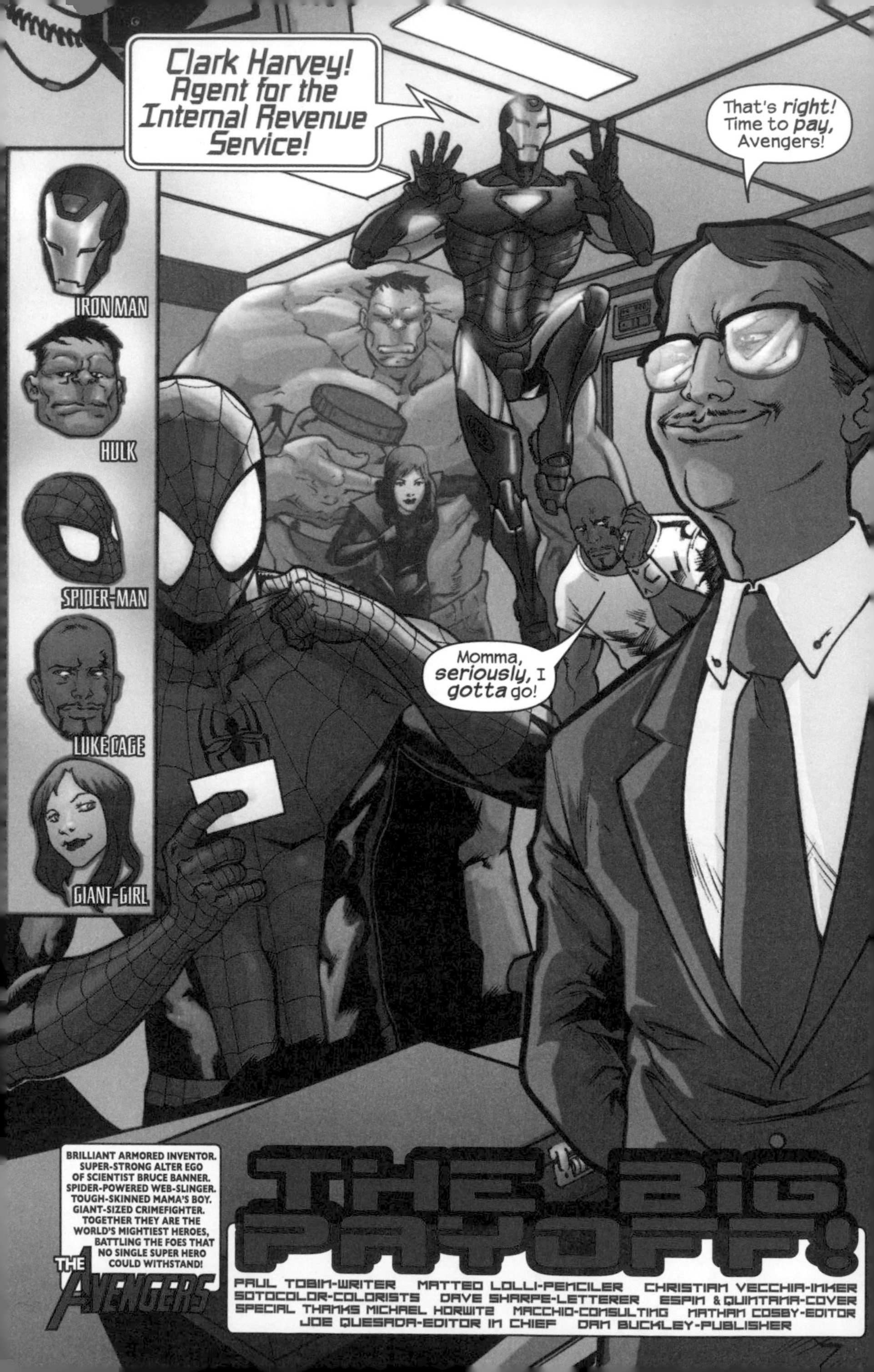

Clark Harvey! Agent for the Internal Revenue Service!
That's right! Time to pay, Avengers!
Momma, seriously, I gotta go!
IRON MAN
HULK
SPIDER-MAN
LUKE CAGE
GIANT-GIRL
BRILLIANT ARMORED INVENTOR.
SUPER-STRONG ALTER EGO OF SCIENTIST BRUCE BANNER.
SPIDER-POWERED WEB-SLINGER.
TOUGH-SKINNED MAMA'S BOY.
GIANT-SIZED CRIMEFIGHTER.
TOGETHER THEY ARE THE WORLD'S MIGHTIEST HEROES, BATTLING THE FOES THAT NO SINGLE SUPER HERO COULD WITHSTAND!
THE AVENGERS
THE BIG PAYOFF!
PAUL TOBIN-WRITER MATTEO LOLLI-PENCILER CHRISTIAN VECCHIA-INKER
SOTOCOLOR-COLORISTS DAVE SHARPE-LETTERER ESPIN & QUINTANA-COVER
SPECIAL THANKS MICHAEL HORWITZ MACCHIO-CONSULTING NATHAN COSBY-EDITOR
JOE QUESADA-EDITOR IN CHIEF DAN BUCKLEY-PUBLISHER

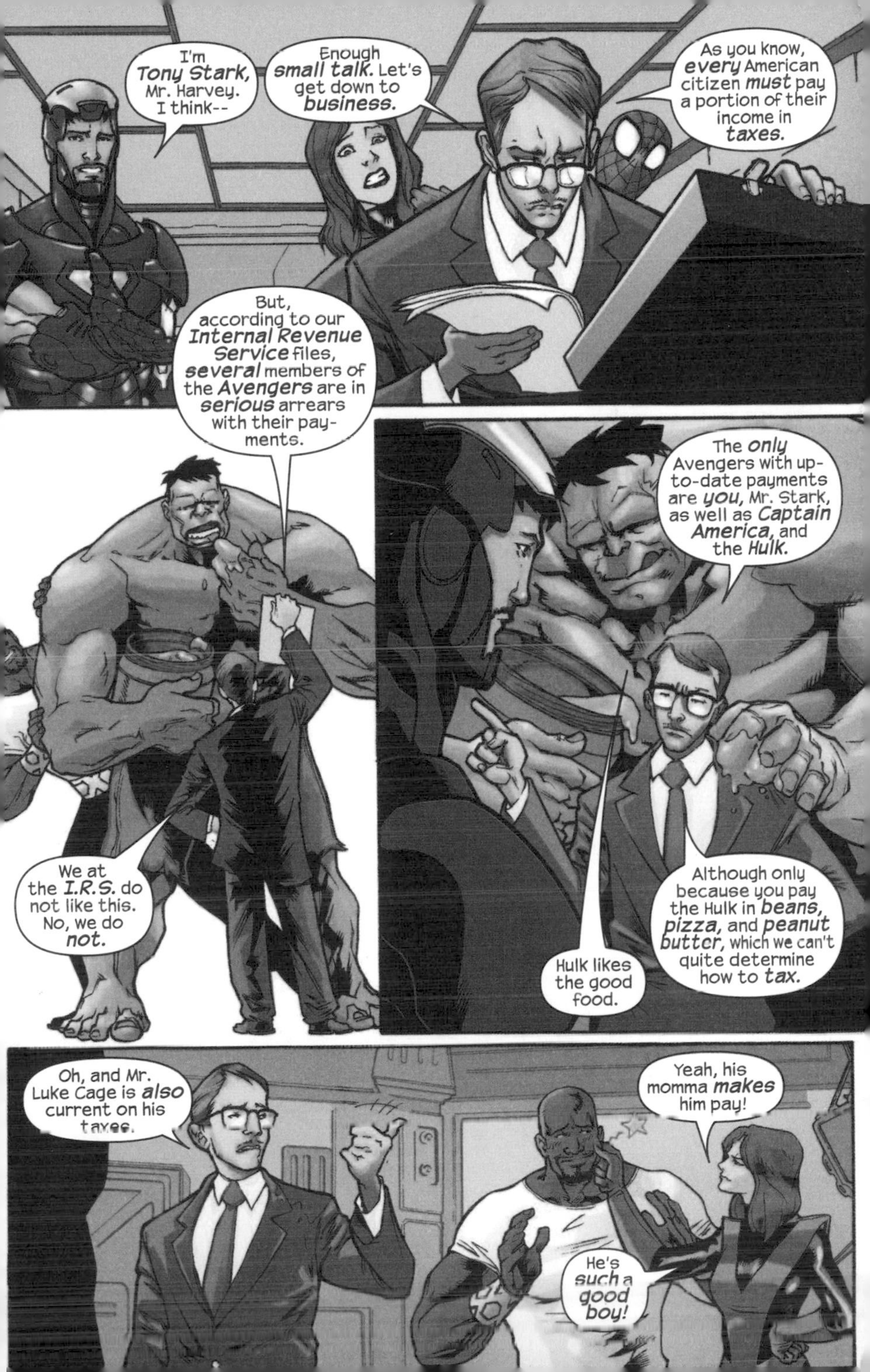

I'm Tony Stark, Mr. Harvey. I think--
Enough small talk. Let's get down to business.
As you know, every American citizen must pay a portion of their income in taxes.
But, according to our Internal Revenue Service files, several members of the Avengers are in serious arrears with their pay-ments.
We at the I.R.S. do not like this. No, we do not.
The only Avengers with up-to-date payments are you, Mr. Stark, as well as Captain America, and the Hulk.
Although only because you pay the Hulk in beans, pizza, and peanut butter, which we can't quite determine how to tax.
Hulk likes the good food.
Oh, and Mr. Luke Cage is also current on his taxes.
Yeah, his momma makes him pay!
He's such a good boy!

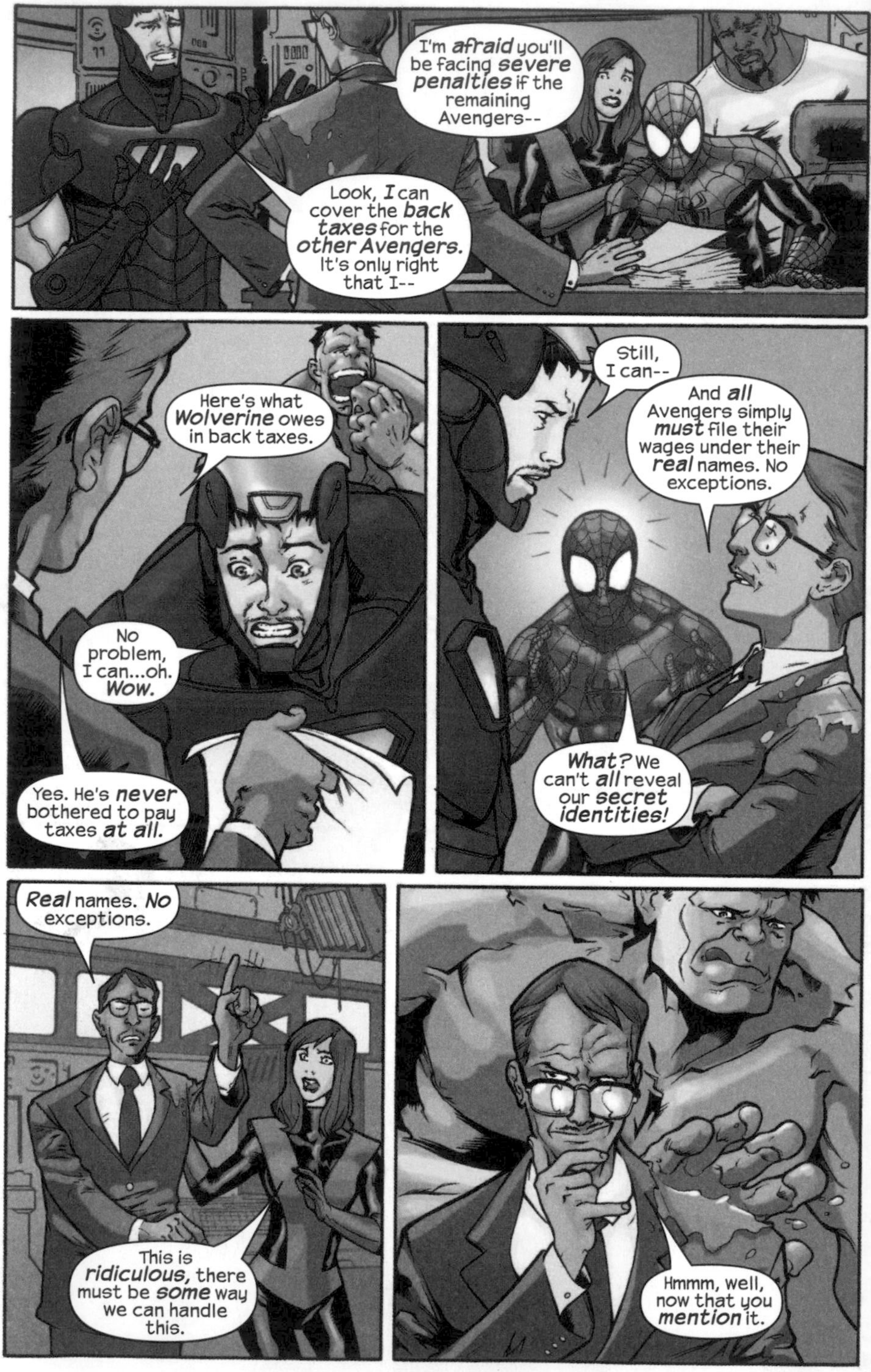
I'm *afraid* you'll be facing *severe penalties* if the remaining Avengers--
Look, *I* can cover the *back taxes* for the *other Avengers.* It's only right that I--
Here's what *Wolverine* owes in back taxes.
No problem, I can...oh. *Wow.*
Yes. He's *never* bothered to pay taxes *at all.*
Still, I can--
And *all* Avengers simply *must* file their wages under their *real* names. No exceptions.
What? We can't *all* reveal our *secret identities!*
Real names. *No* exceptions.
This is *ridiculous,* there must be *some* way we can handle this.
Hmmm, well, now that you *mention* it.

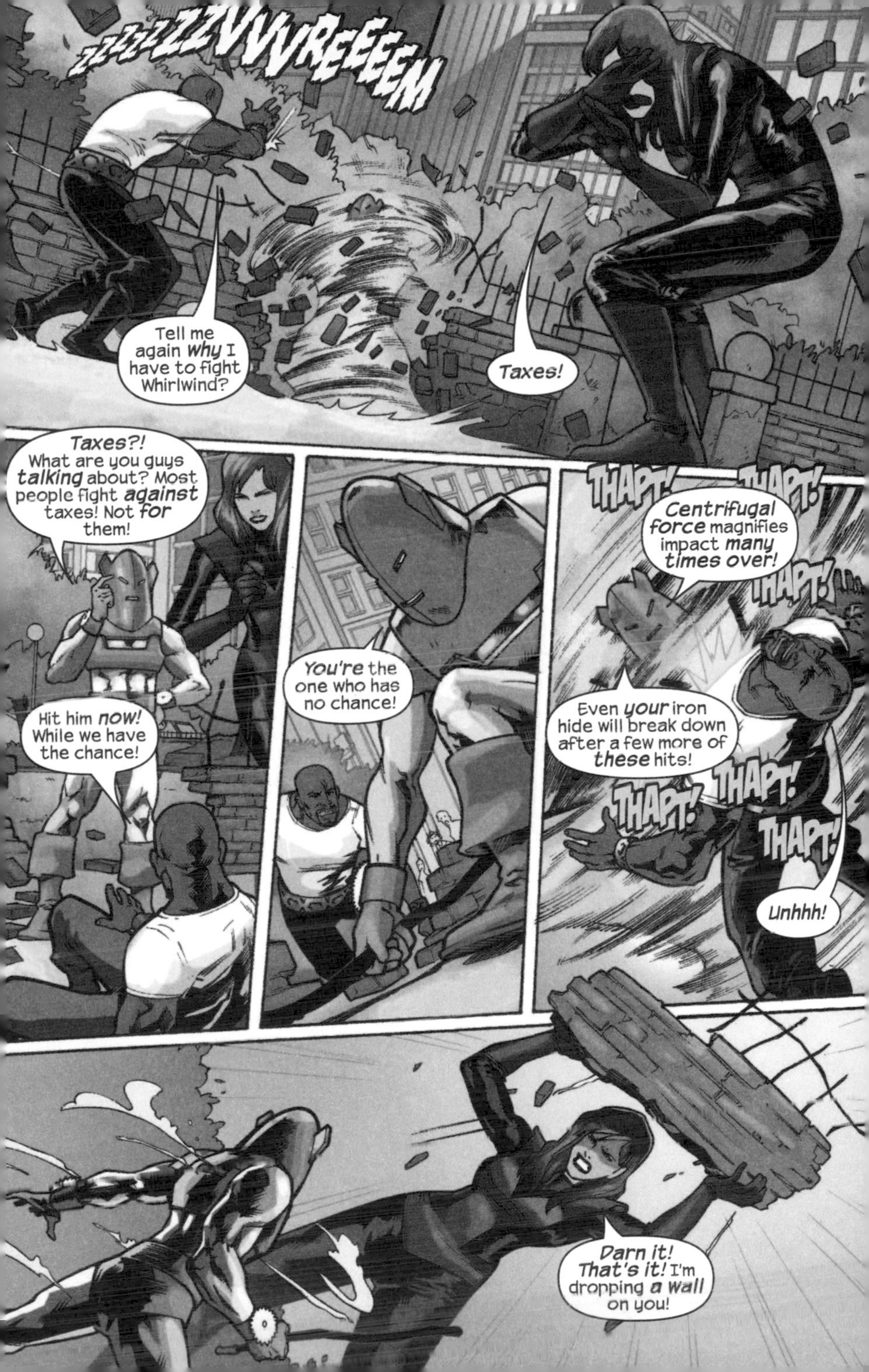
ZZZZZZZZVVVVREEEEEM
Tell me again why I have to fight Whirlwind?
Taxes!
Taxes?! What are you guys talking about? Most people fight against taxes! Not for them!
Hit him now! While we have the chance!
You're the one who has no chance!
THAPT! THAPT!
Centrifugal force magnifies impact many times over!
THAPT!
Even your iron hide will break down after a few more of these hits!
THAPT! THAPT! THAPT!
Unhhh!
Darn it! That's it! I'm dropping a wall on you!

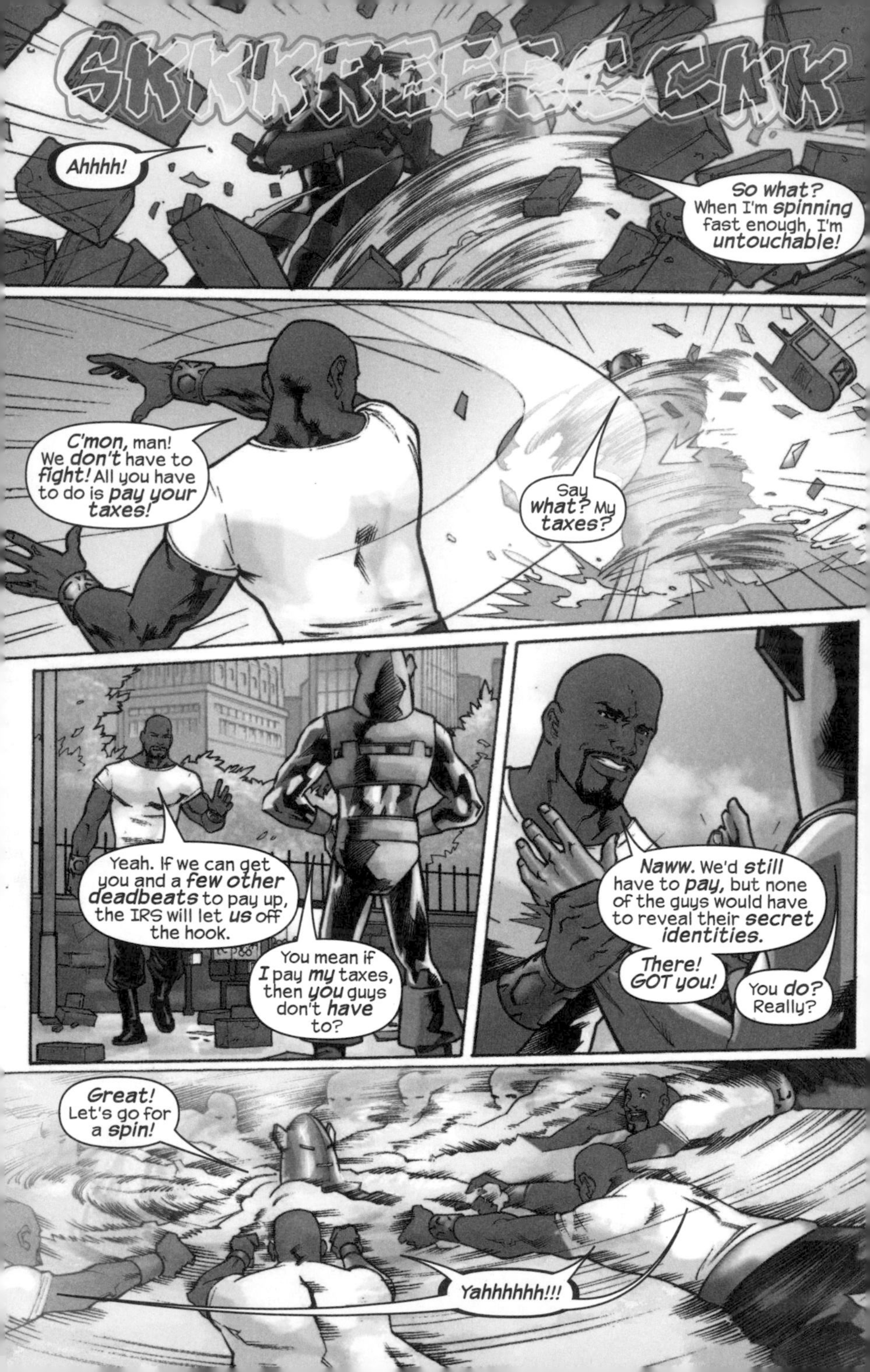
SKKKREEECCHK
Ahhhh!
So what? When I'm spinning fast enough, I'm untouchable!
C'mon, man! We don't have to fight! All you have to do is pay your taxes!
Say what? My taxes?
Yeah. If we can get you and a few other deadbeats to pay up, the IRS will let us off the hook.
You mean if I pay my taxes, then you guys don't have to?
Naww. We'd still have to pay, but none of the guys would have to reveal their secret identities.
There! GOT you!
You do? Really?
Great! Let's go for a spin!
Yahhhhhh!!!

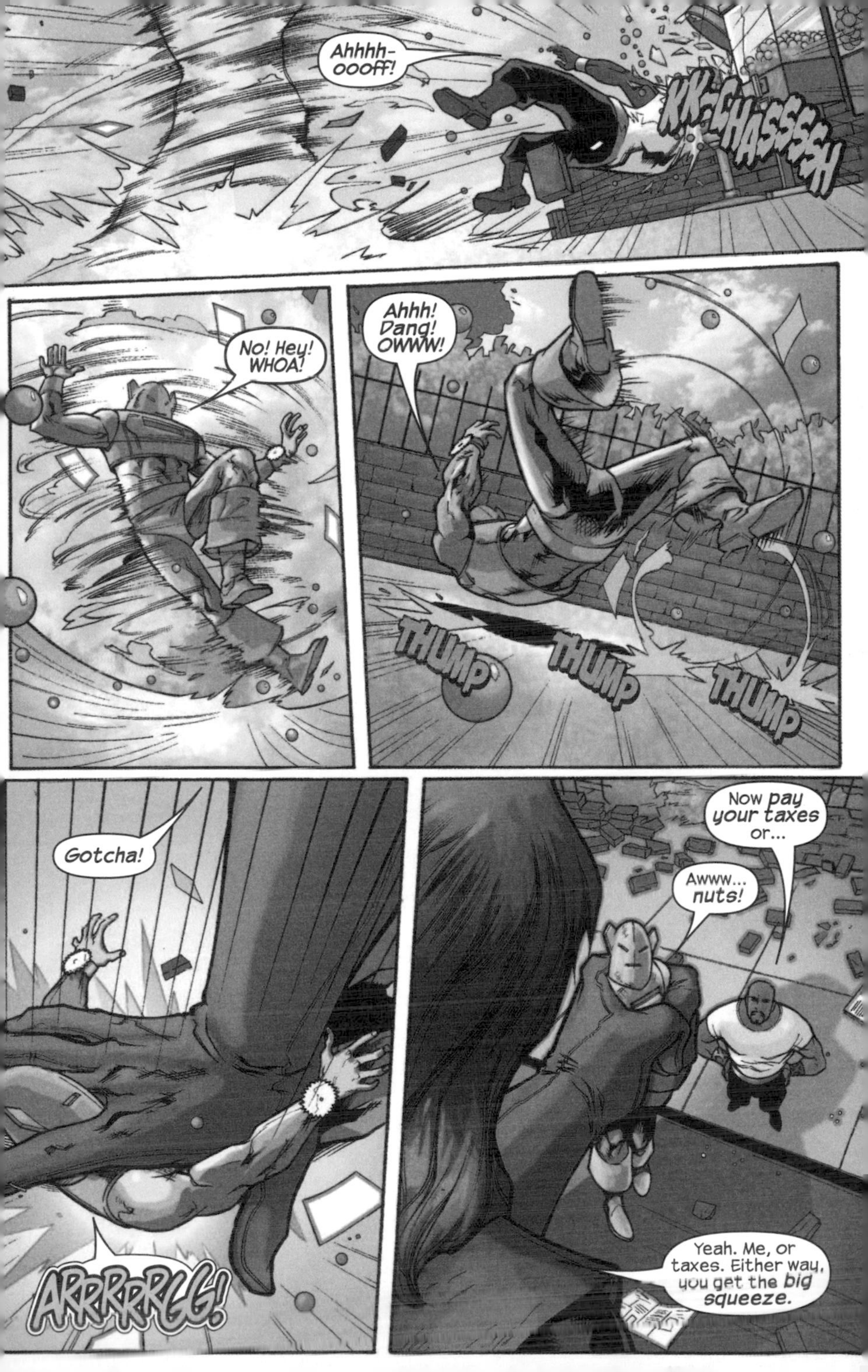
Ahhhh-
oooff!
KK-CHASSSSH
No! Hey!
WHOA!
Ahhh!
Dang!
OWWW!
THUMP
THUMP
THUMP
Gotcha!
ARRRRRGG!
Now pay
your taxes
or...
Awww...
nuts!
Yeah. Me, or
taxes. Either way,
you get the big
squeeze.

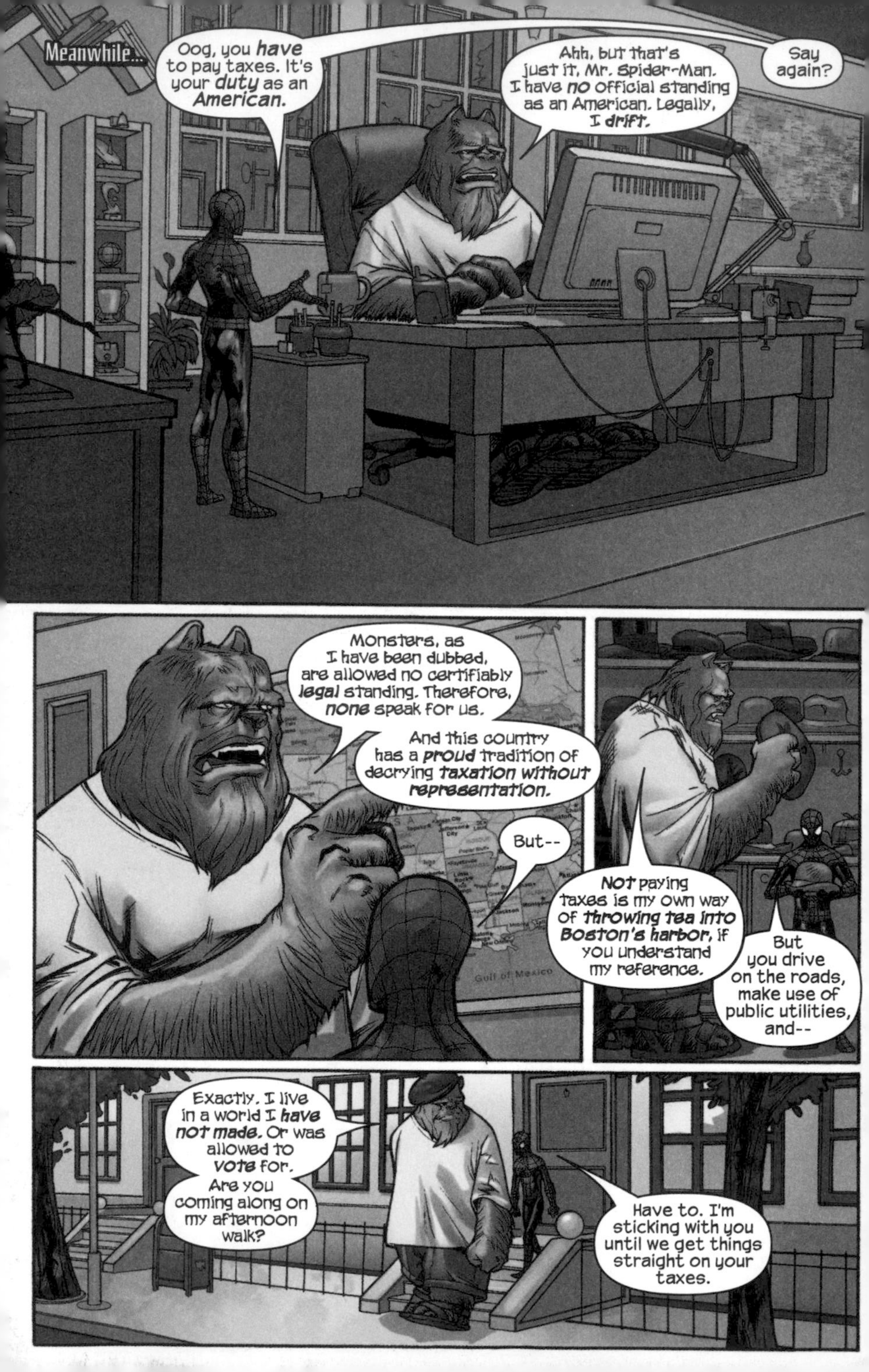

Meanwhile...
Oog, you have to pay taxes. It's your duty as an American.
Ahh, but that's just it, Mr. Spider-Man. I have no official standing as an American. Legally, I drift.
Say again?
Monsters, as I have been dubbed, are allowed no certifiably legal standing. Therefore, none speak for us.
And this country has a proud tradition of decrying taxation without representation.
But--
NOT paying taxes is my own way of throwing tea into Boston's harbor, if you understand my reference.
But you drive on the roads, make use of public utilities, and--
Exactly. I live in a world I have not made. Or was allowed to vote for.
Are you coming along on my afternoon walk?
Have to. I'm sticking with you until we get things straight on your taxes.

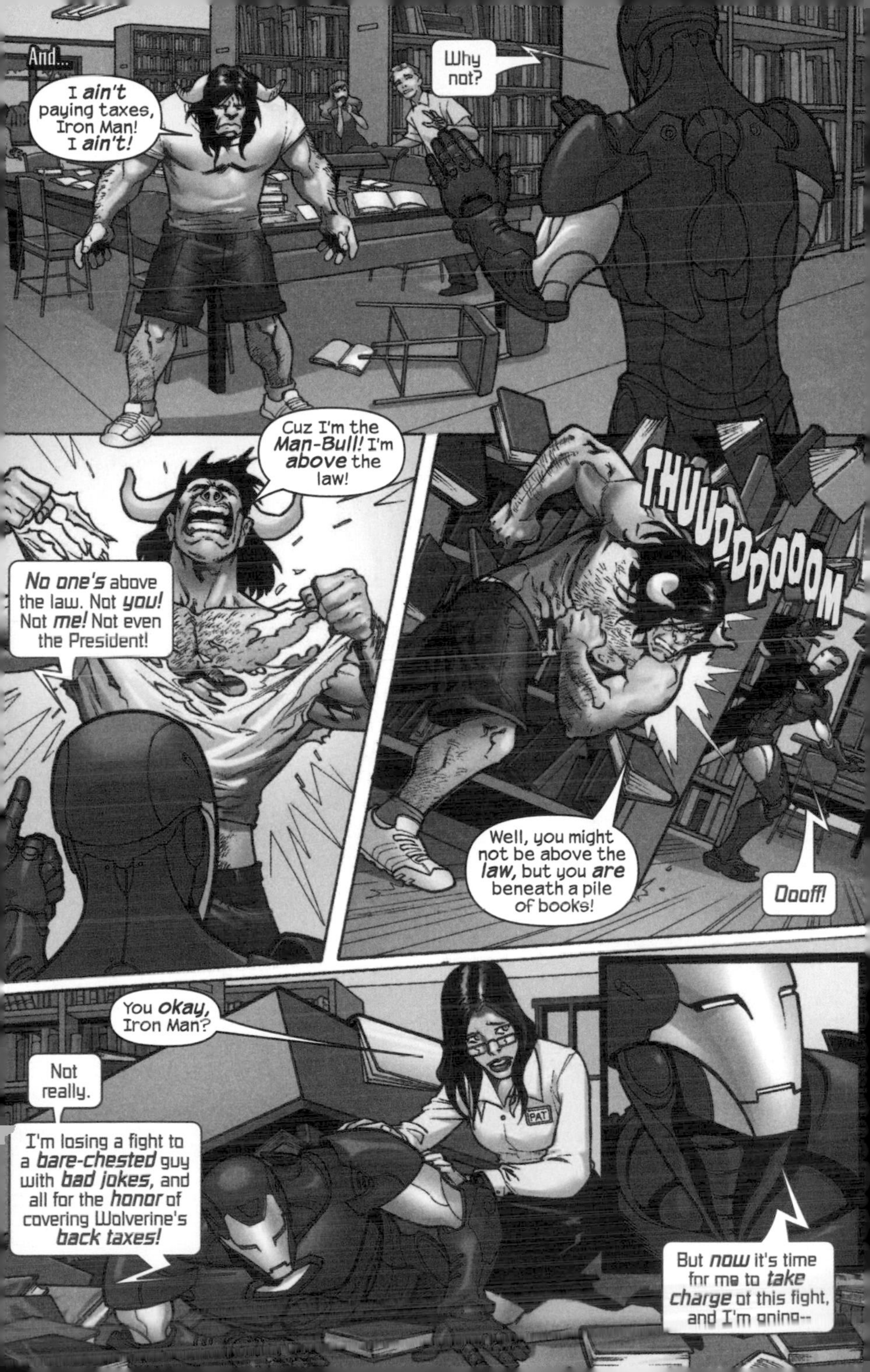
And...
I ain't paying taxes, Iron Man! I ain't!
Why not?
Cuz I'm the Man-Bull! I'm above the law!
No one's above the law. Not you! Not me! Not even the President!
THUUDDDOOOM
Well, you might not be above the law, but you are beneath a pile of books!
Oooff!
You okay, Iron Man?
Not really.
I'm losing a fight to a bare-chested guy with bad jokes, and all for the honor of covering Wolverine's back taxes!
PAT
But now it's time for me to take charge of this fight, and I'm going--

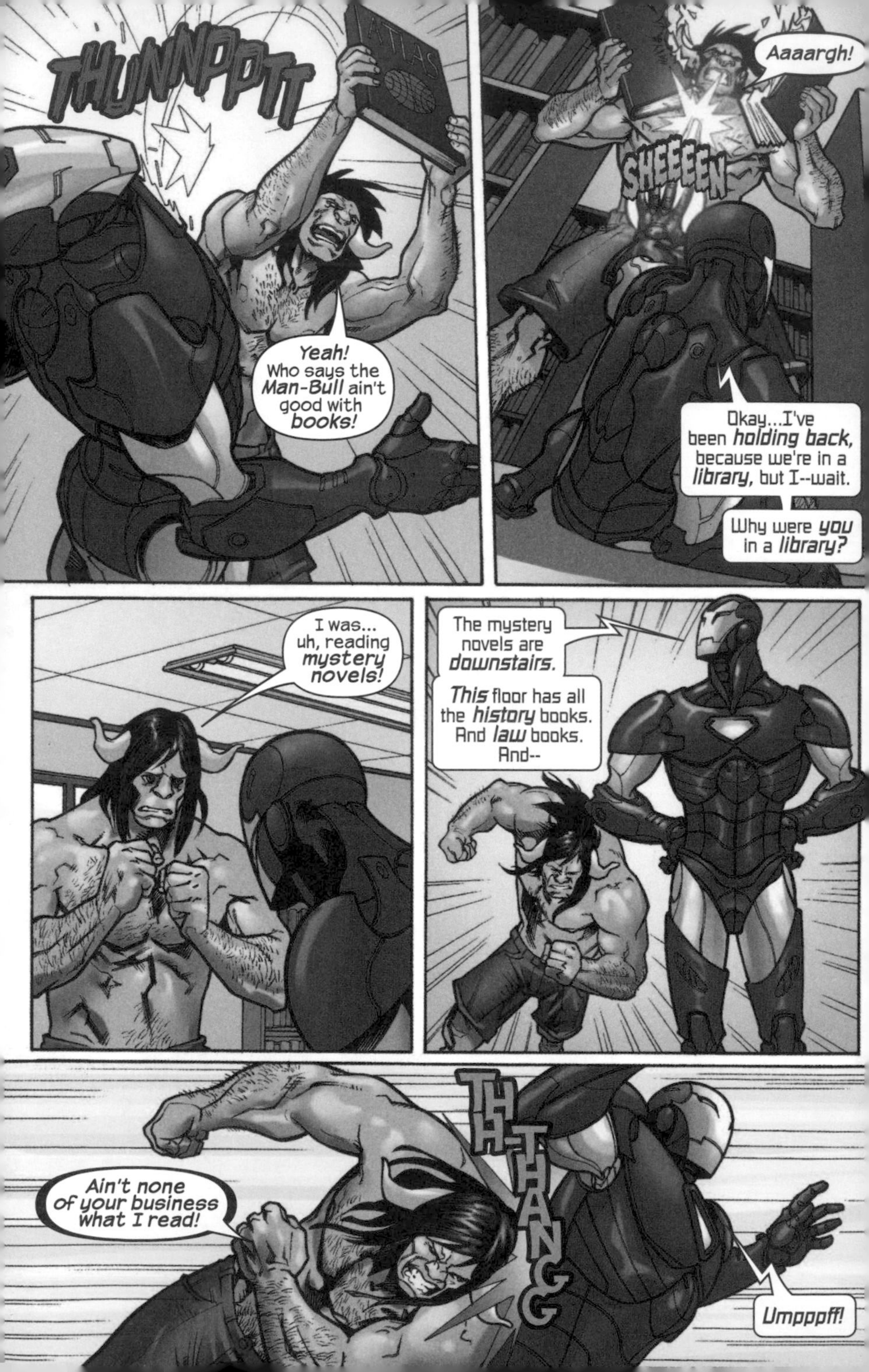
THUNNPPTT
Yeah! Who says the Man-Bull ain't good with books!
Aaaargh!
SHEEEEN
Okay...I've been holding back, because we're in a library, but I--wait.
Why were you in a library?
I was... uh, reading mystery novels!
The mystery novels are downstairs.
This floor has all the history books. And law books. And--
TH-THANGG
Ain't none of your business what I read!
Umpppff!

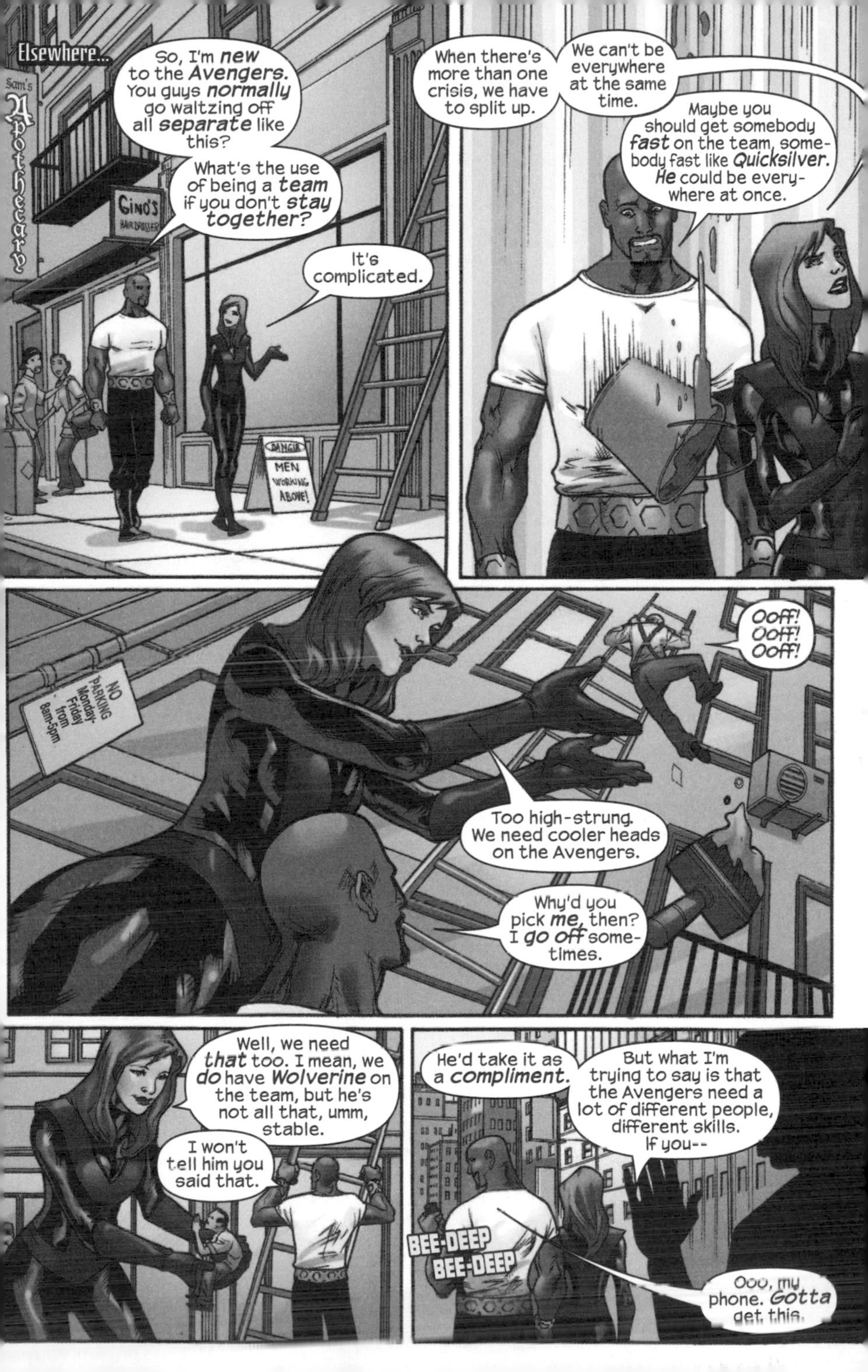

Elsewhere...
Sam's Apothecary
So, I'm new to the Avengers. You guys normally go waltzing off all separate like this?
What's the use of being a team if you don't stay together?
GINO'S HAIRDRESSER
It's complicated.
DANGER MEN WORKING ABOVE!
When there's more than one crisis, we have to split up.
We can't be everywhere at the same time.
Maybe you should get somebody fast on the team, somebody fast like Quicksilver. He could be everywhere at once.
NO PARKING Monday-Friday from 8am-5pm
Ooff! Ooff! Ooff!
Too high-strung. We need cooler heads on the Avengers.
Why'd you pick me, then? I go off sometimes.
Well, we need that too. I mean, we do have Wolverine on the team, but he's not all that, umm, stable.
I won't tell him you said that.
He'd take it as a compliment.
But what I'm trying to say is that the Avengers need a lot of different people, different skills. If you--
BEE-DEEP BEE-DEEP
Ooo, my phone. Gotta get this.

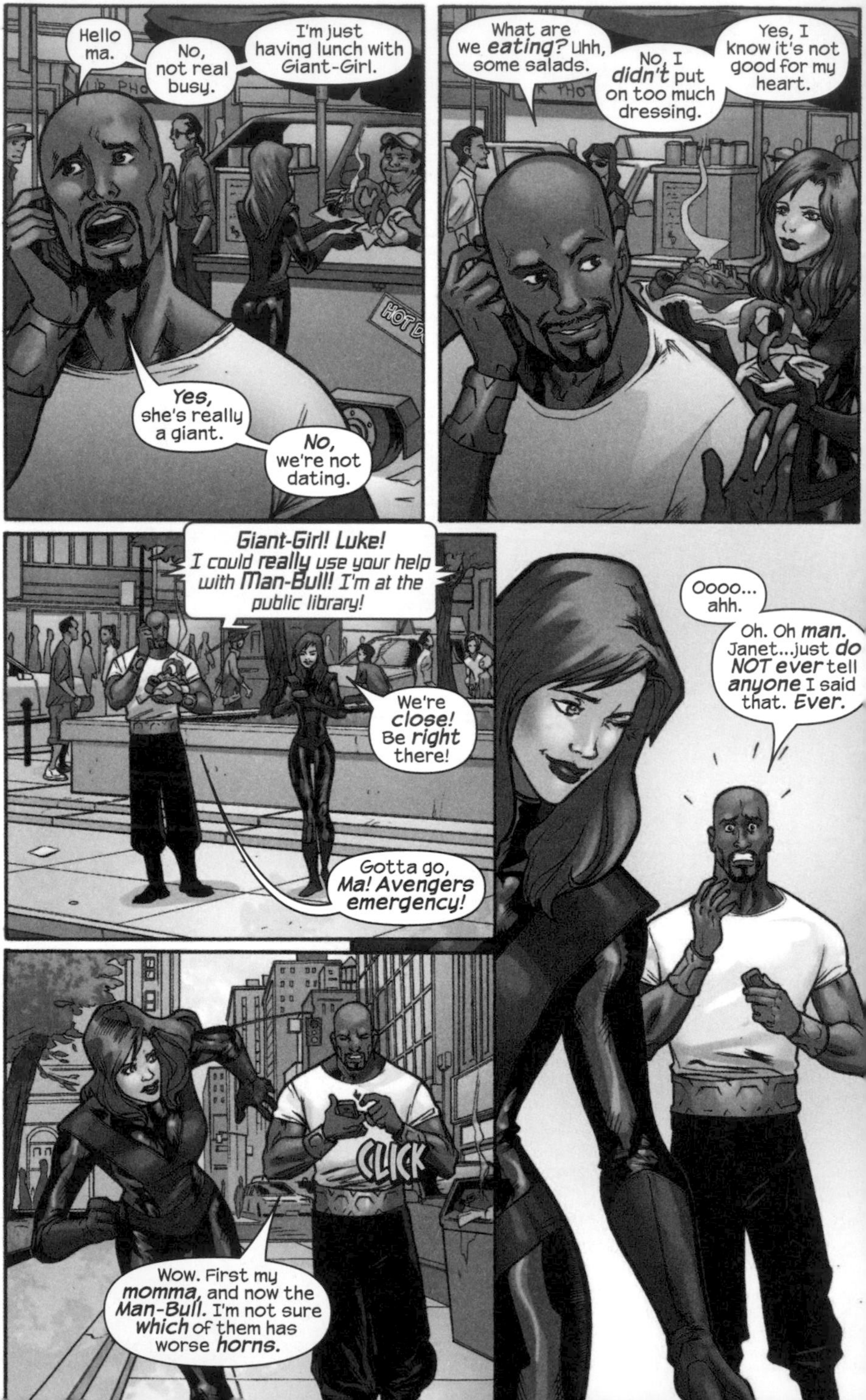

Hello ma.
No, not real busy.
I'm just having lunch with Giant-Girl.
Yes, she's really a giant.
No, we're not dating.
What are we *eating?* Uhh, some salads.
No, I *didn't* put on too much dressing.
Yes, I know it's not good for my heart.
Giant-Girl! Luke! I could *really* use your help with Man-Bull! I'm at the public library!
We're *close!* Be *right* there!
Gotta go, *Ma! Avengers emergency!*
CLICK
Wow. First my *momma,* and now the *Man-Bull.* I'm not sure *which* of them has worse *horns.*
Oooo... ahh.
Oh. Oh *man.* Janet...just *do NOT ever* tell *anyone* I said that. *Ever.*

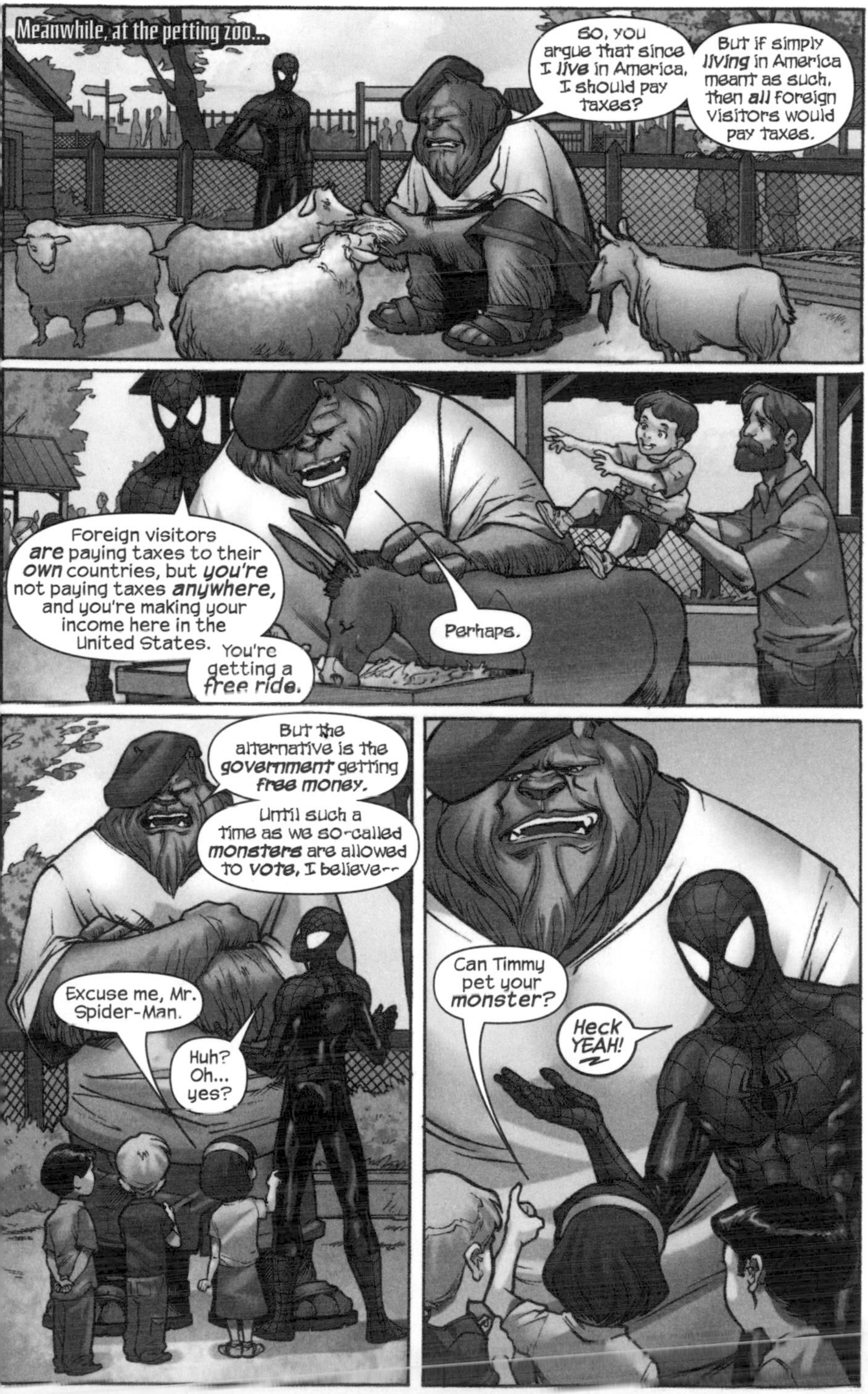
Meanwhile, at the petting zoo...
SO, YOU argue that since I live in America, I should pay taxes?
But if simply living in America meant as such, then all foreign visitors would pay taxes.
Foreign visitors are paying taxes to their own countries, but you're not paying taxes anywhere, and you're making your income here in the United States.
You're getting a free ride.
Perhaps.
But the alternative is the government getting free money.
Until such a time as we so-called monsters are allowed to vote, I believe--
Excuse me, Mr. Spider-Man.
Huh? Oh... yes?
Can Timmy pet your monster?
Heck YEAH!

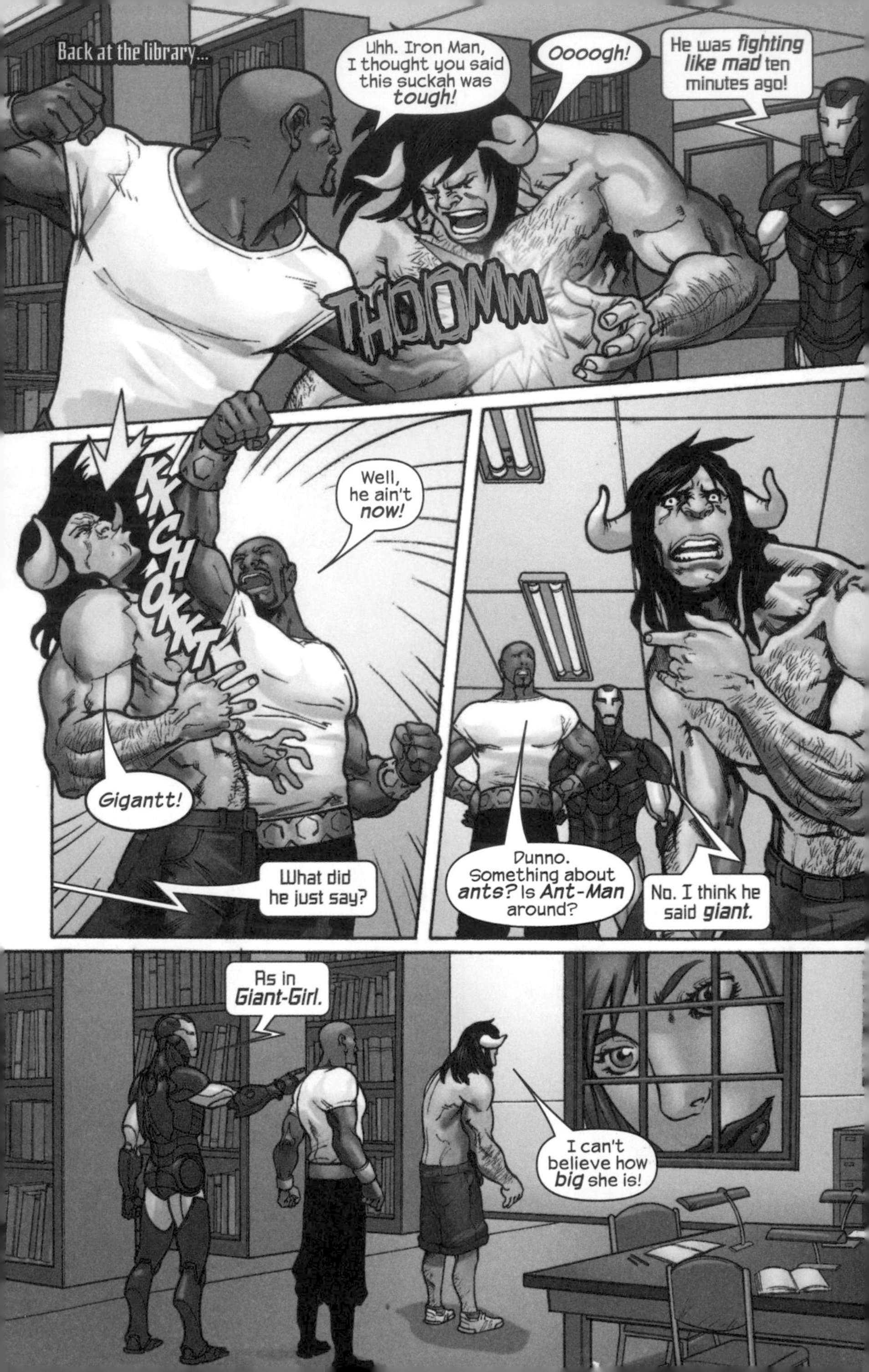
Back at the library...
Uhh. Iron Man, I thought you said this suckah was tough!
Oooogh!
He was fighting like mad ten minutes ago!
THOOMM
KKCHOKKT
Well, he ain't now!
Gigantt!
What did he just say?
Dunno. Something about ants? Is Ant-Man around?
No. I think he said giant.
As in Giant-Girl.
I can't believe how big she is!

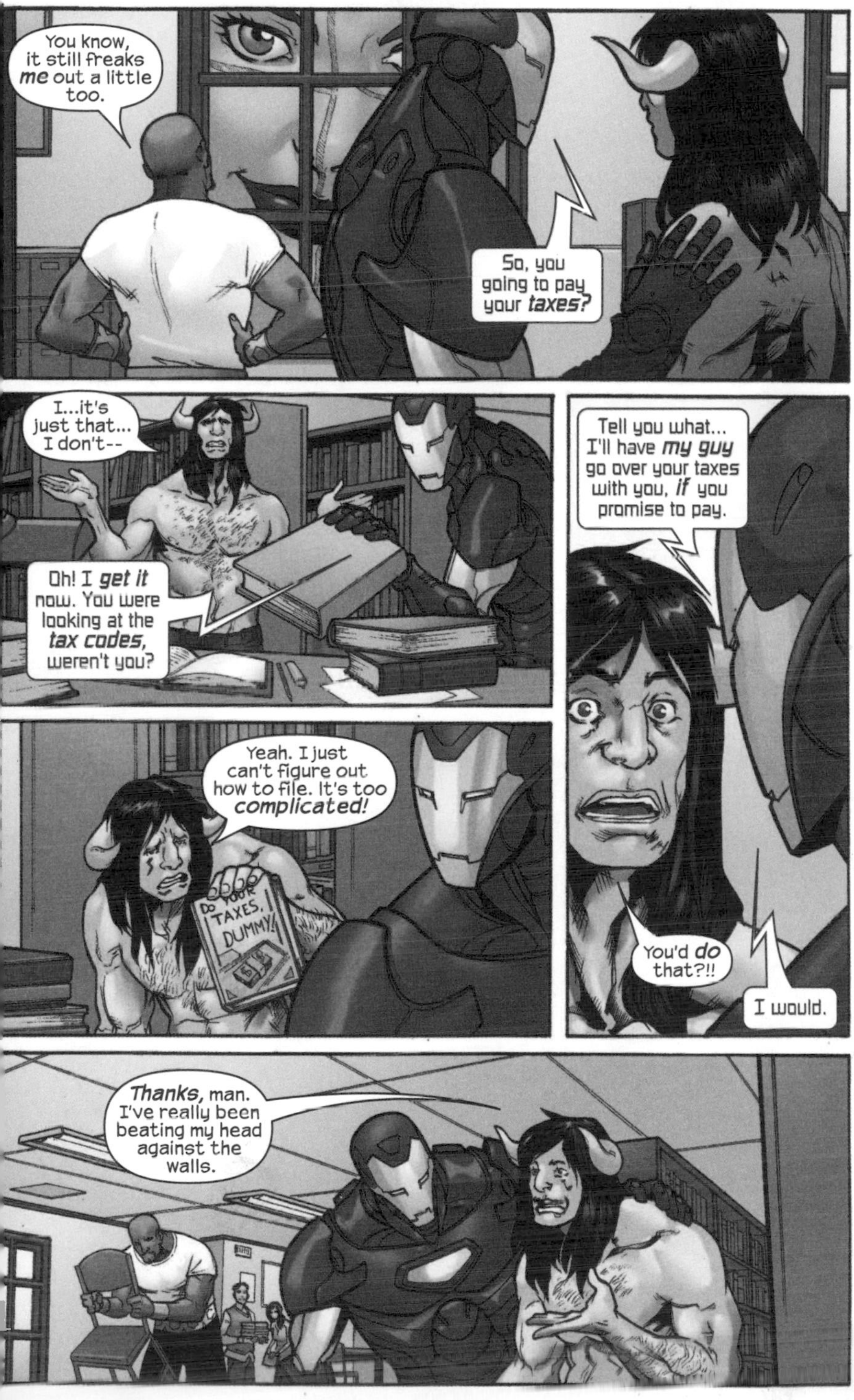
You know, it still freaks *me* out a little too.
So, you going to pay your *taxes?*
I...it's just that... I don't--
Oh! I *get it* now. You were looking at the *tax codes,* weren't you?
Yeah. I just can't figure out how to file. It's too *complicated!*
DO YOUR TAXES, DUMMY!
Tell you what... I'll have *my guy* go over your taxes with you, *if* you promise to pay.
You'd *do* that?!!
I would.
Thanks, man. I've really been beating my head against the walls.

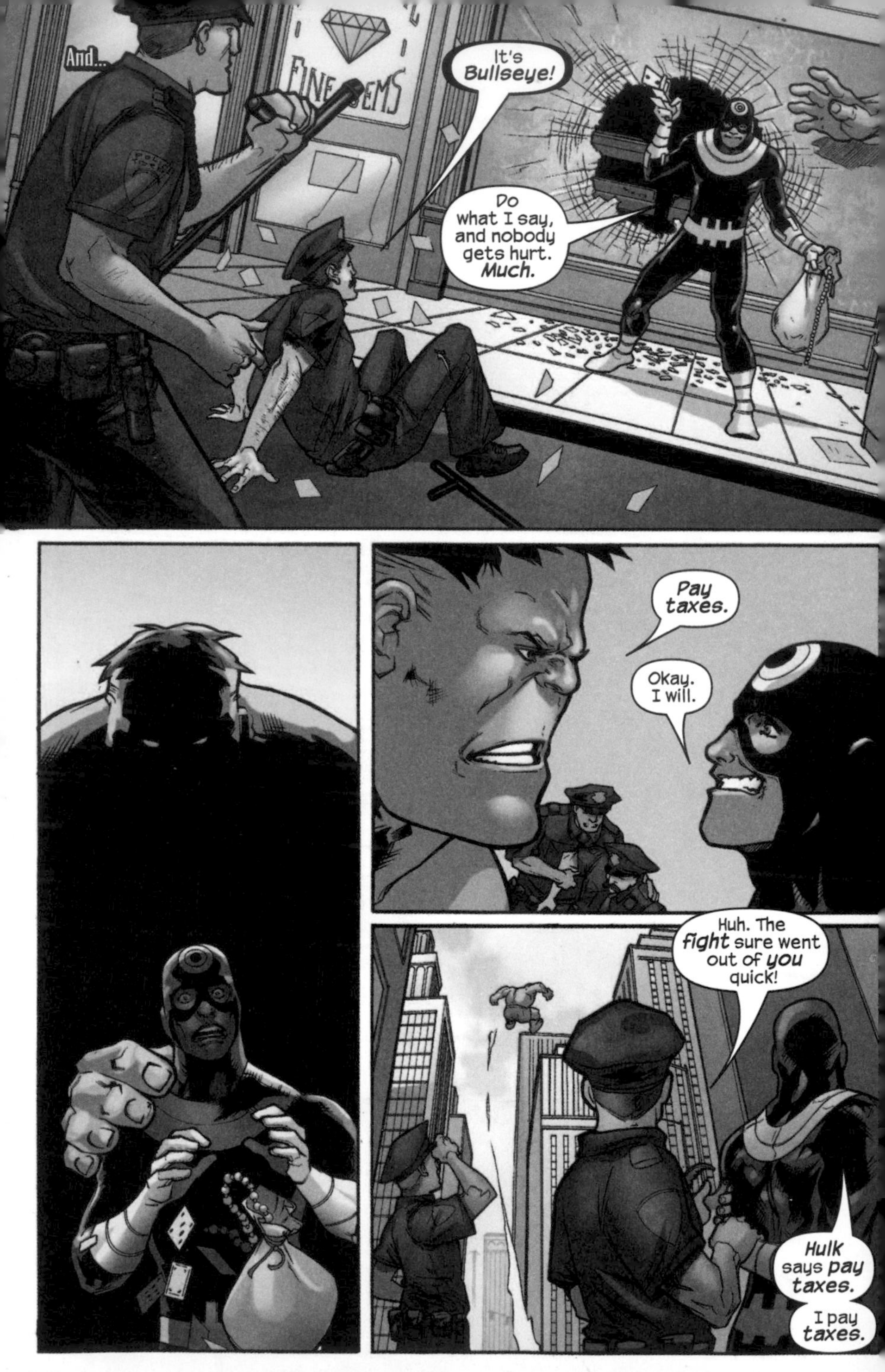
And...
It's Bullseye!
Do what I say, and nobody gets hurt. Much.
Pay taxes.
Okay. I will.
Huh. The fight sure went out of you quick!
Hulk says pay taxes.
I pay taxes.

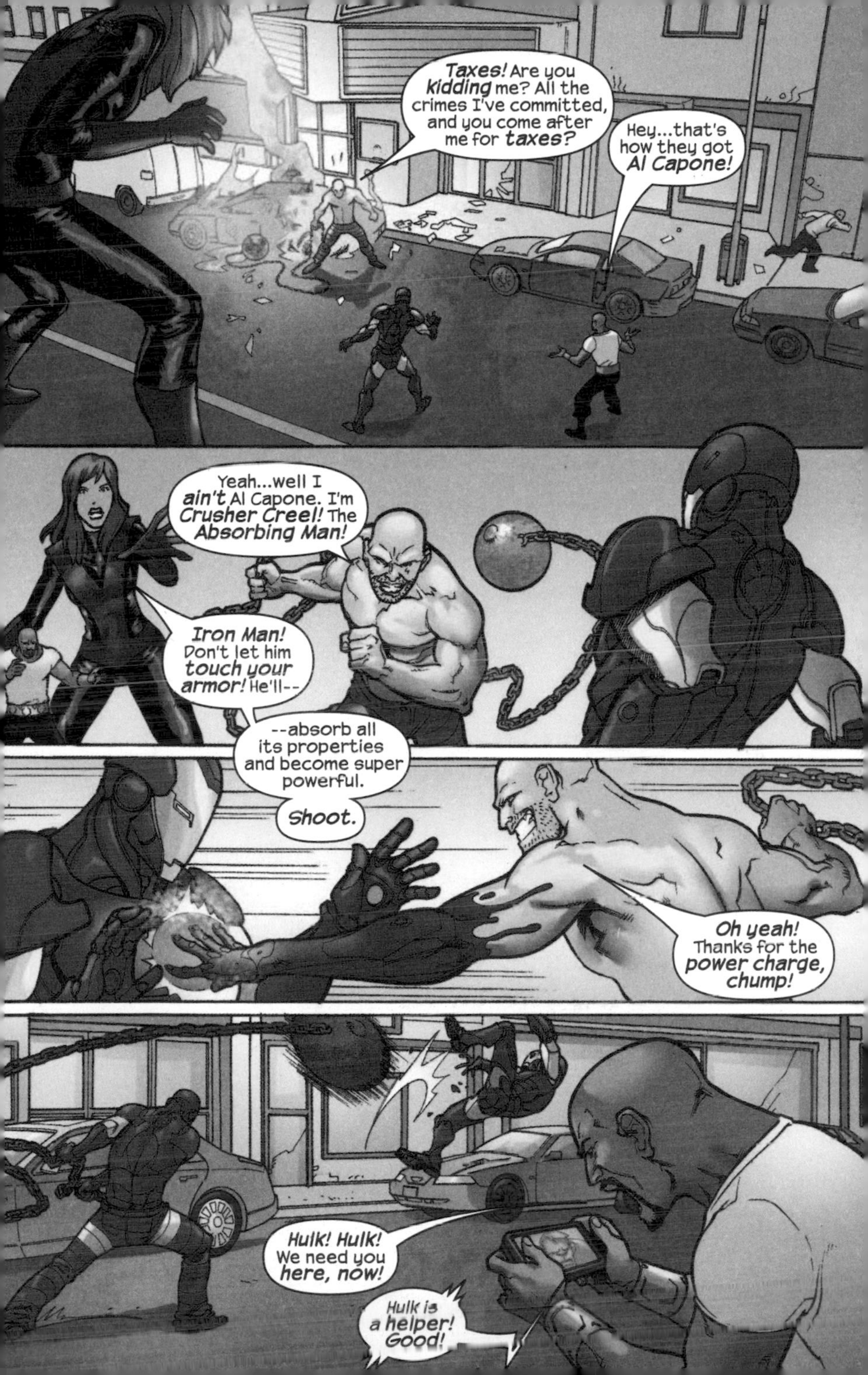
Taxes! Are you kidding me? All the crimes I've committed, and you come after me for taxes?
Hey...that's how they got Al Capone!
Yeah...well I ain't Al Capone. I'm Crusher Creel! The Absorbing Man!
Iron Man! Don't let him touch your armor! He'll--
--absorb all its properties and become super powerful.
Shoot.
Oh yeah! Thanks for the power charge, chump!
Hulk! Hulk! We need you here, now!
Hulk is a helper! Good!

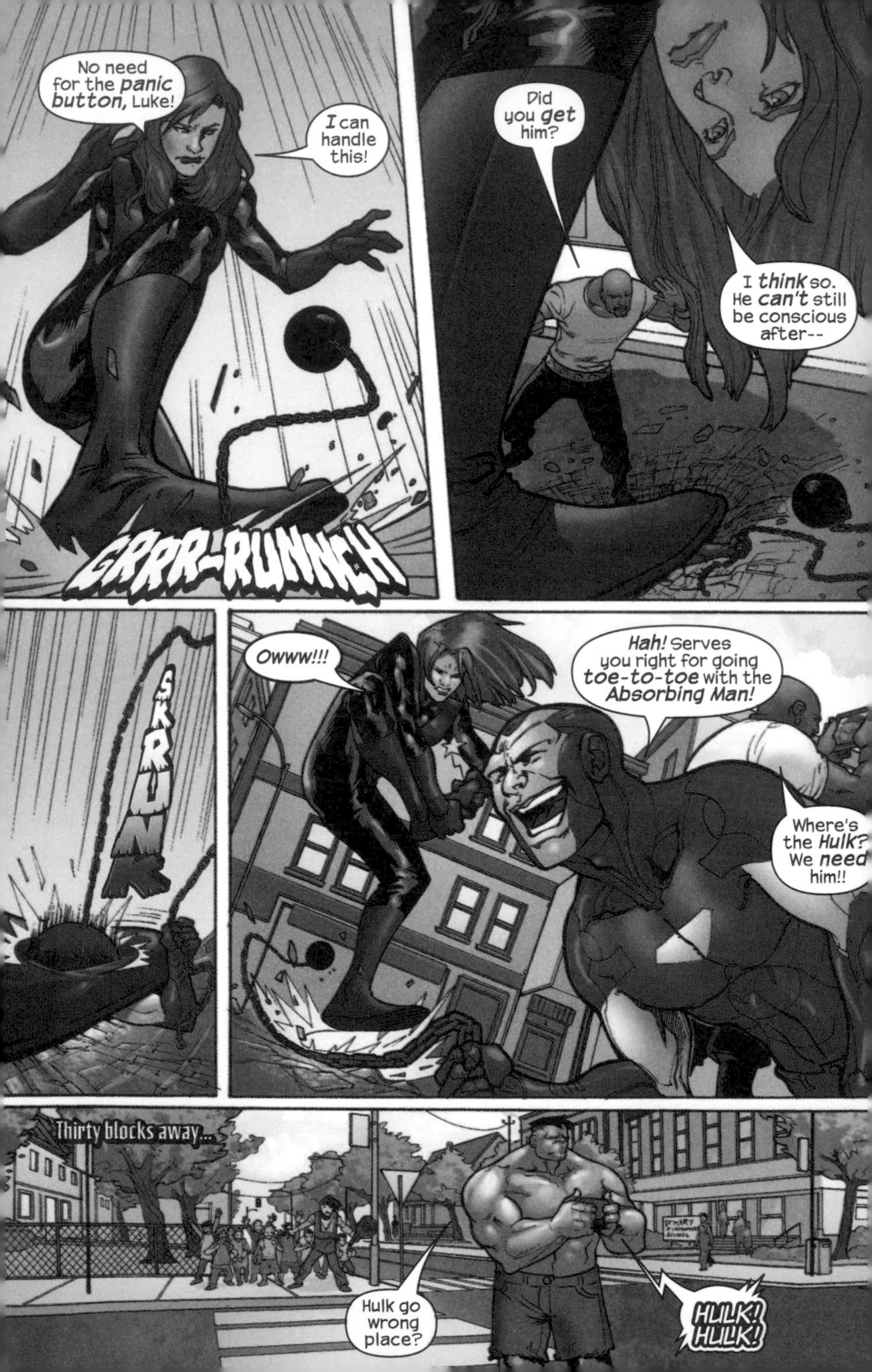

No need for the panic button, Luke!
I can handle this!
GRRR-RUNNCH
Did you get him?
I think so. He can't still be conscious after--
SKRUNK
Owww!!!
Hah! Serves you right for going toe-to-toe with the Absorbing Man!
Where's the Hulk? We need him!!
Thirty blocks away...
Hulk go wrong place?
HULK! HULK!

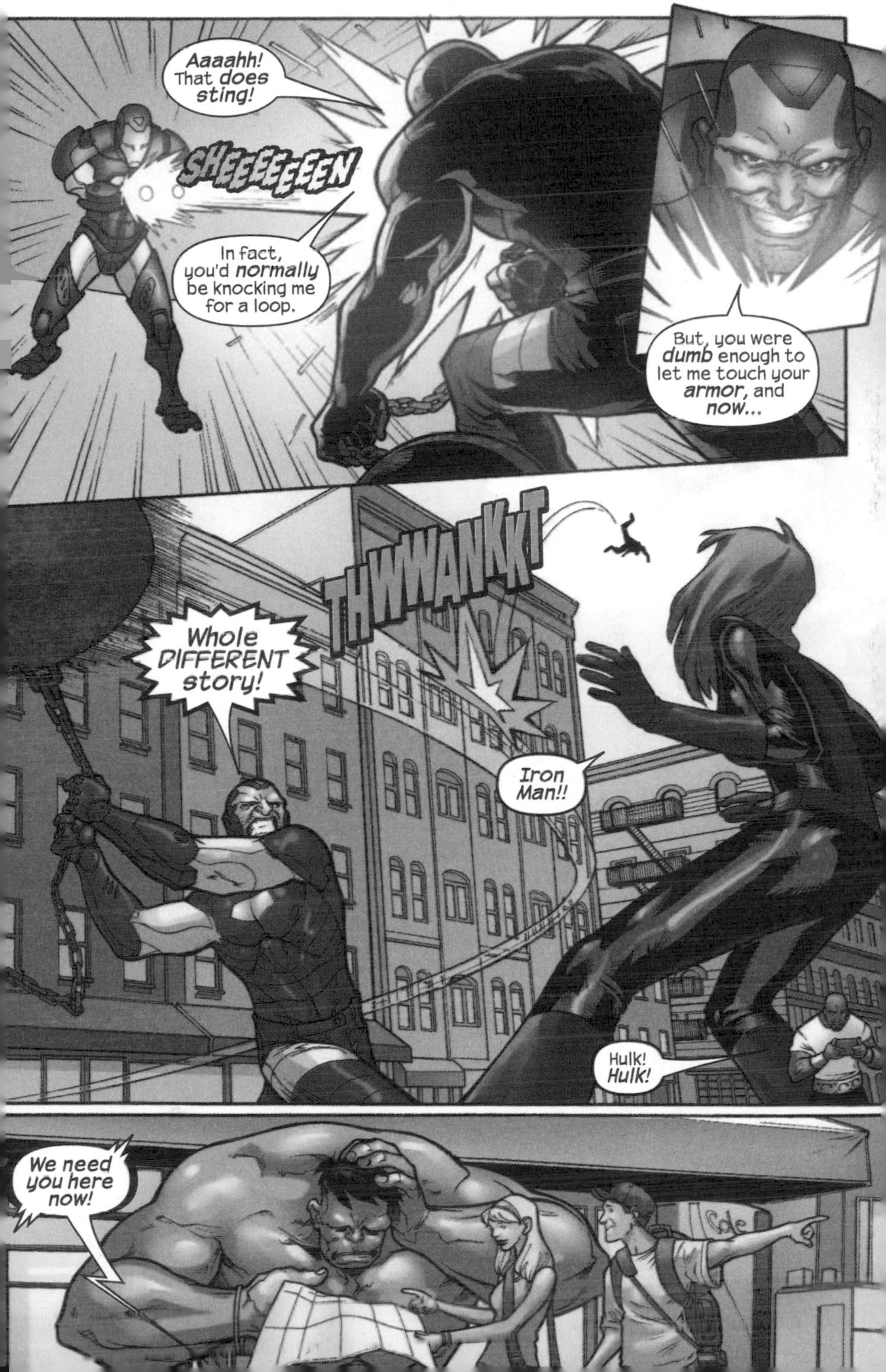

Aaaahh! That does sting!
SHEEEEEEEN
In fact, you'd normally be knocking me for a loop.
But, you were dumb enough to let me touch your armor, and now...
THWWANKKT
Whole DIFFERENT story!
Iron Man!!
Hulk! Hulk!
We need you here now!

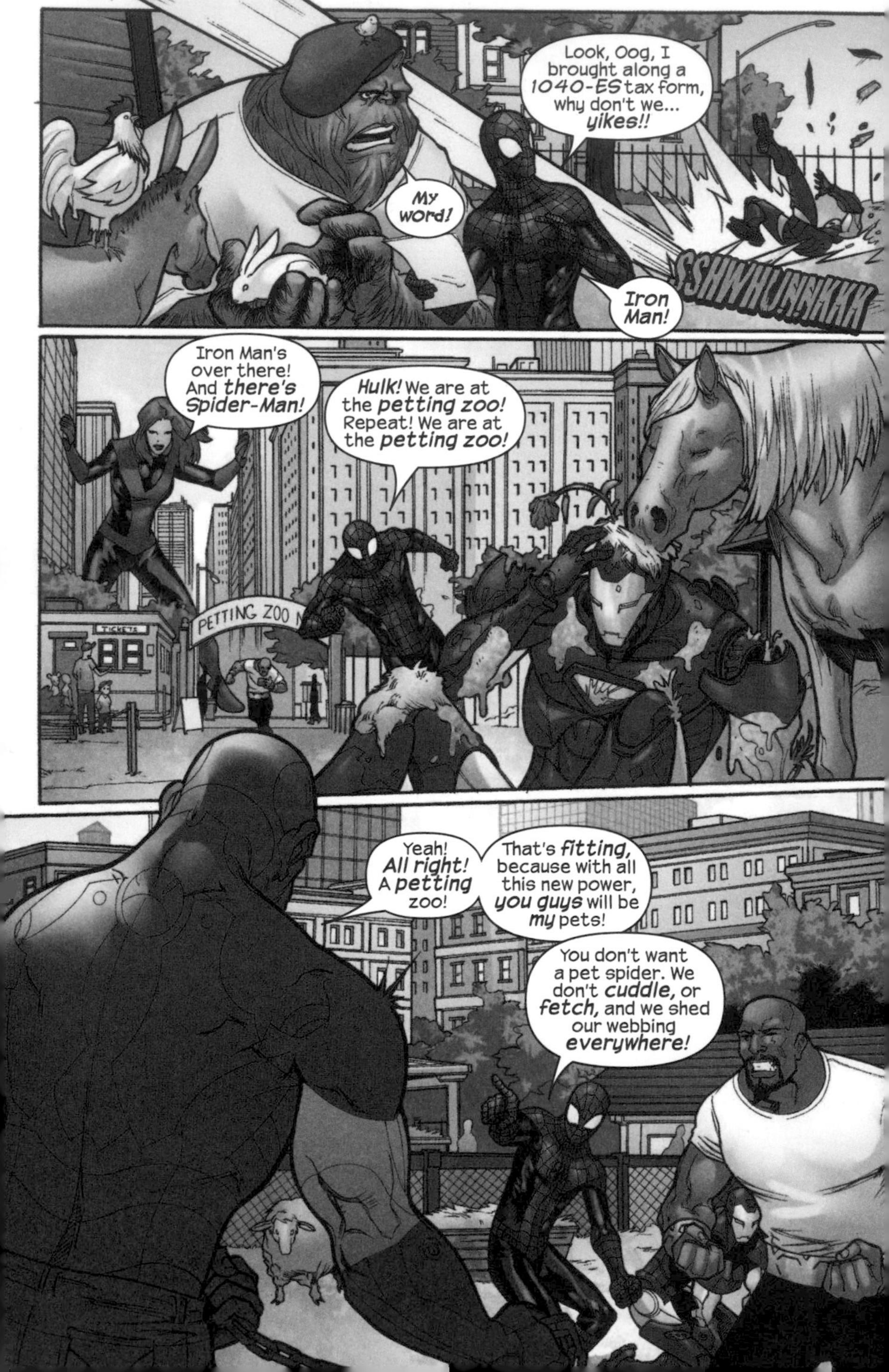

Look, Oog, I brought along a 1040-ES tax form, why don't we... yikes!!
My word!
SSHWHUNNKKK
Iron Man!
Iron Man's over there! And there's Spider-Man!
Hulk! We are at the petting zoo! Repeat! We are at the petting zoo!
PETTING ZOO
TICKETS
Yeah! All right! A petting zoo!
That's fitting, because with all this new power, you guys will be my pets!
You don't want a pet spider. We don't cuddle, or fetch, and we shed our webbing everywhere!

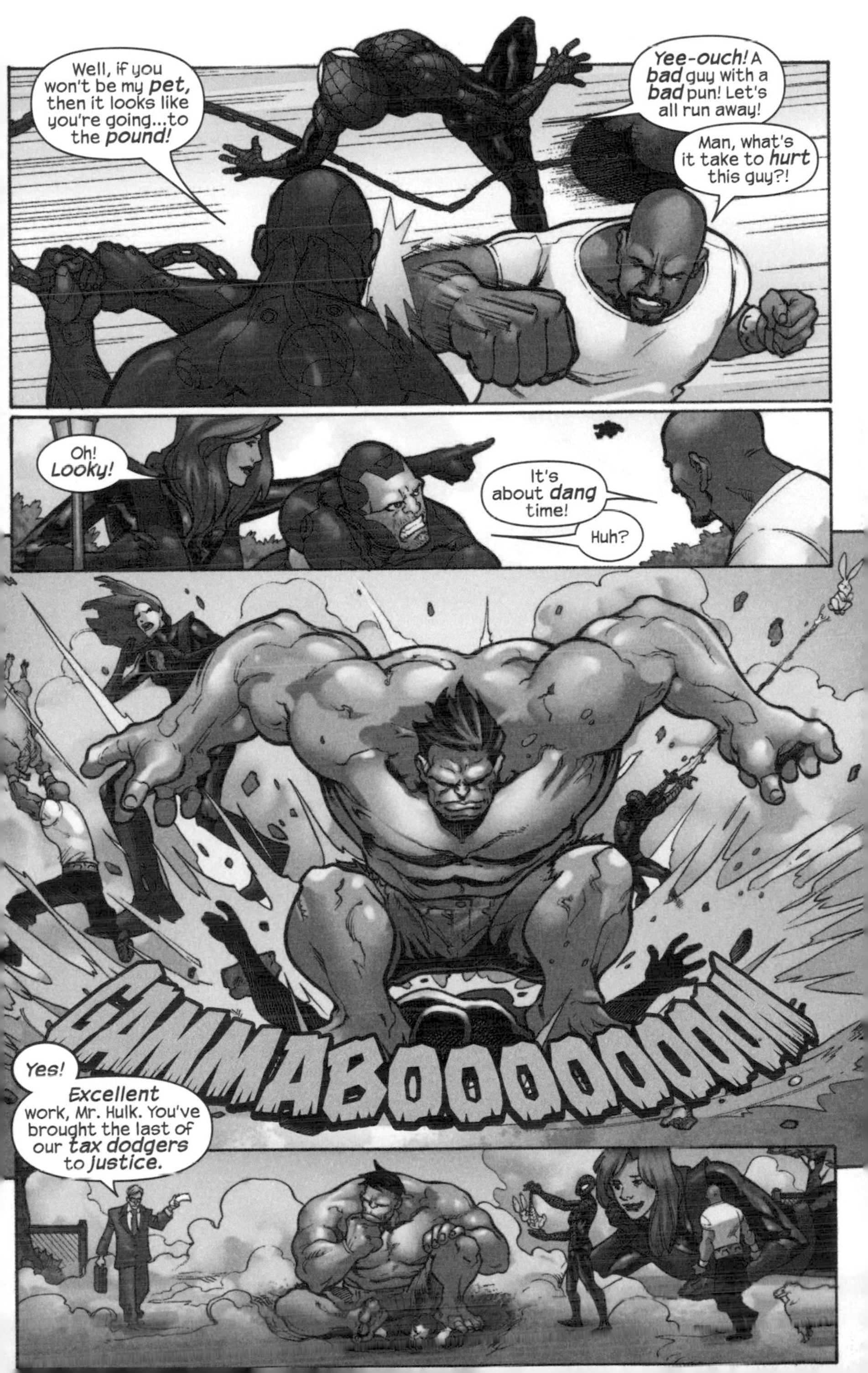

Well, if you won't be my *pet,* then it looks like you're going...to the *pound!*
Yee-ouch! A *bad* guy with a *bad* pun! Let's all run away!
Man, what's it take to *hurt* this guy?!
Oh! *Looky!*
It's about *dang* time!
Huh?
GAMMABOOOOOOOOM
Yes! *Excellent* work, Mr. Hulk. You've brought the last of our *tax dodgers* to *justice.*

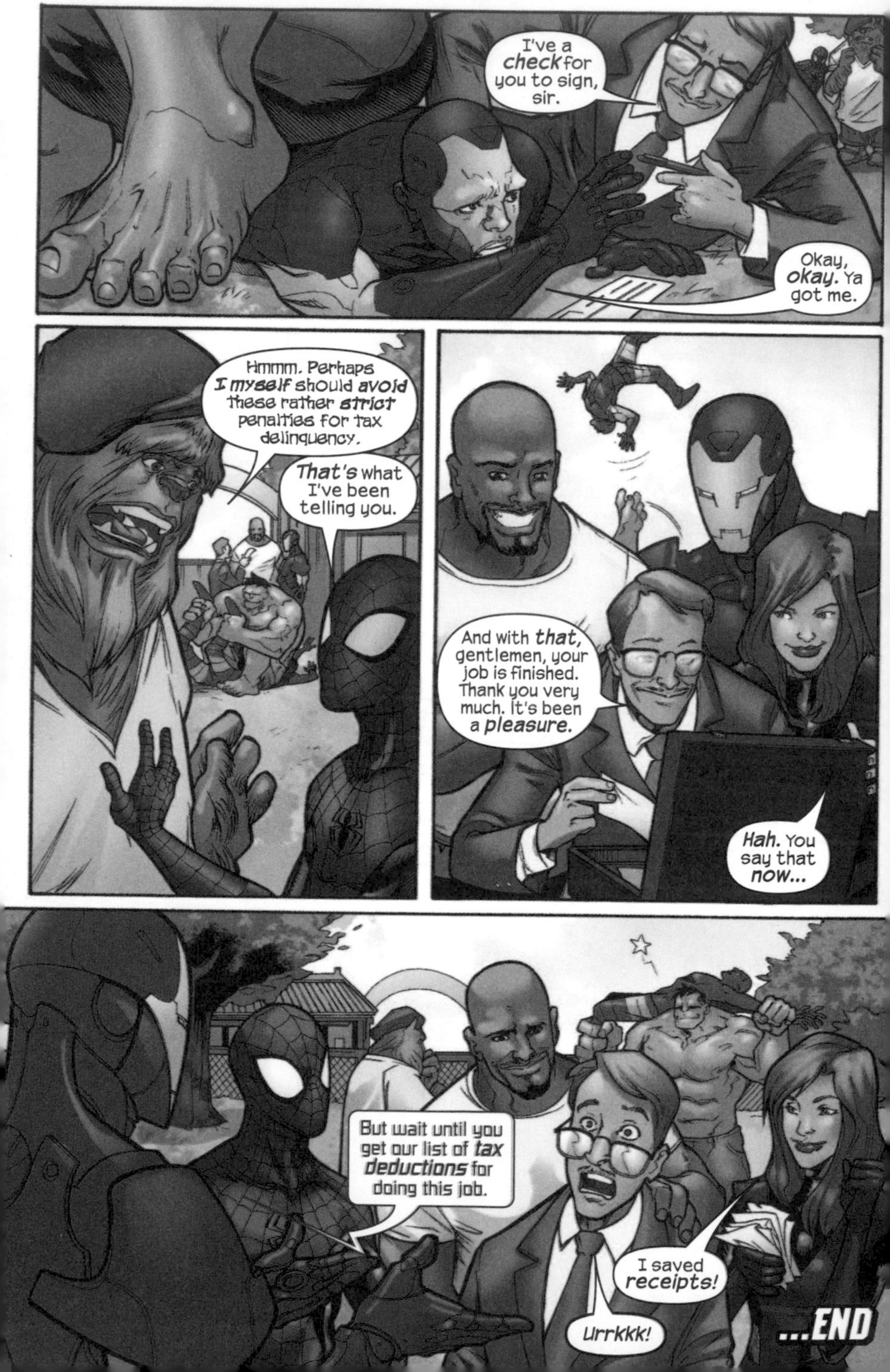
I've a check for you to sign, sir.
Okay, okay. Ya got me.
Hmmm. Perhaps I myself should avoid these rather strict penalties for tax delinquency.
That's what I've been telling you.
And with that, gentlemen, your job is finished. Thank you very much. It's been a pleasure.
Hah. You say that now...
But wait until you get our list of tax deductions for doing this job.
I saved receipts!
Urrkkk!
...END

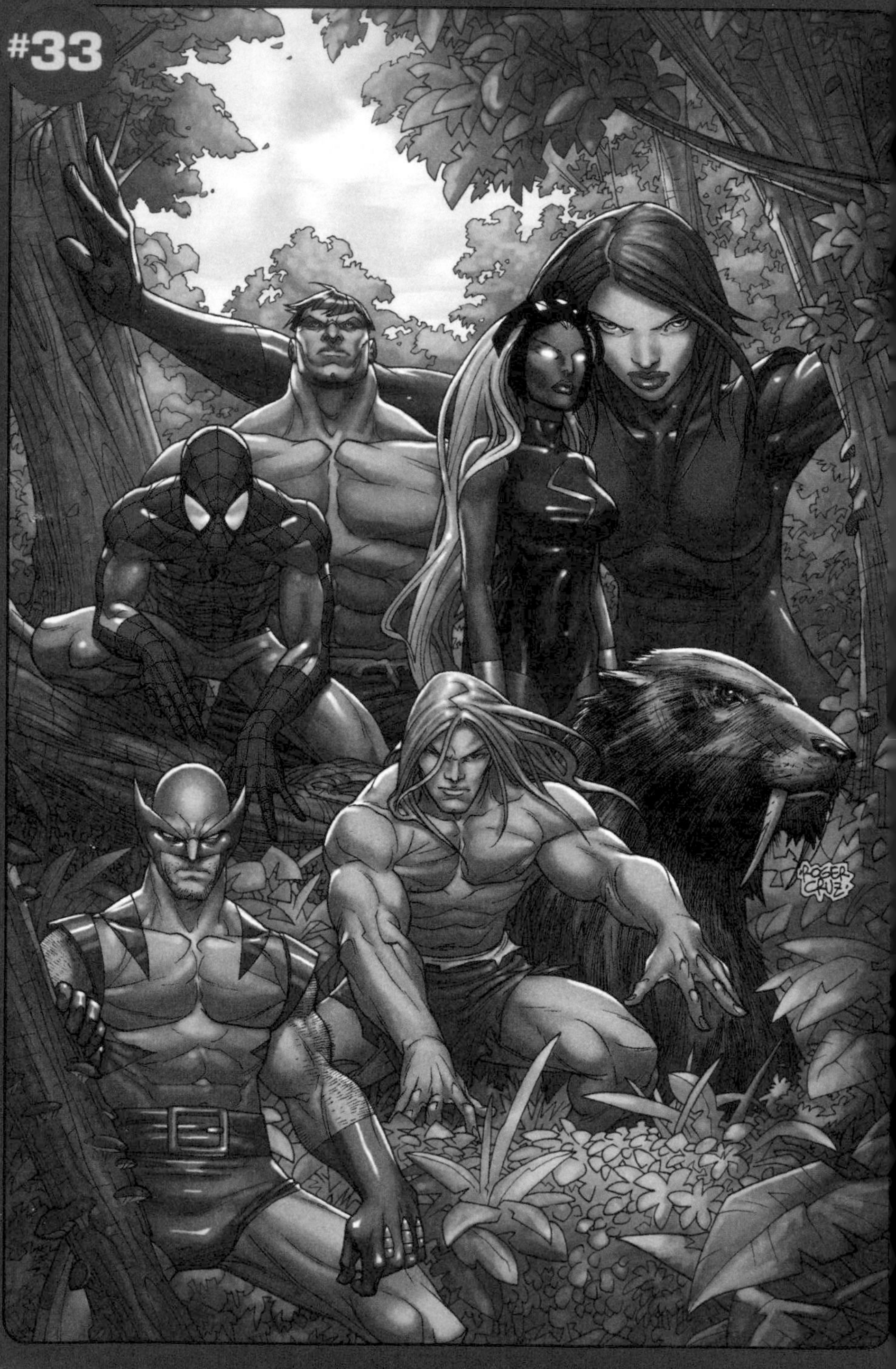
#33
ROGER CRUZ

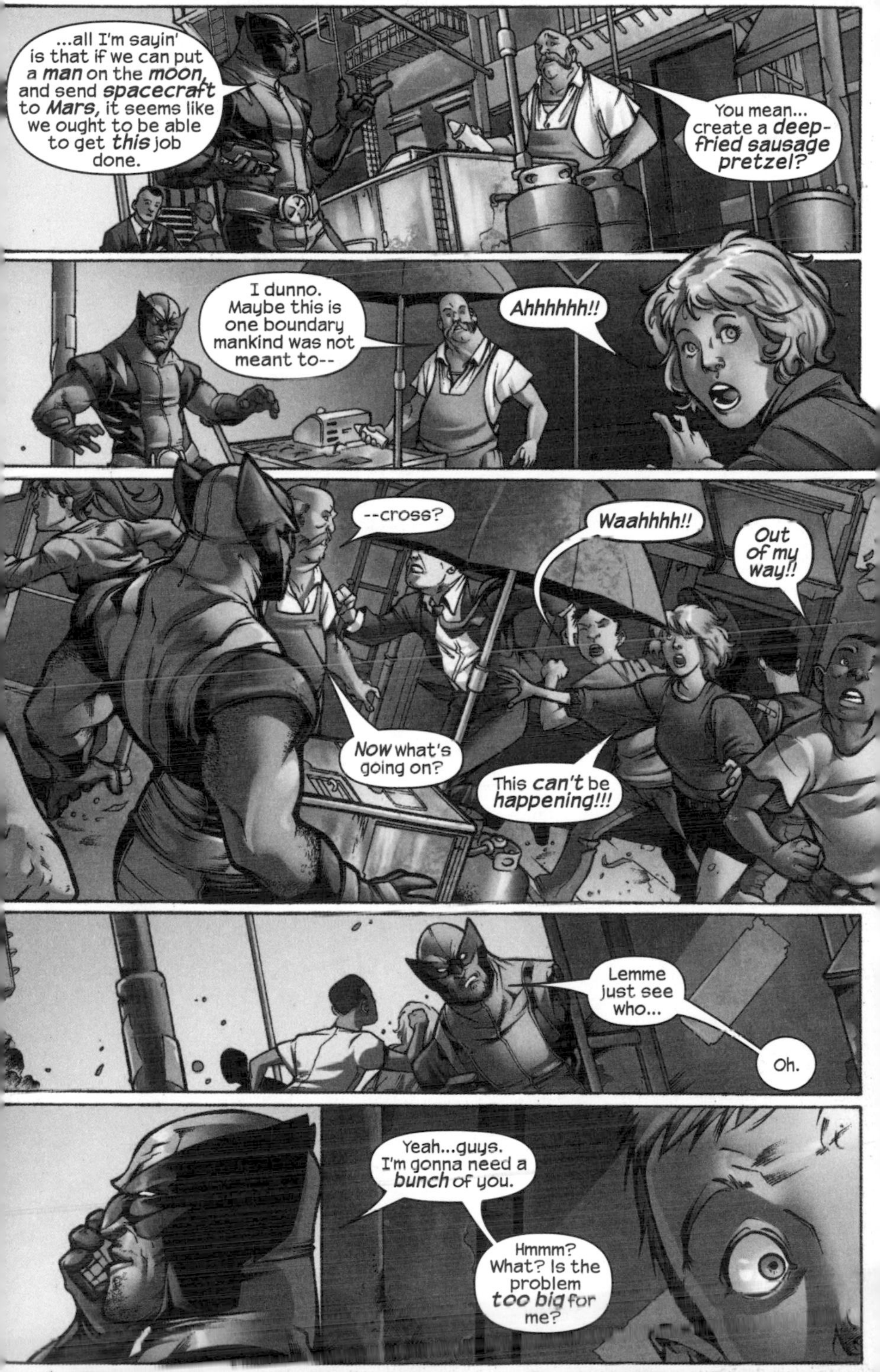
...all I'm sayin' is that if we can put a *man* on the *moon*, and send *spacecraft* to *Mars*, it seems like we ought to be able to get *this* job done.
You mean... create a *deep-fried sausage pretzel?*
I dunno. Maybe this is one boundary mankind was not meant to--
Ahhhhhh!!
--cross?
Waahhhh!!
Out of my way!!
Now what's going on?
This *can't* be *happening!!!*
Lemme just see who...
Oh.
Yeah...guys. I'm gonna need a *bunch* of you.
Hmmm? What? Is the problem *too big* for me?

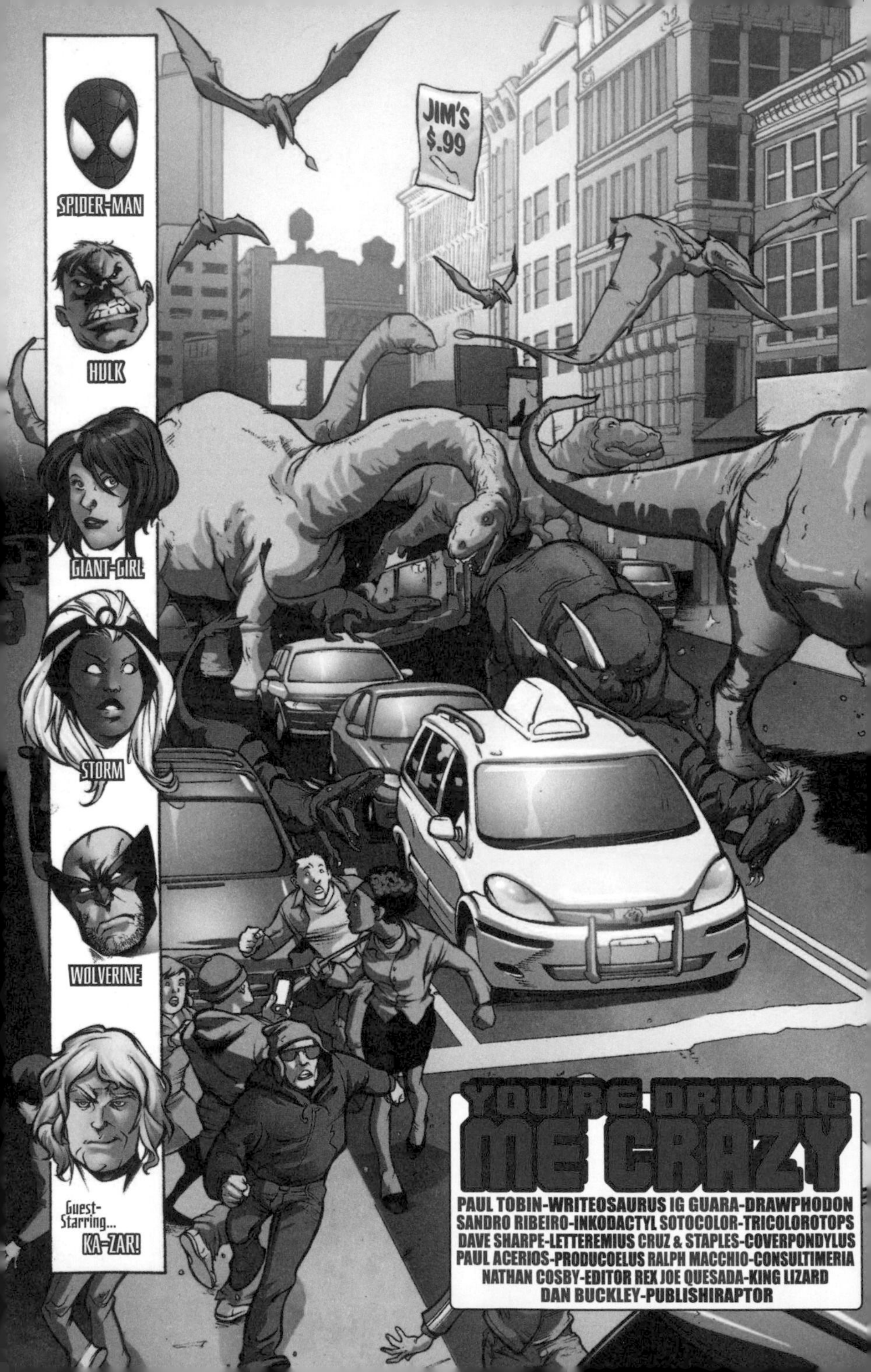

JIM'S $.99
SPIDER-MAN
HULK
GIANT-GIRL
STORM
WOLVERINE
Guest-Starring... KA-ZAR!
YOU'RE DRIVING ME CRAZY
PAUL TOBIN-WRITEOSAURUS IG GUARA-DRAWPHODON
SANDRO RIBEIRO-INKODACTYL SOTOCOLOR-TRICOLOROTOPS
DAVE SHARPE-LETTEREMIUS CRUZ & STAPLES-COVERPONDYLUS
PAUL ACERIOS-PRODUCOELUS RALPH MACCHIO-CONSULTIMERIA
NATHAN COSBY-EDITOR REX JOE QUESADA-KING LIZARD
DAN BUCKLEY-PUBLISHIRAPTOR

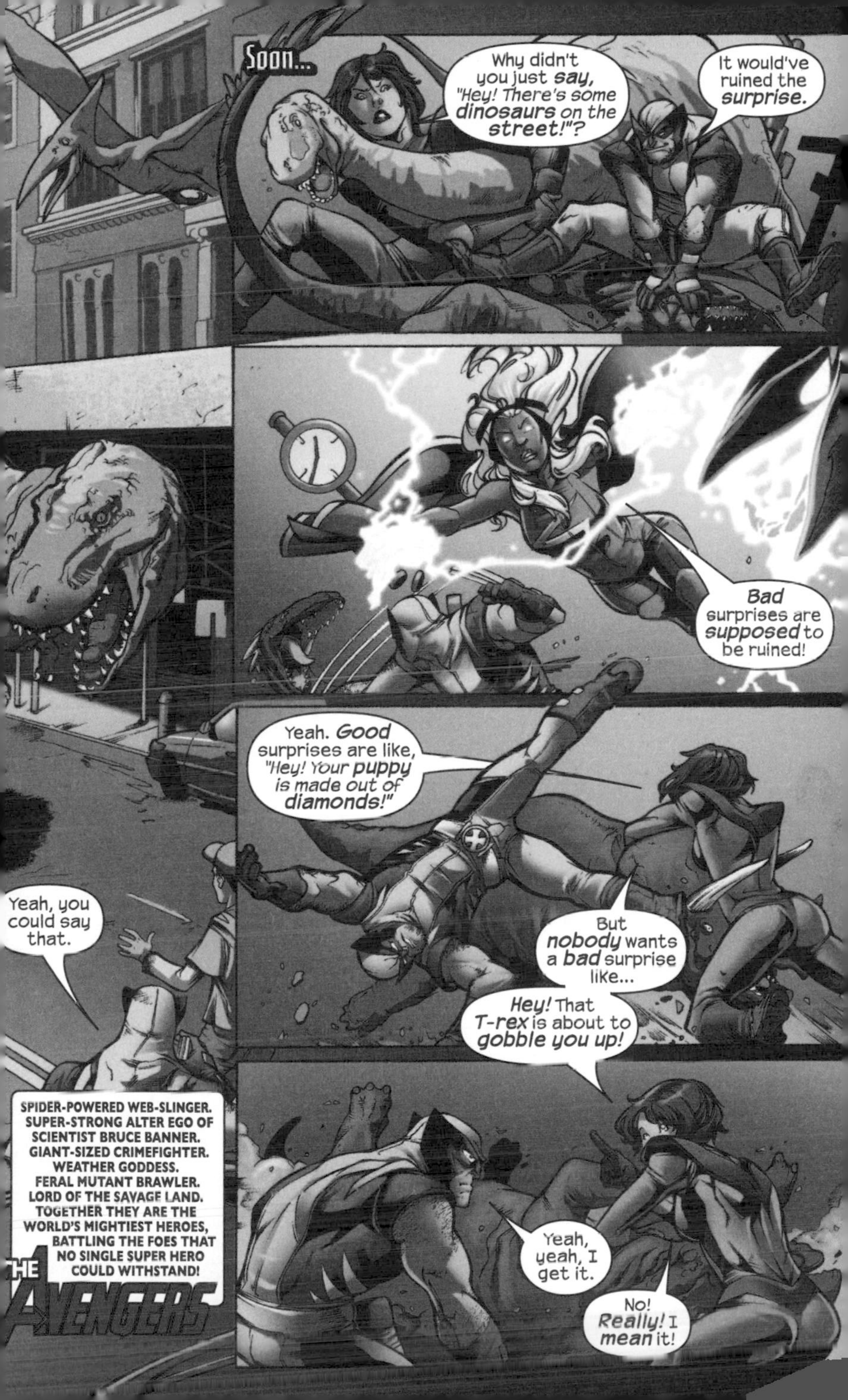
Soon...
Why didn't you just say, "Hey! There's some dinosaurs on the street!"?
It would've ruined the surprise.
Bad surprises are supposed to be ruined!
Yeah. Good surprises are like, "Hey! Your puppy is made out of diamonds!"
Yeah, you could say that.
But nobody wants a bad surprise like...
Hey! That T-rex is about to gobble you up!
SPIDER-POWERED WEB-SLINGER. SUPER-STRONG ALTER EGO OF SCIENTIST BRUCE BANNER. GIANT-SIZED CRIMEFIGHTER. WEATHER GODDESS. FERAL MUTANT BRAWLER. LORD OF THE SAVAGE LAND. TOGETHER THEY ARE THE WORLD'S MIGHTIEST HEROES, BATTLING THE FOES THAT NO SINGLE SUPER HERO COULD WITHSTAND!
THE AVENGERS
Yeah, yeah, I get it.
No! Really! I mean it!

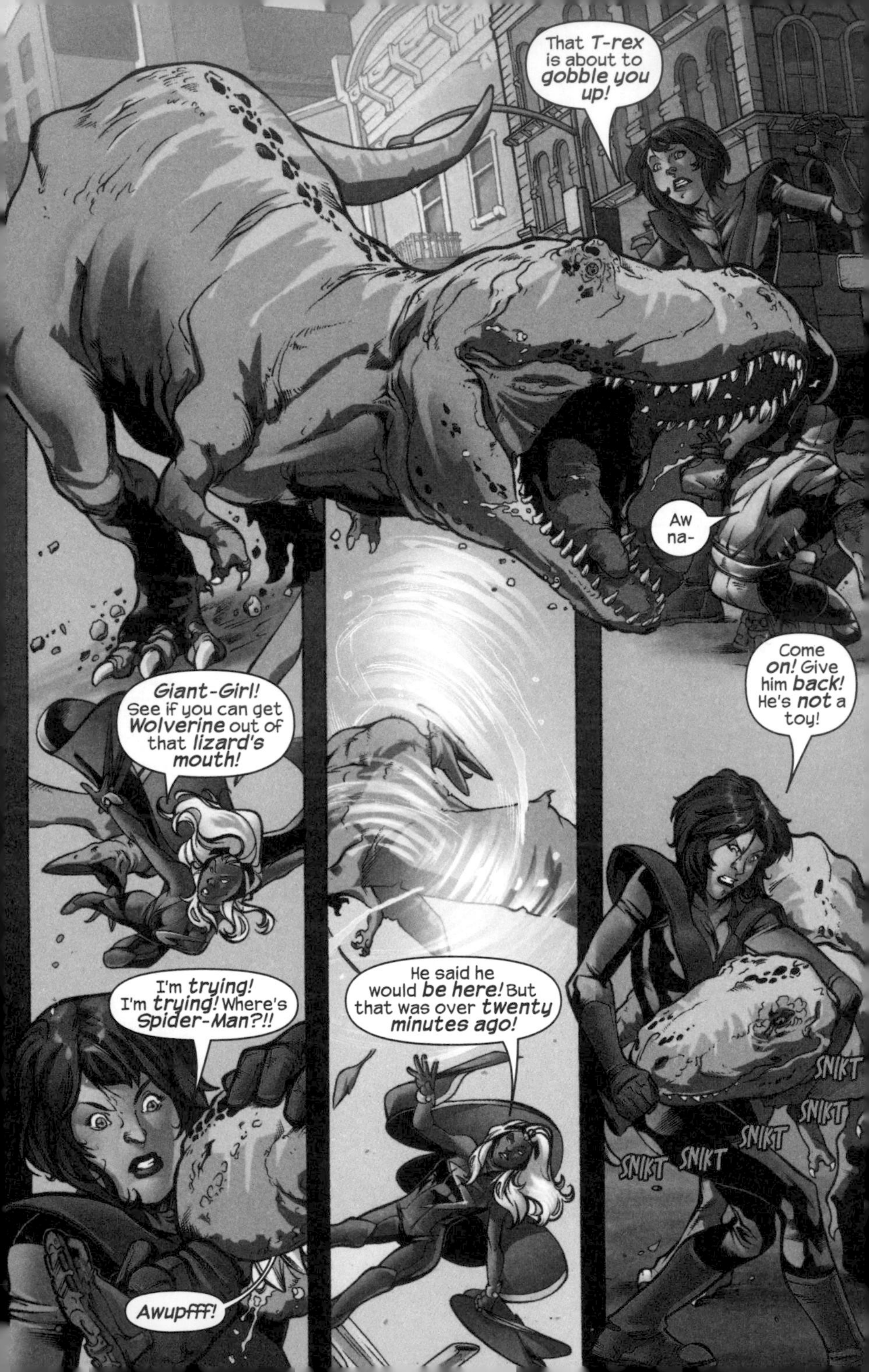
That T-rex is about to gobble you up!
Aw na-
Giant-Girl! See if you can get Wolverine out of that lizard's mouth!
I'm trying! I'm trying! Where's Spider-Man?!!
Awupfff!
He said he would be here! But that was over twenty minutes ago!
Come on! Give him back! He's not a toy!
SNIKT
SNIKT
SNIKT
SNIKT
SNIKT

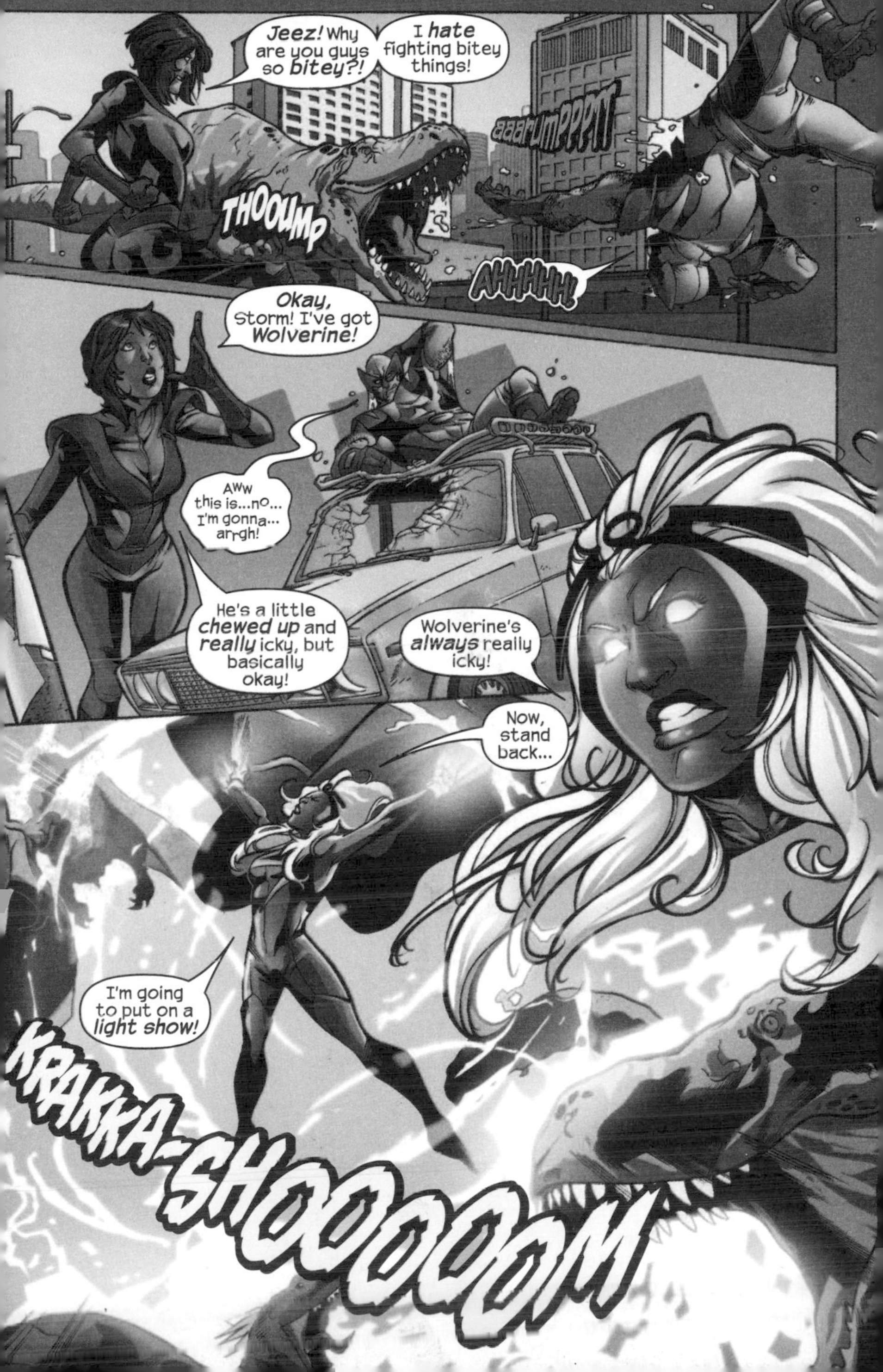
Jeez! Why are you guys so bitey?!
I hate fighting bitey things!
THOOUMP
aaarumPPPT
AHHHHH!
Okay, Storm! I've got Wolverine!
Aww this is...no... I'm gonna... arrgh!
He's a little chewed up and really icky, but basically okay!
Wolverine's always really icky!
Now, stand back...
I'm going to put on a light show!
KRAKKA-SHOOOOOM

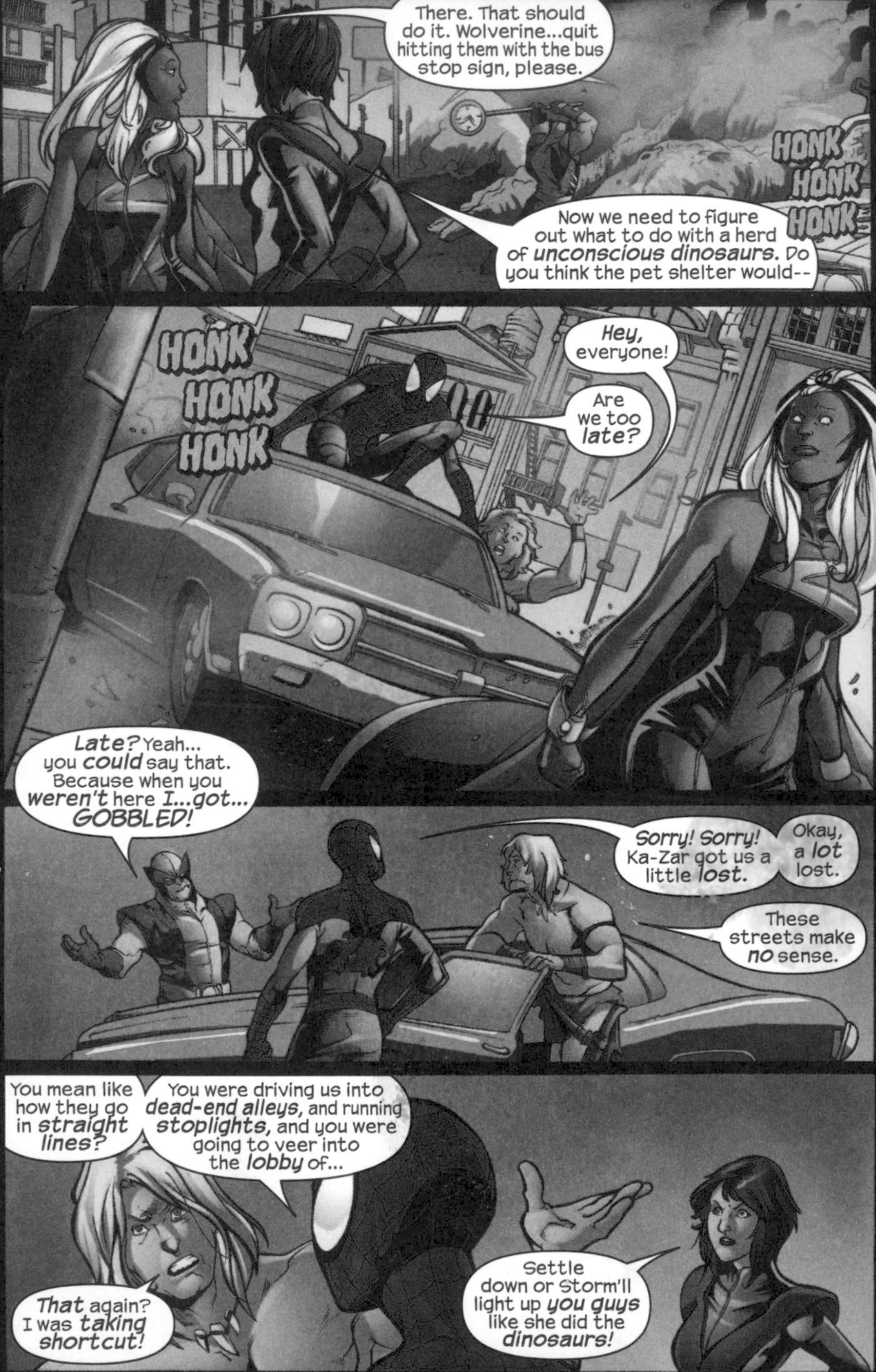
There. That should do it. Wolverine...quit hitting them with the bus stop sign, please.
HONK HONK HONK
Now we need to figure out what to do with a herd of *unconscious dinosaurs.* Do you think the pet shelter would--
HONK HONK HONK
Hey, everyone!
Are we too *late?*
Late? Yeah... you **could** say that. Because when you *weren't* here *I...got... GOBBLED!*
Sorry! Sorry! Ka-Zar got us a little *lost.*
Okay, a *lot* lost.
These streets make **NO** sense.
You mean like how they go in *straight lines?*
You were driving us into *dead-end alleys,* and running *stoplights,* and you were going to veer into the *lobby* of...
That again? I was *taking shortcut!*
Settle down or Storm'll light up *you guys* like she did the *dinosaurs!*

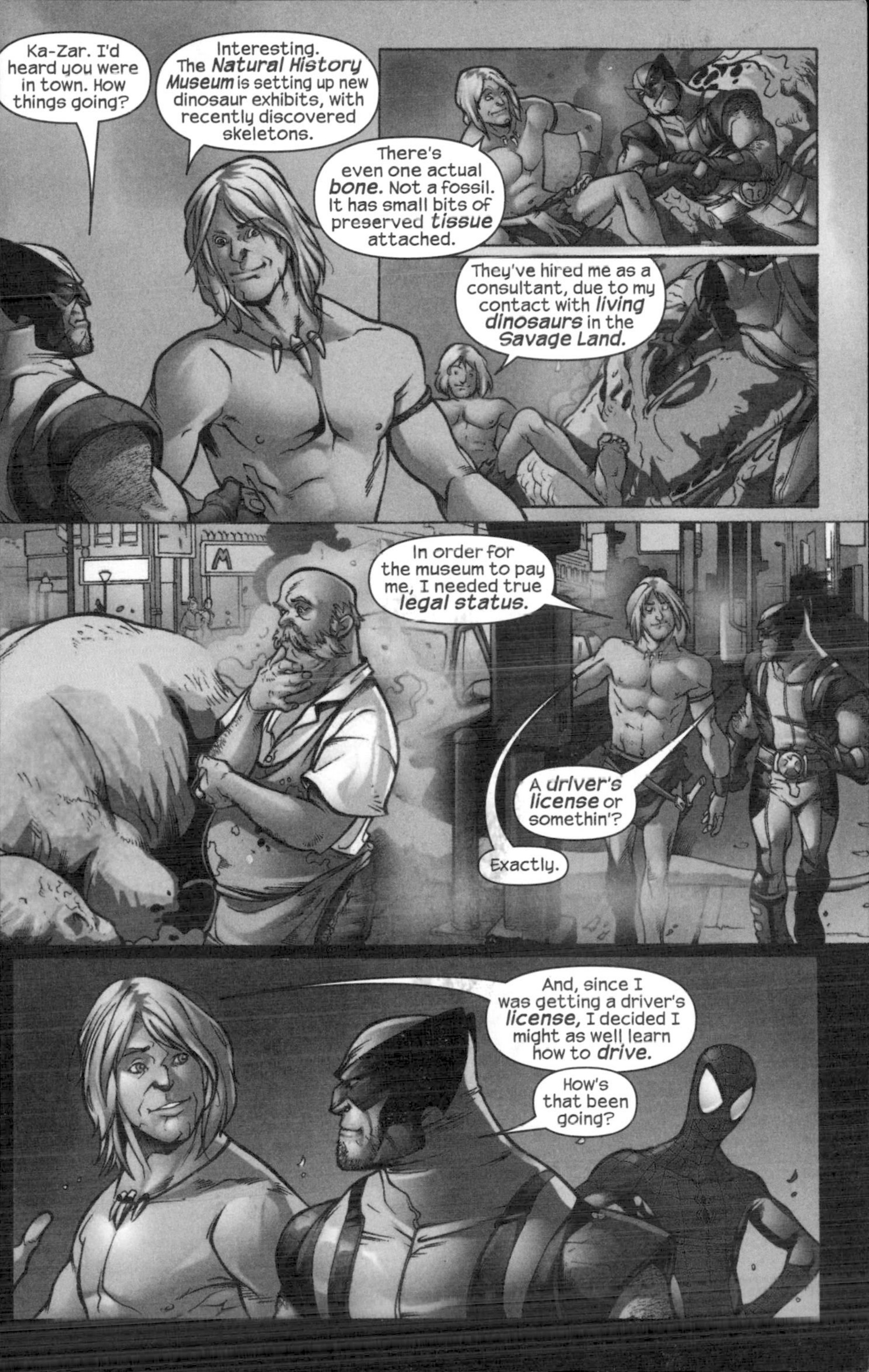
Ka-Zar. I'd heard you were in town. How things going?
Interesting. The *Natural History Museum* is setting up new dinosaur exhibits, with recently discovered skeletons.
There's even one actual *bone.* Not a fossil. It has small bits of preserved *tissue* attached.
They've hired me as a consultant, due to my contact with *living dinosaurs* in the *Savage Land.*
In order for the museum to pay me, I needed true *legal status.*
A *driver's license* or somethin'?
Exactly.
And, since I was getting a driver's *license,* I decided I might as well learn how to *drive.*
How's that been going?

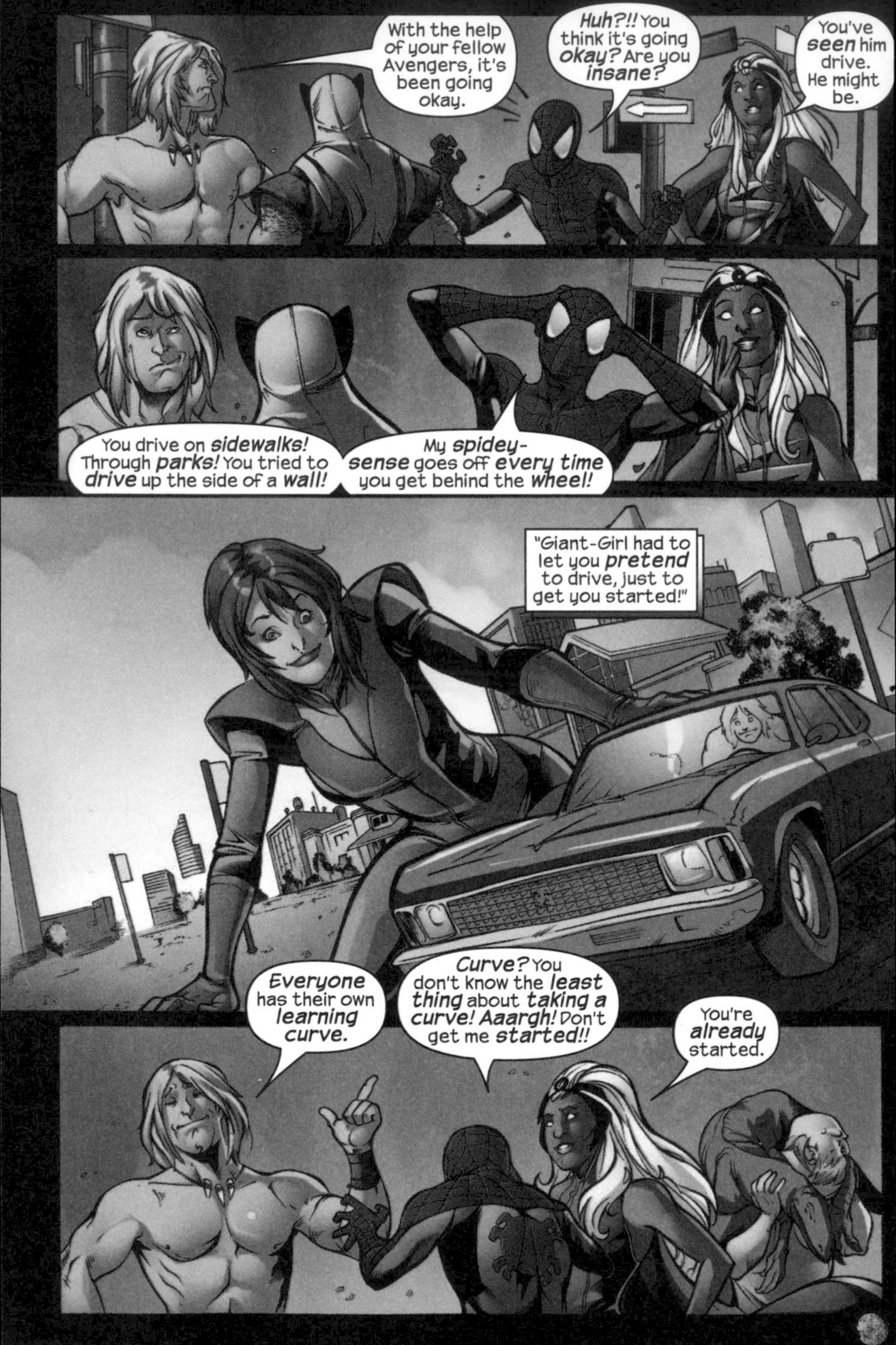
With the help of your fellow Avengers, it's been going okay.
Huh?!! You think it's going okay? Are you insane?
You've seen him drive. He might be.
You drive on sidewalks! Through parks! You tried to drive up the side of a wall!
My spidey-sense goes off every time you get behind the wheel!
"Giant-Girl had to let you pretend to drive, just to get you started!"
Everyone has their own learning curve.
Curve? You don't know the least thing about taking a curve! Aaargh! Don't get me started!!
You're already started.

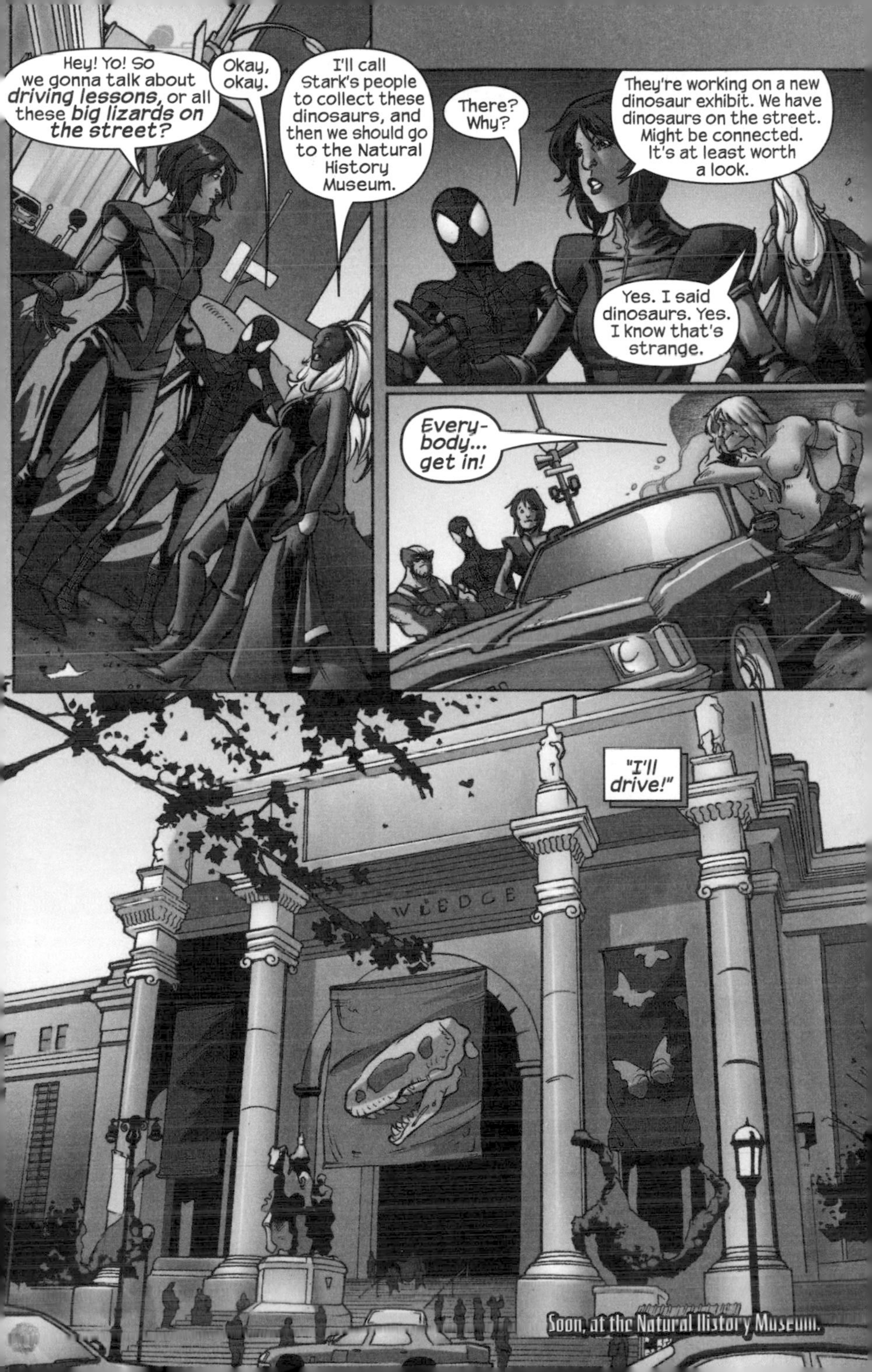
Hey! Yo! So we gonna talk about driving lessons, or all these big lizards on the street?
Okay, okay.
I'll call Stark's people to collect these dinosaurs, and then we should go to the Natural History Museum.
There? Why?
They're working on a new dinosaur exhibit. We have dinosaurs on the street. Might be connected. It's at least worth a look.
Yes. I said dinosaurs. Yes. I know that's strange.
Every-body... get in!
"I'll drive!"
Soon, at the Natural History Museum.

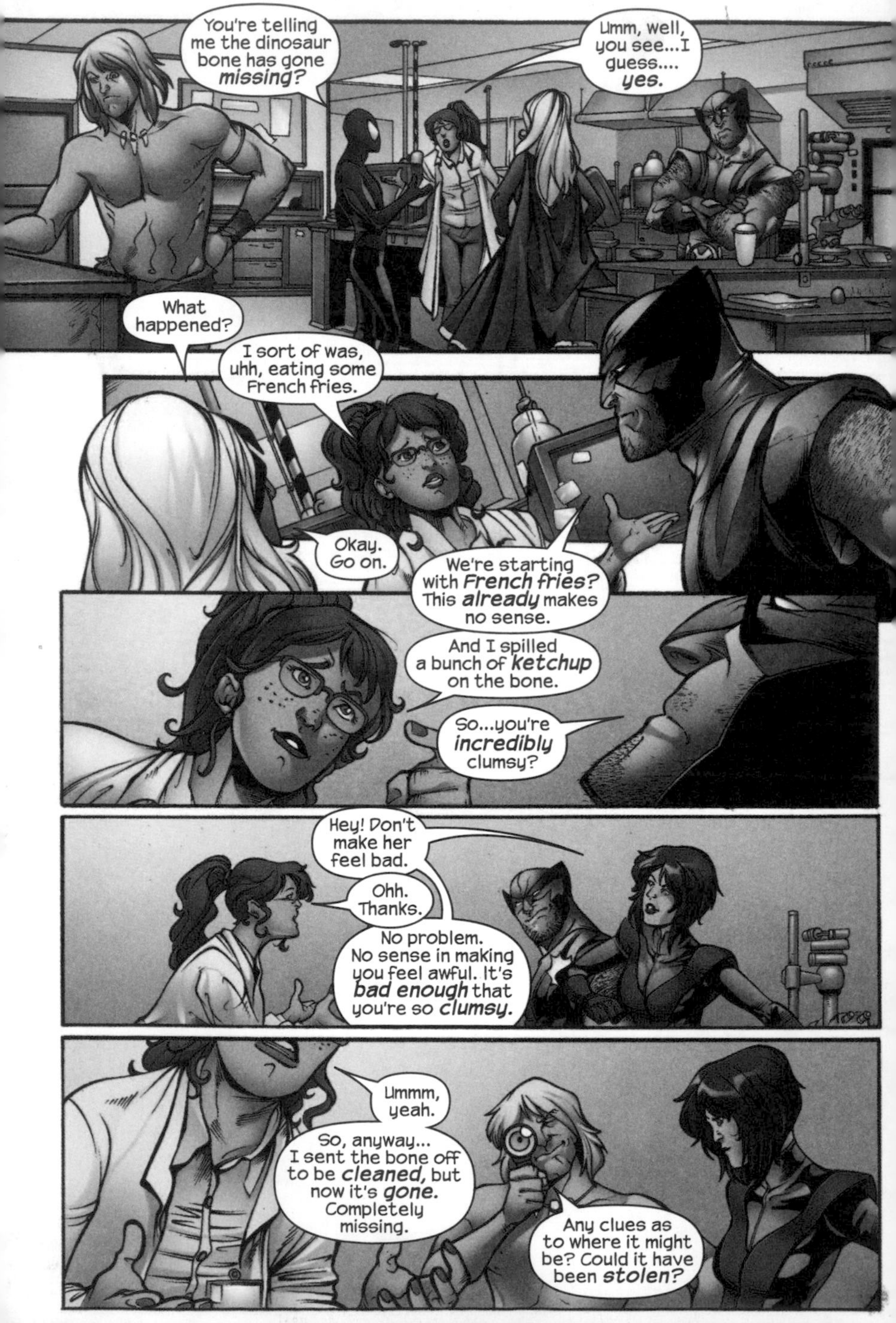
You're telling me the dinosaur bone has gone *missing?*
Umm, well, you see...I guess.... *yes.*
What happened?
I sort of was, uhh, eating some French fries.
Okay. Go on.
We're starting with *French fries?* This *already* makes no sense.
And I spilled a bunch of *ketchup* on the bone.
So...you're *incredibly* clumsy?
Hey! Don't make her feel bad.
Ohh. Thanks.
No problem. No sense in making you feel awful. It's *bad enough* that you're so *clumsy.*
Ummm, yeah.
So, anyway... I sent the bone off to be *cleaned,* but now it's *gone.* Completely missing.
Any clues as to where it might be? Could it have been *stolen?*

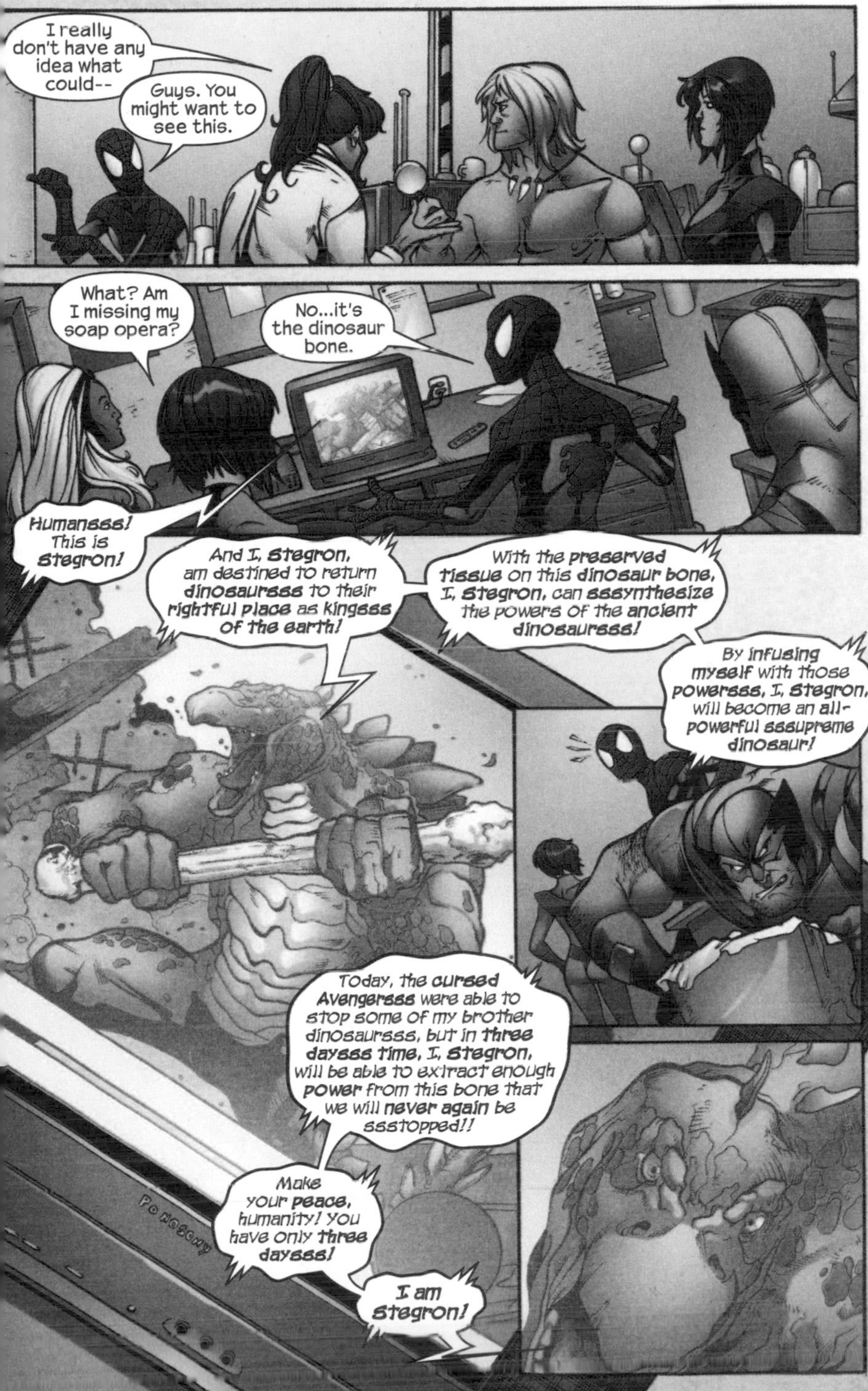

I really don't have any idea what could--
Guys. You might want to see this.
What? Am I missing my soap opera?
No...it's the dinosaur bone.
Humansss! This is Stegron!
And I, Stegron, am destined to return dinosaursss to their rightful place as kingsss of the earth!
With the preserved tissue on this dinosaur bone, I, Stegron, can sssynthesize the powers of the ancient dinosaursss!
By infusing myself with those powersss, I, Stegron, will become an all-powerful sssupreme dinosaur!
Today, the cursed Avengersss were able to stop some of my brother dinosaursss, but in three daysss time, I, Stegron, will be able to extract enough power from this bone that we will never again be ssstopped!!
Make your peace, humanity! You have only three daysss!
I am Stegron!

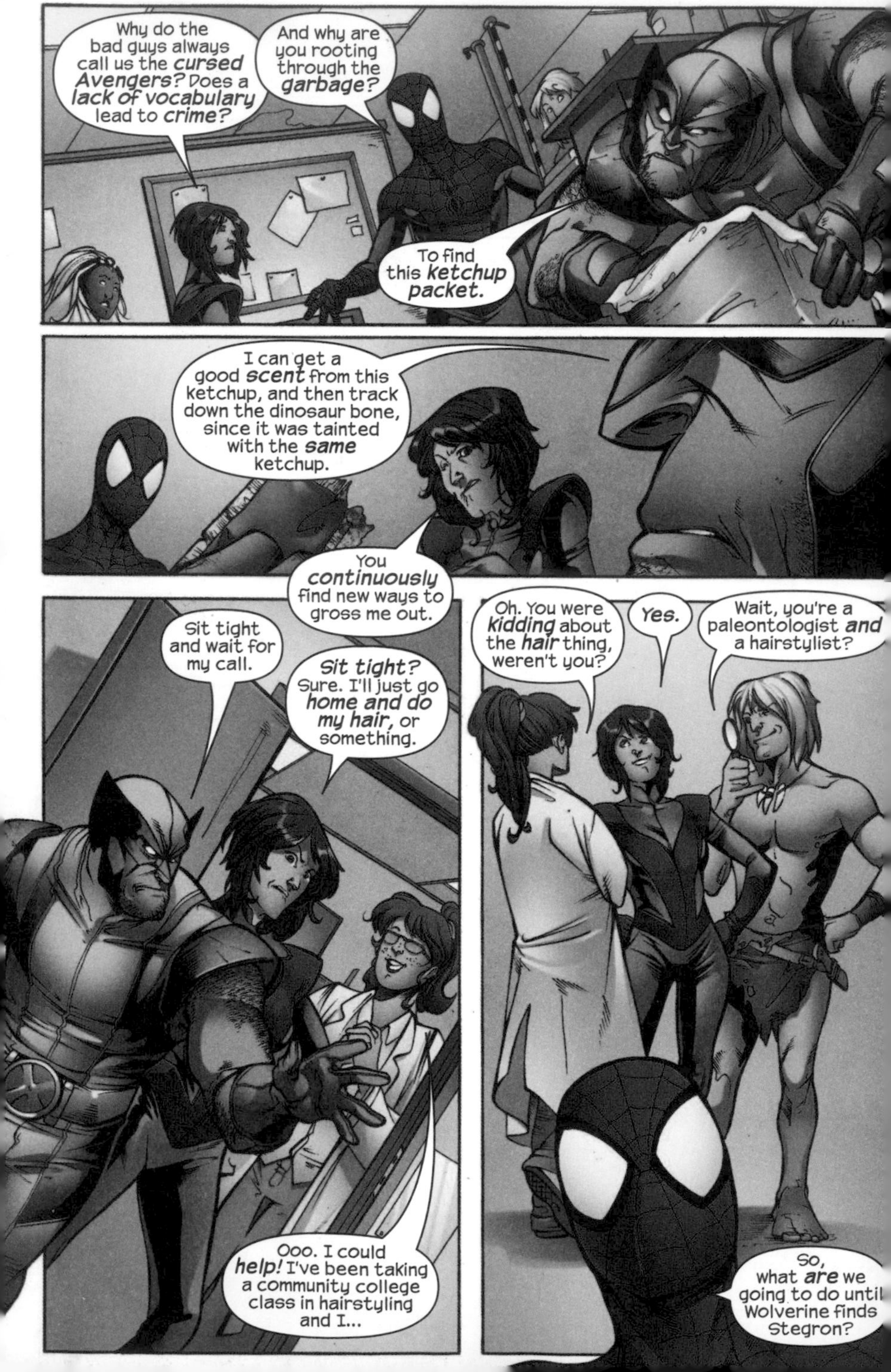

Why do the bad guys always call us the *cursed Avengers?* Does a *lack of vocabulary* lead to *crime?*
And why are you rooting through the *garbage?*
To find this *ketchup packet.*
I can get a good *scent* from this ketchup, and then track down the dinosaur bone, since it was tainted with the *same* ketchup.
You *continuously* find new ways to gross me out.
Sit tight and wait for my call.
Sit tight? Sure. I'll just go *home and do my hair,* or something.
Ooo. I could *help!* I've been taking a community college class in hairstyling and I...
Oh. You were *kidding* about the *hair* thing, weren't you?
Yes.
Wait, you're a paleontologist *and* a hairstylist?
So, what *are* we going to do until Wolverine finds Stegron?

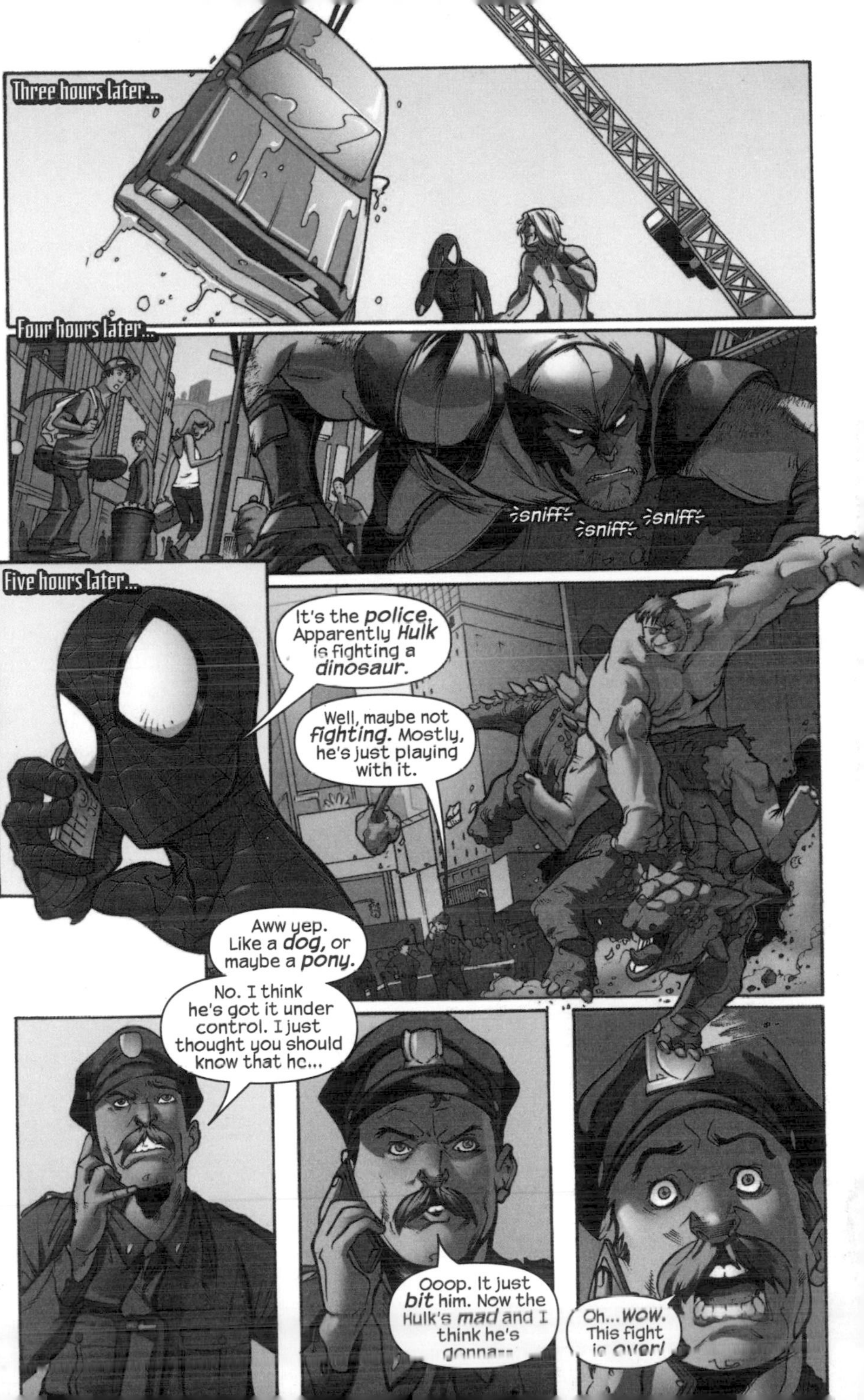

Three hours later...
Four hours later...
sniff
sniff
sniff
Five hours later...
It's the police. Apparently Hulk is fighting a dinosaur.
Well, maybe not fighting. Mostly, he's just playing with it.
Aww yep. Like a dog, or maybe a pony.
No. I think he's got it under control. I just thought you should know that he...
Ooop. It just bit him. Now the Hulk's mad and I think he's gonna--
Oh... WOW. This fight is over!

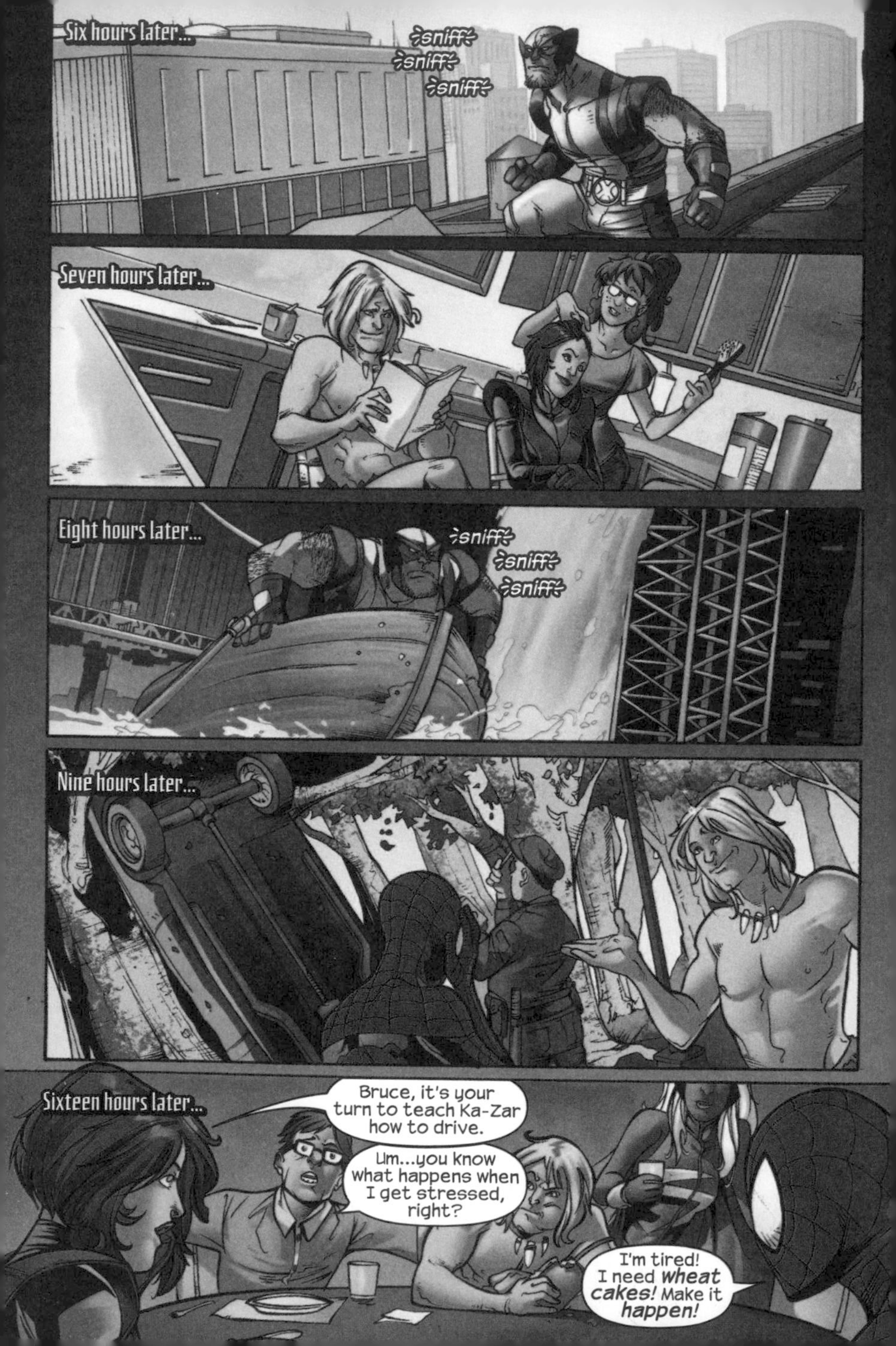
Six hours later...
sniff
sniff
sniff
Seven hours later...
Eight hours later...
sniff
sniff
sniff
Nine hours later...
Sixteen hours later...
Bruce, it's your turn to teach Ka-Zar how to drive.
Um...you know what happens when I get stressed, right?
I'm tired! I need *wheat cakes!* Make it *happen!*

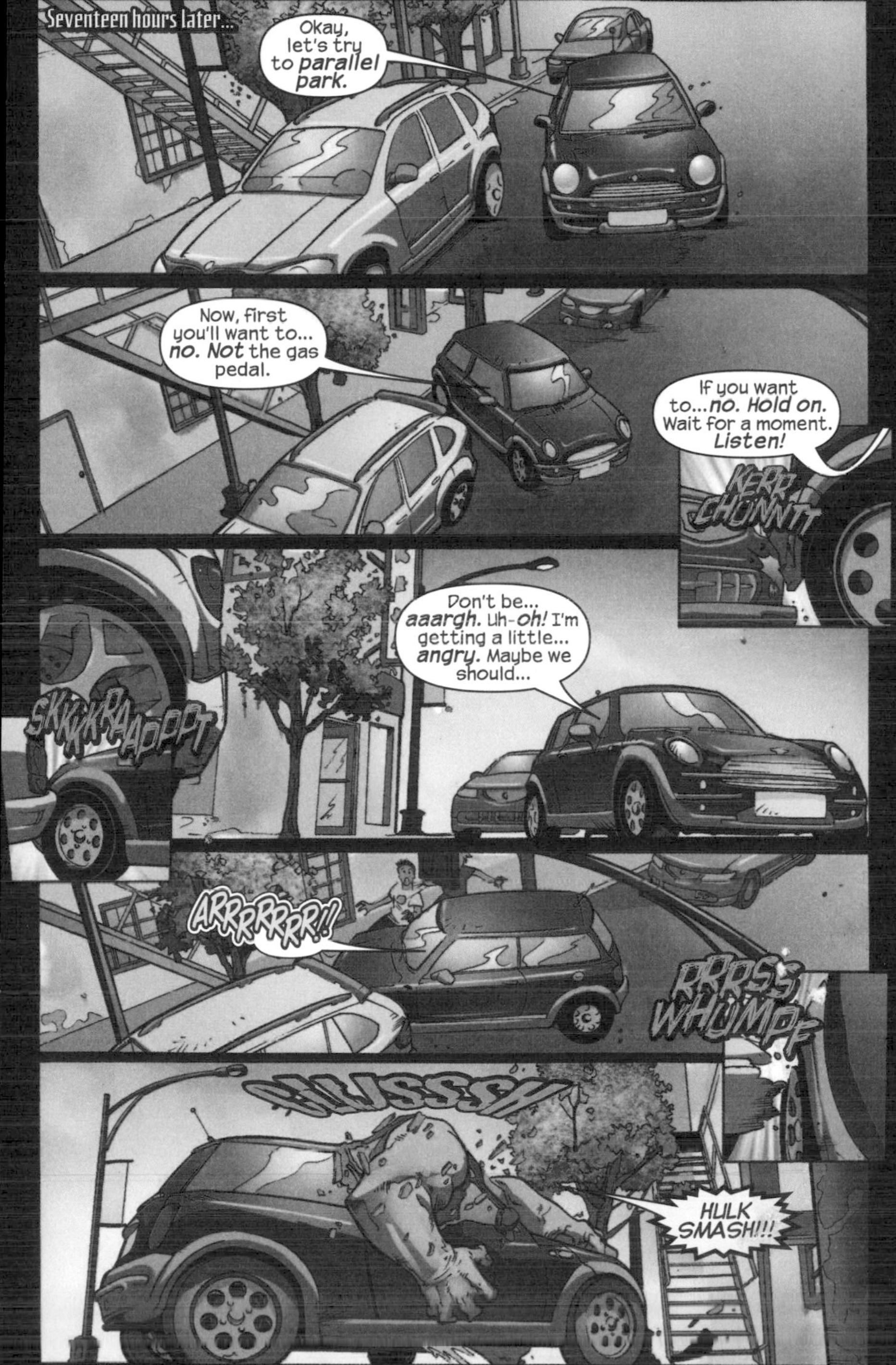
Seventeen hours later...
Okay, let's try to parallel park.
Now, first you'll want to... no. Not the gas pedal.
If you want to...no. Hold on. Wait for a moment. Listen!
KERR CHUNNTT
Don't be... aaargh. Uh-oh! I'm getting a little... angry. Maybe we should...
SKKKKRAADPPT
ARRRRRRR!!
RRRSS WHUMPF
HULK SMASH!!!

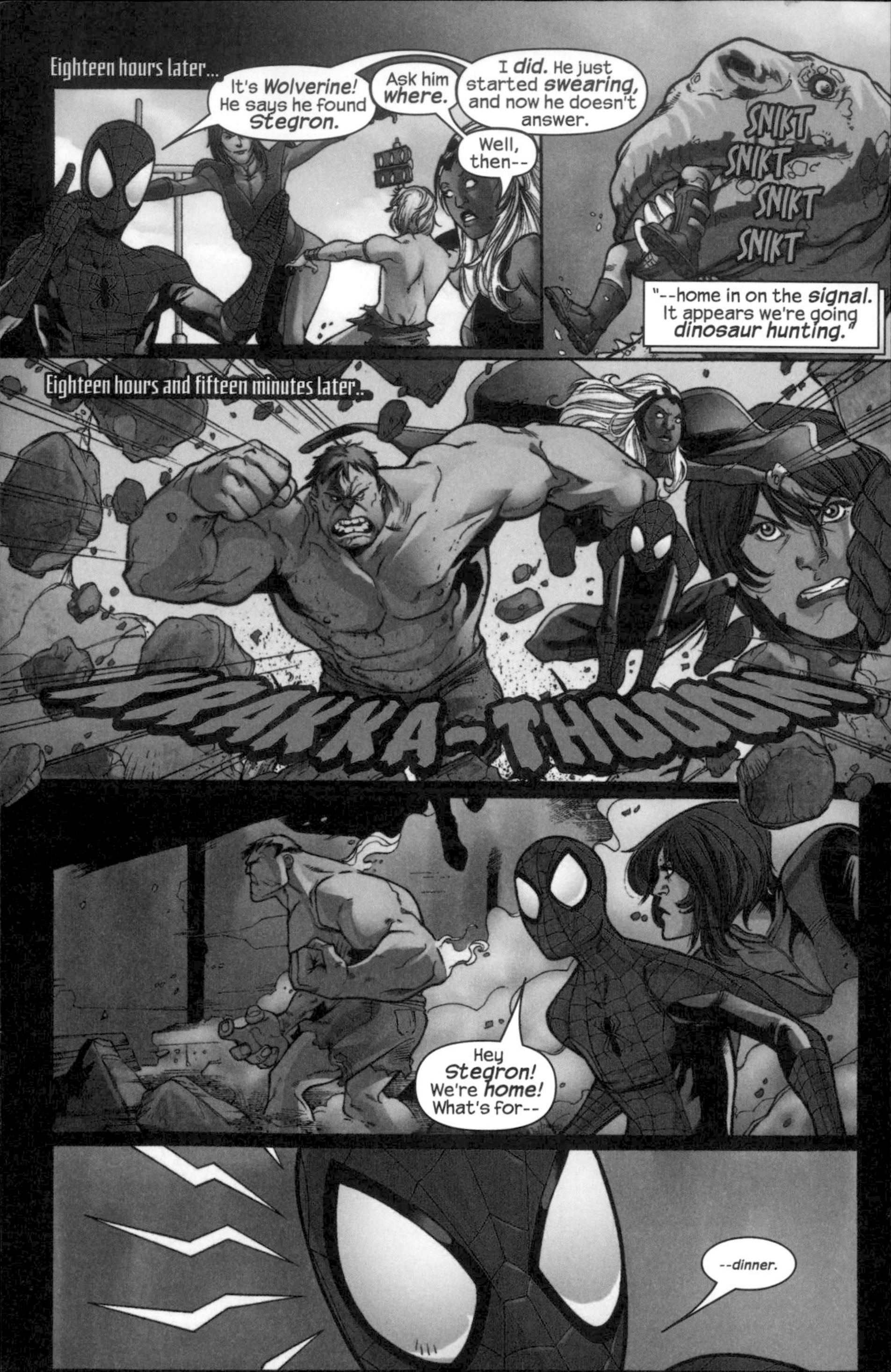
Eighteen hours later...
It's Wolverine! He says he found Stegron.
Ask him where.
I did. He just started swearing, and now he doesn't answer.
Well, then--
SNIKT SNIKT SNIKT SNIKT
"--home in on the signal. It appears we're going dinosaur hunting."
Eighteen hours and fifteen minutes later..
KRAKKA-THOOOM
Hey Stegron! We're home! What's for--
--dinner.

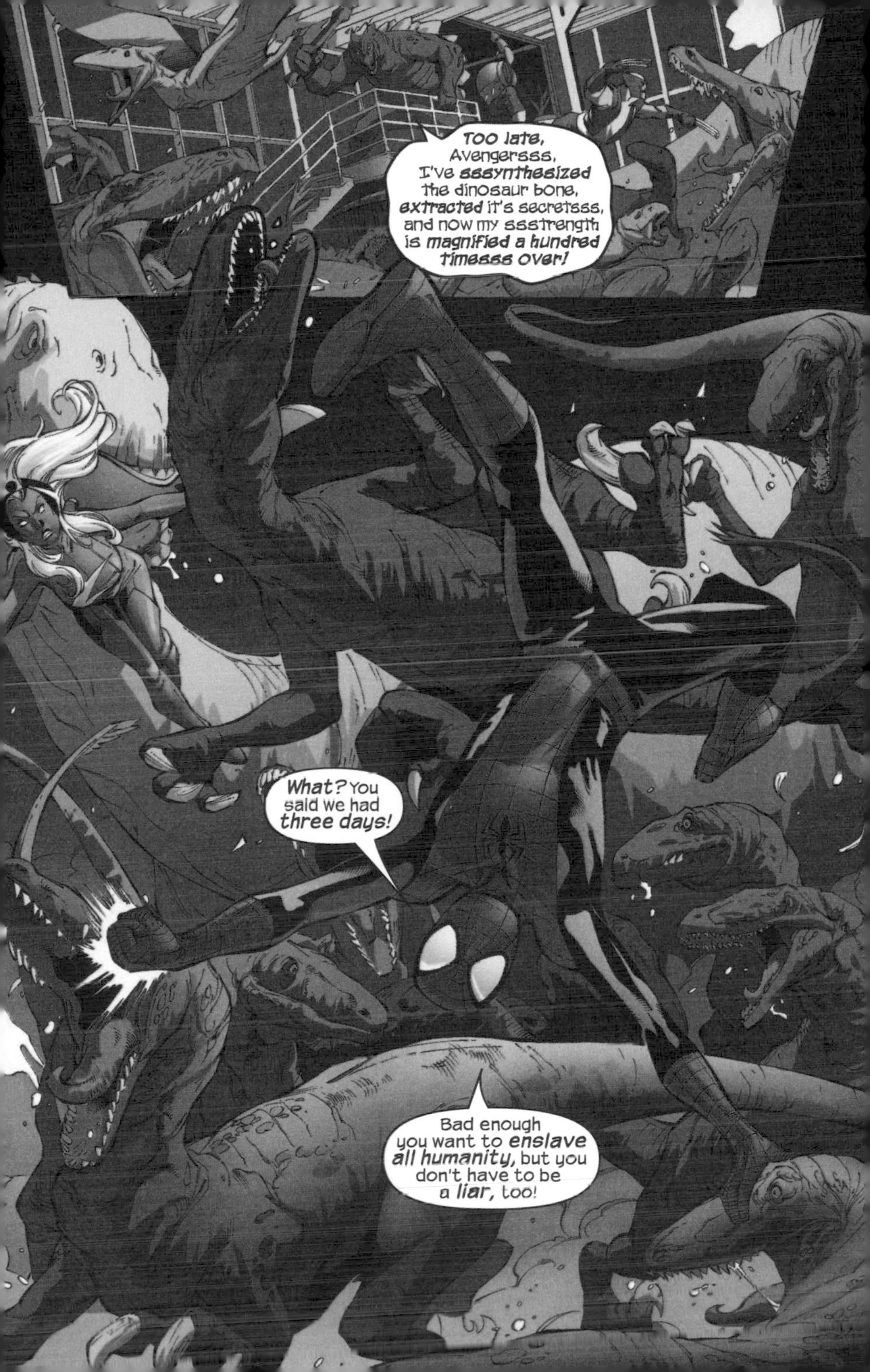
TOO late, Avengersss, I've sssynthesized the dinosaur bone, extracted it's secretsss, and now my ssstrength is magnified a hundred timesss over!
What? You said we had three days!
Bad enough you want to enslave all humanity, but you don't have to be a liar, too!

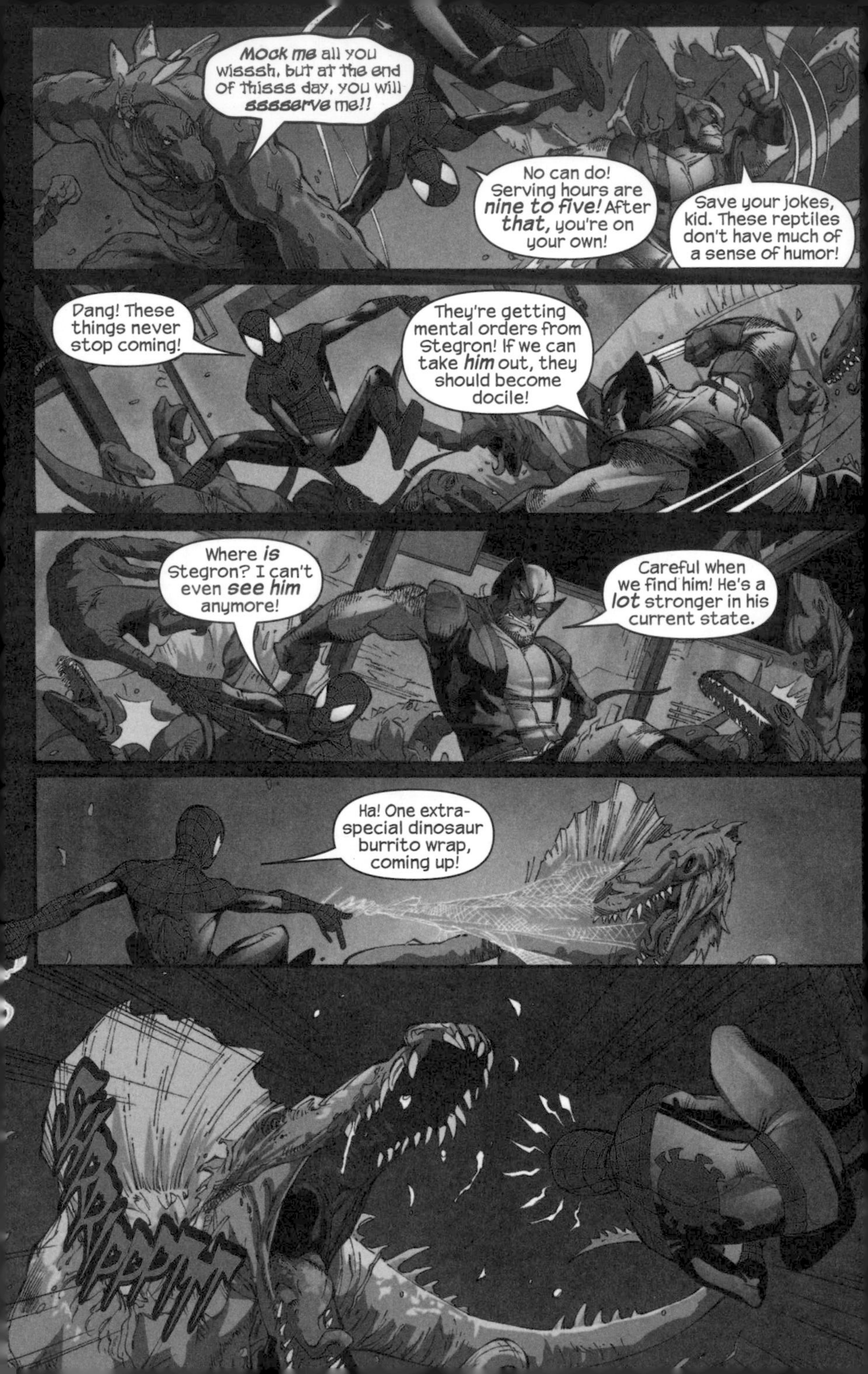

Mock me all you wisssh, but at the end of thisss day, you will ssssserve me!!
No can do! Serving hours are nine to five! After that, you're on your own!
Save your jokes, kid. These reptiles don't have much of a sense of humor!
Dang! These things never stop coming!
They're getting mental orders from Stegron! If we can take him out, they should become docile!
Where is Stegron? I can't even see him anymore!
Careful when we find him! He's a lot stronger in his current state.
Ha! One extra-special dinosaur burrito wrap, coming up!
SHRRIPPPPT

Yikes yikes yikes! Mommy! Look what followed me home!
Can we... GET RID OF HIM??!!
My lightning is not stopping them this time! Stegron must have increased their powers along with his own!!
Hulk! We could use some help here!
You're the only one worthy of my notice, but our numbers will overwhelm you!
Scaly man is strong!!
Why isn't Ka-Zar here?!! Ain't he our dinosaur expert?!
He was out shopping for a used car when we called him! Said he'd drive right on over!
He's driving? Oh great! He's probably in Idaho by now!

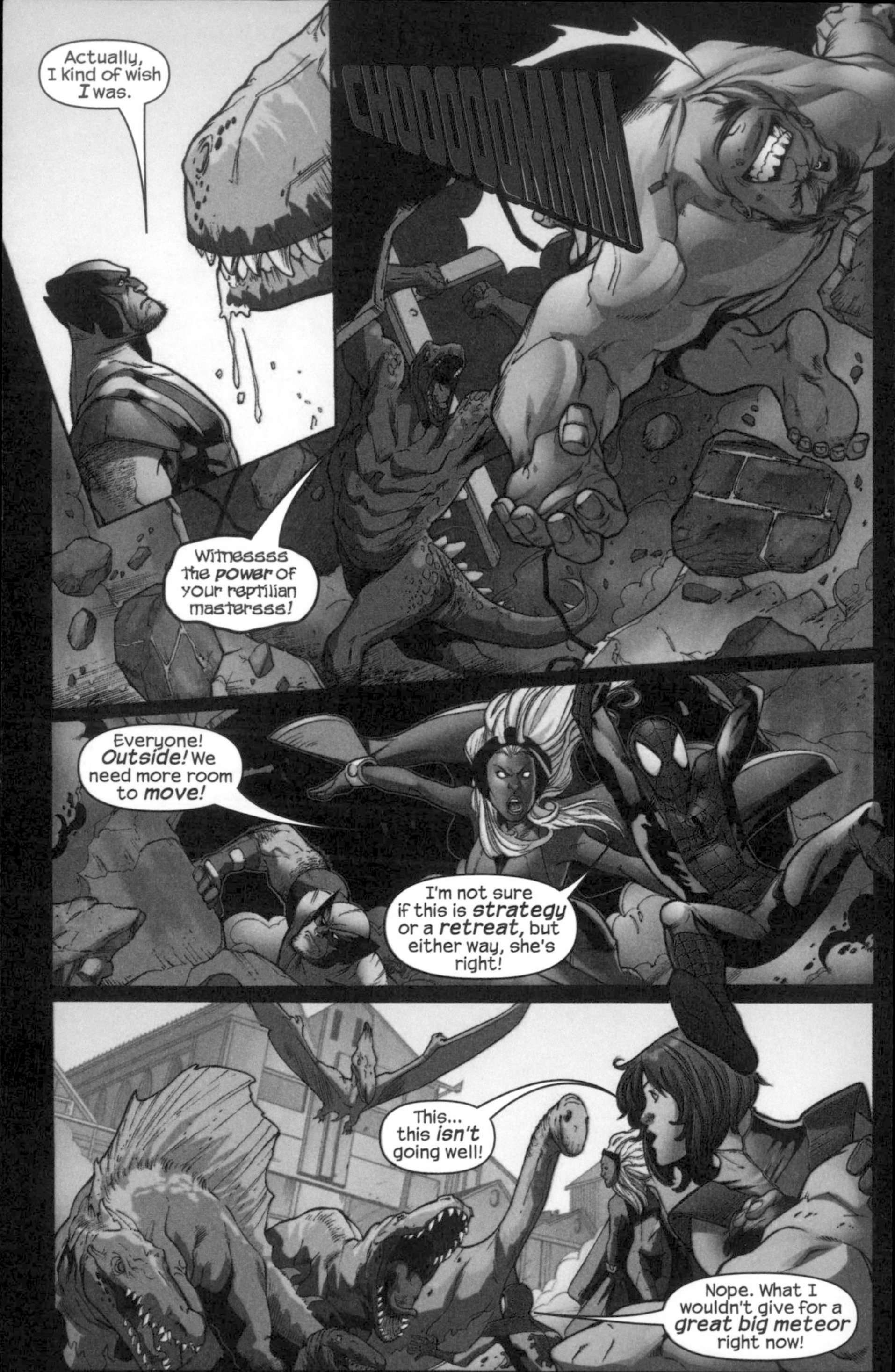
Actually, I kind of wish I was.
CHOOOOOMMM
Witnessss the power of your reptilian mastersss!
Everyone! Outside! We need more room to move!
I'm not sure if this is strategy or a retreat, but either way, she's right!
This... this isn't going well!
Nope. What I wouldn't give for a great big meteor right now!

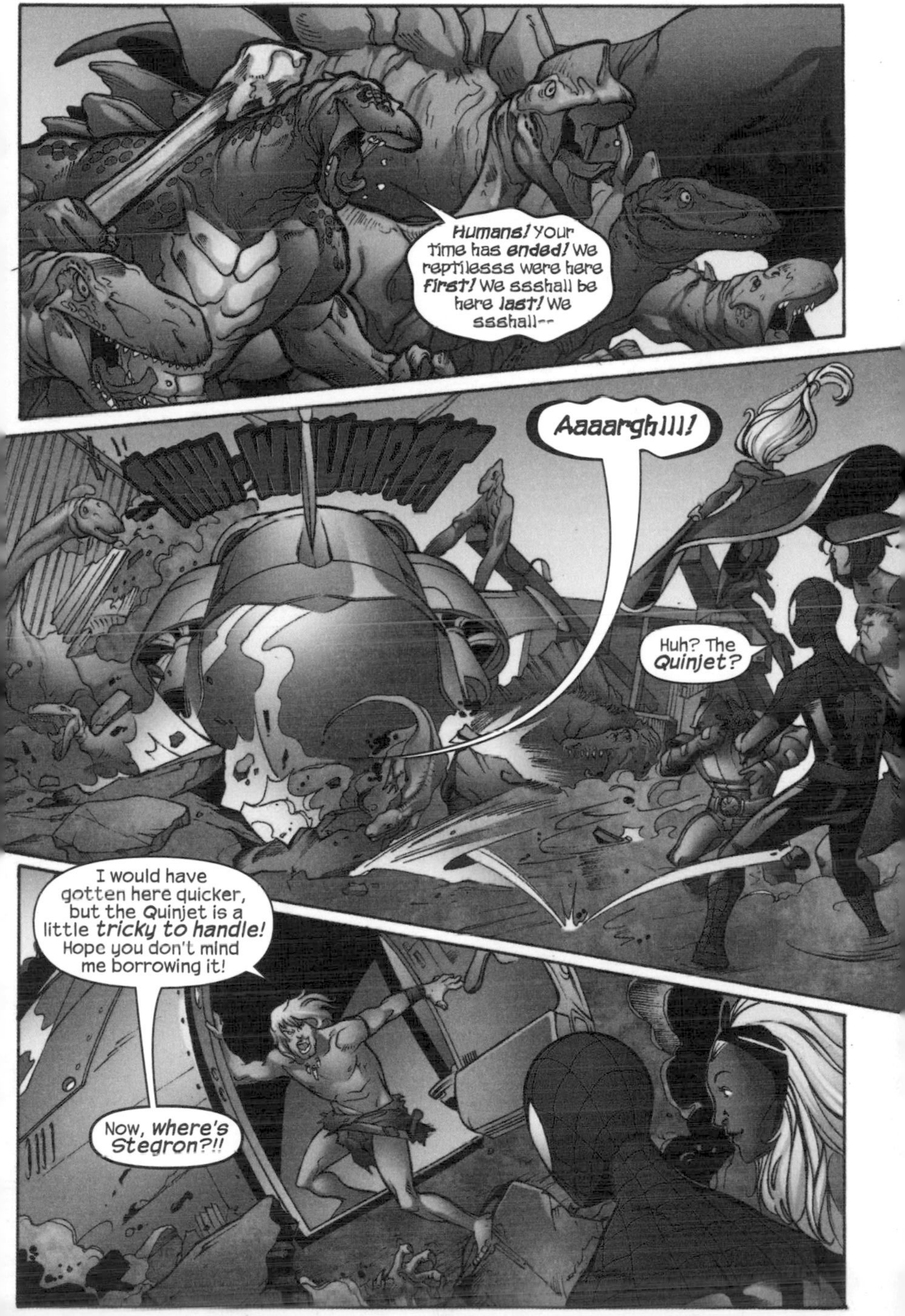

Humans! Your time has ended! We reptilesss were here first! We ssshall be here last! We ssshall--
Aaaargh!!!!
Huh? The Quinjet?
I would have gotten here quicker, but the Quinjet is a little tricky to handle! Hope you don't mind me borrowing it!
Now, where's Stegron?!!

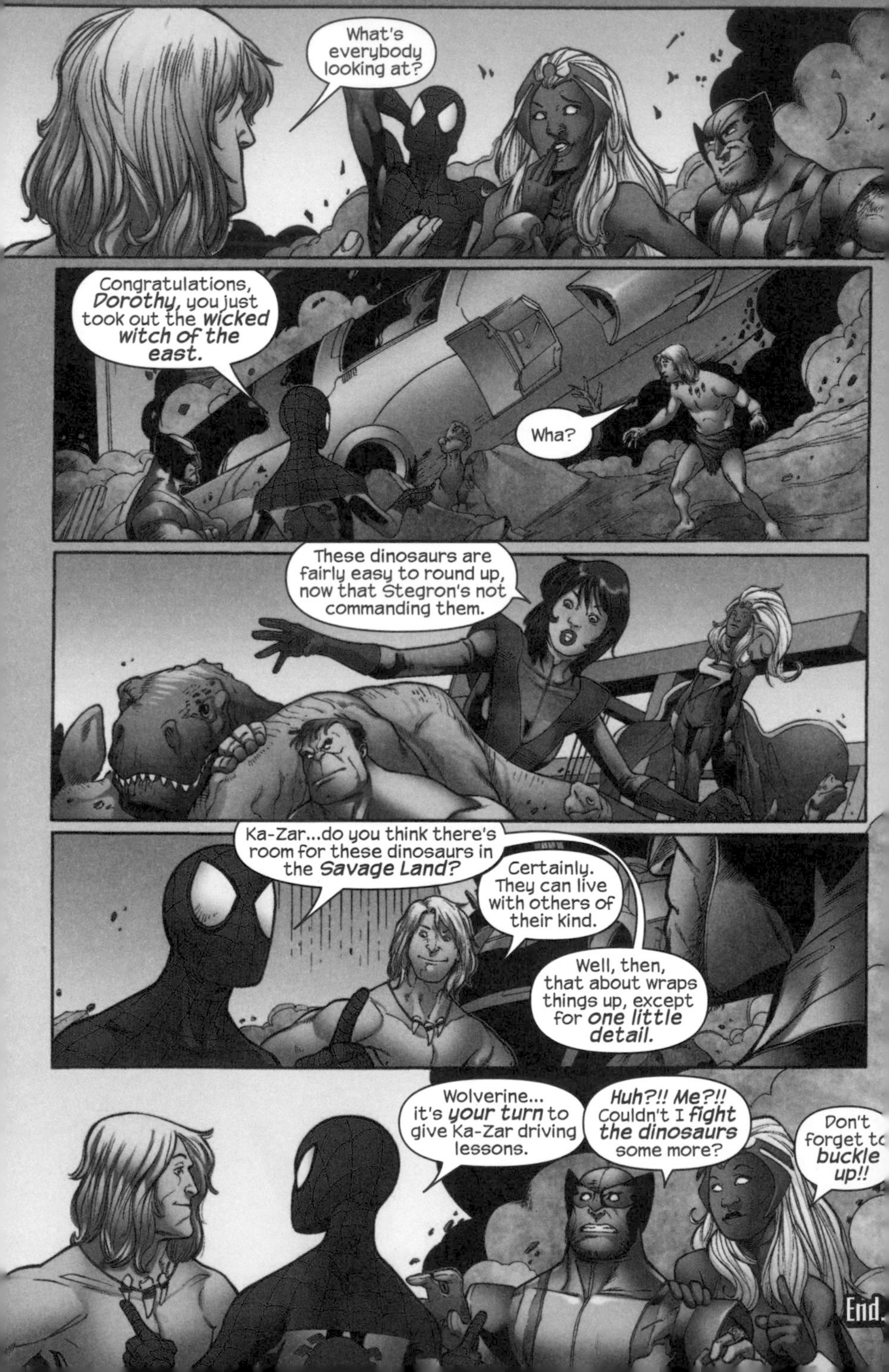
What's everybody looking at?
Congratulations, Dorothy, you just took out the wicked witch of the east.
Wha?
These dinosaurs are fairly easy to round up, now that Stegron's not commanding them.
Ka-Zar...do you think there's room for these dinosaurs in the Savage Land?
Certainly. They can live with others of their kind.
Well, then, that about wraps things up, except for one little detail.
Wolverine... it's your turn to give Ka-Zar driving lessons.
Huh?!! Me?!! Couldn't I fight the dinosaurs some more?
Don't forget to buckle up!!
End.

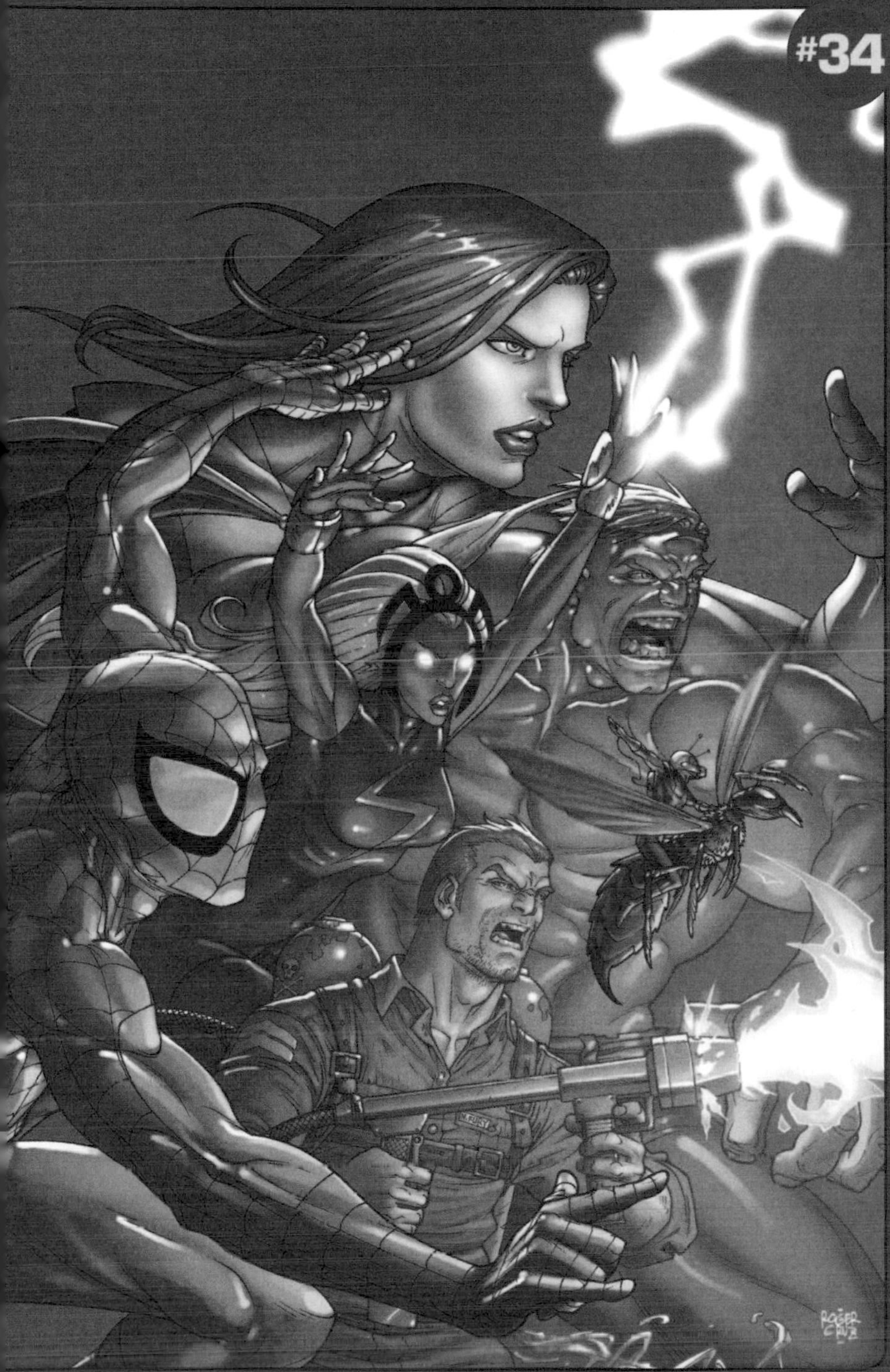
#34
ROGER CRUZ

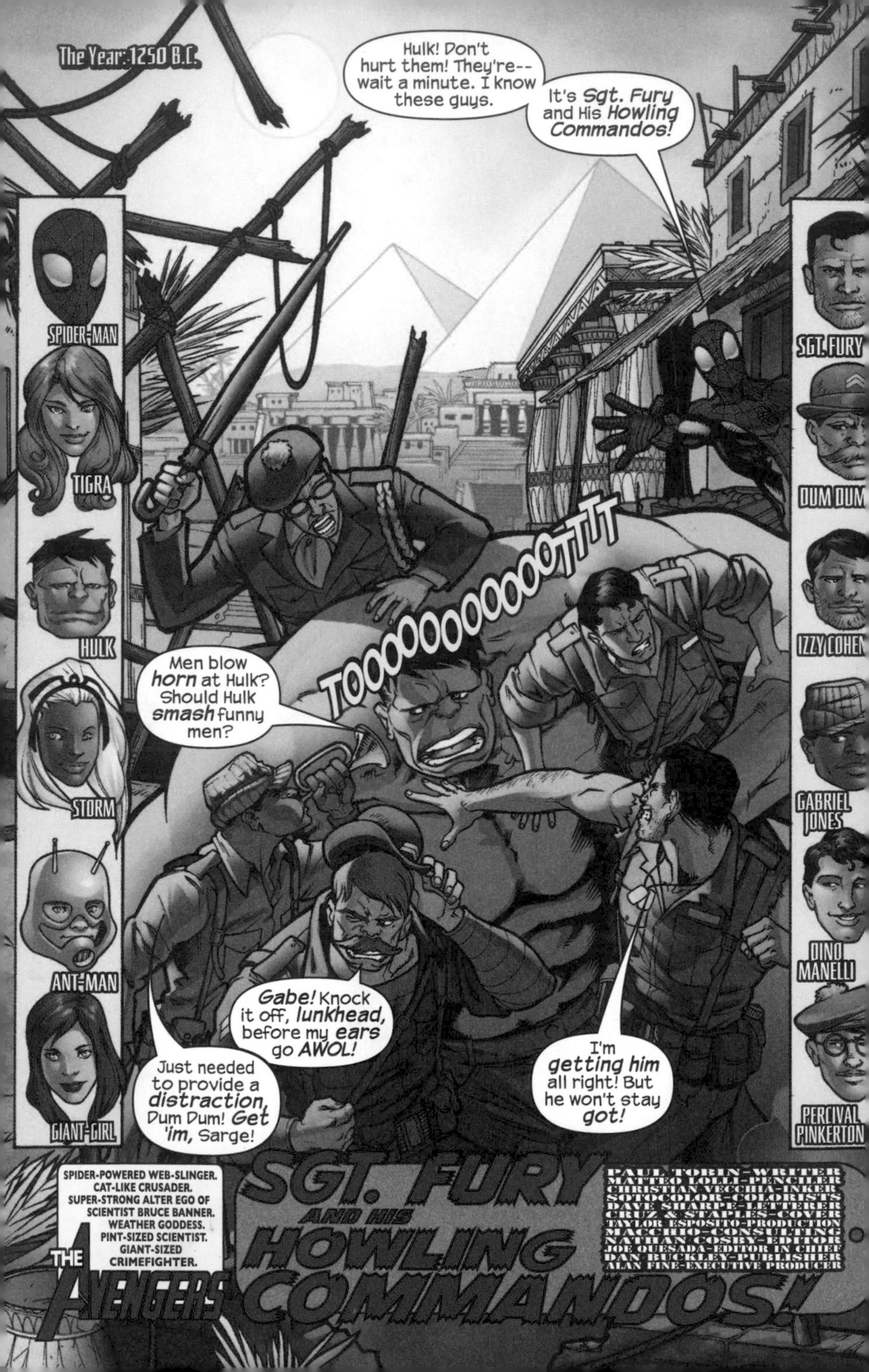
The Year: 1250 B.C.
Hulk! Don't hurt them! They're-- wait a minute. I know these guys.
It's Sgt. Fury and His Howling Commandos!
TOOOOOOOOOOOTTTT
Men blow horn at Hulk? Should Hulk smash funny men?
Gabe! Knock it off, lunkhead, before my ears go AWOL!
Just needed to provide a distraction, Dum Dum! Get 'im, Sarge!
I'm getting him all right! But he won't stay got!
SPIDER-MAN
TIGRA
HULK
STORM
ANT-MAN
GIANT-GIRL
SGT. FURY
DUM DUM
IZZY COHEN
GABRIEL JONES
DINO MANELLI
PERCIVAL PINKERTON
SPIDER-POWERED WEB-SLINGER.
CAT-LIKE CRUSADER.
SUPER-STRONG ALTER EGO OF SCIENTIST BRUCE BANNER.
WEATHER GODDESS.
PINT-SIZED SCIENTIST.
GIANT-SIZED CRIMEFIGHTER.
THE AVENGERS
SGT. FURY AND HIS HOWLING COMMANDOS!
PAUL TOBIN-WRITER
MATTEO LOLLI-PENCILER
CHRISTIAN VECCHIA-INKER
SOTOCOLOR-COLORISTS
DAVE SHARPE-LETTERER
CRUZ & STAPLES-COVER
TAYLOR ESPOSITO-PRODUCTION
MACCHIO-CONSULTING
NATHAN COSBY-EDITOR
JOE QUESADA-EDITOR IN CHIEF
DAN BUCKLEY-PUBLISHER
ALAN FINE-EXECUTIVE PRODUCER

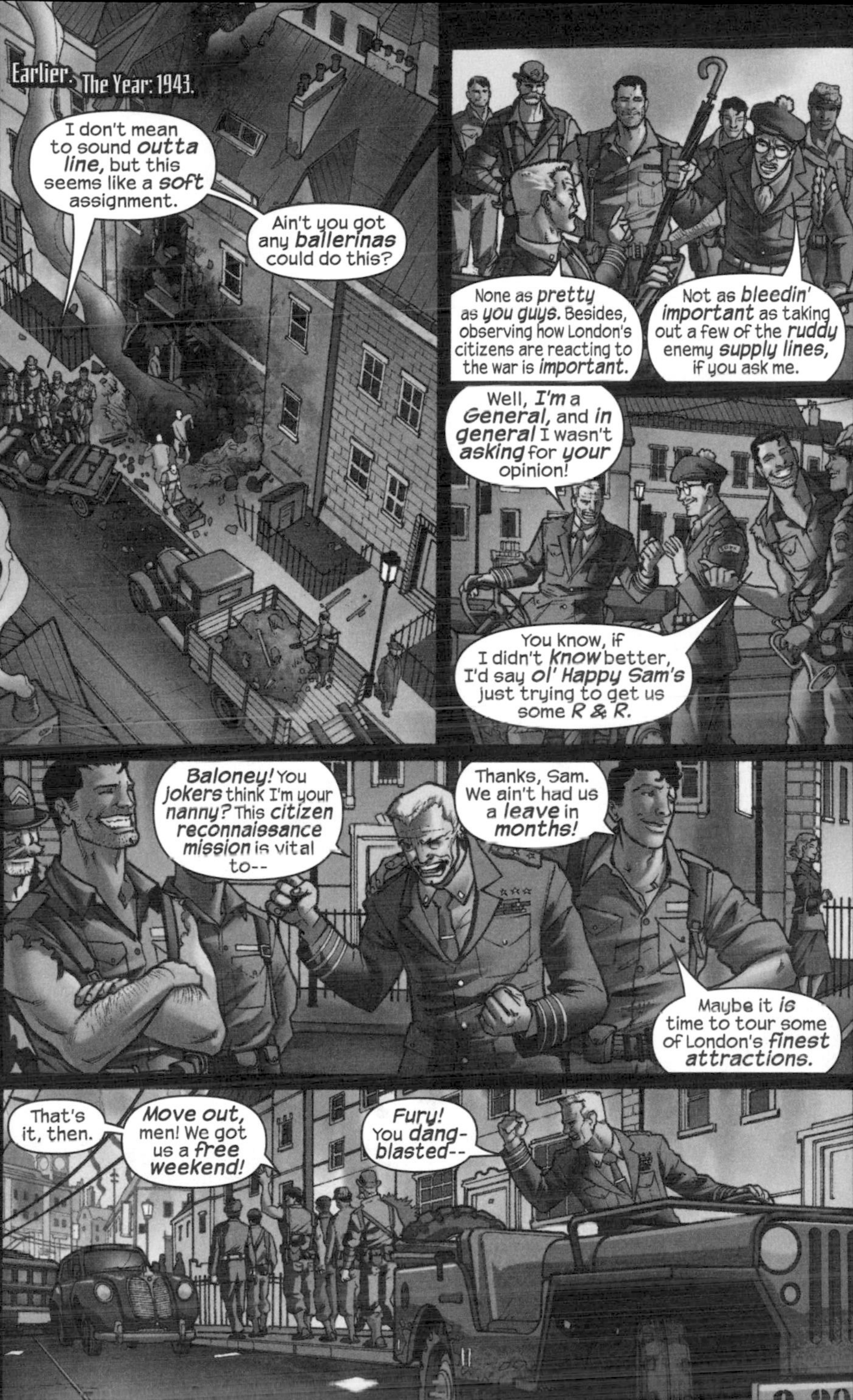

Earlier. The Year: 1943.
I don't mean to sound outta line, but this seems like a soft assignment.
Ain't you got any ballerinas could do this?
None as pretty as you guys. Besides, observing how London's citizens are reacting to the war is important.
Not as bleedin' important as taking out a few of the ruddy enemy supply lines, if you ask me.
Well, I'm a General, and in general I wasn't asking for your opinion!
You know, if I didn't know better, I'd say ol' Happy Sam's just trying to get us some R & R.
Baloney! You jokers think I'm your nanny? This citizen reconnaissance mission is vital to--
Thanks, Sam. We ain't had us a leave in months!
Maybe it is time to tour some of London's finest attractions.
That's it, then.
Move out, men! We got us a free weekend!
Fury! You dang-blasted--

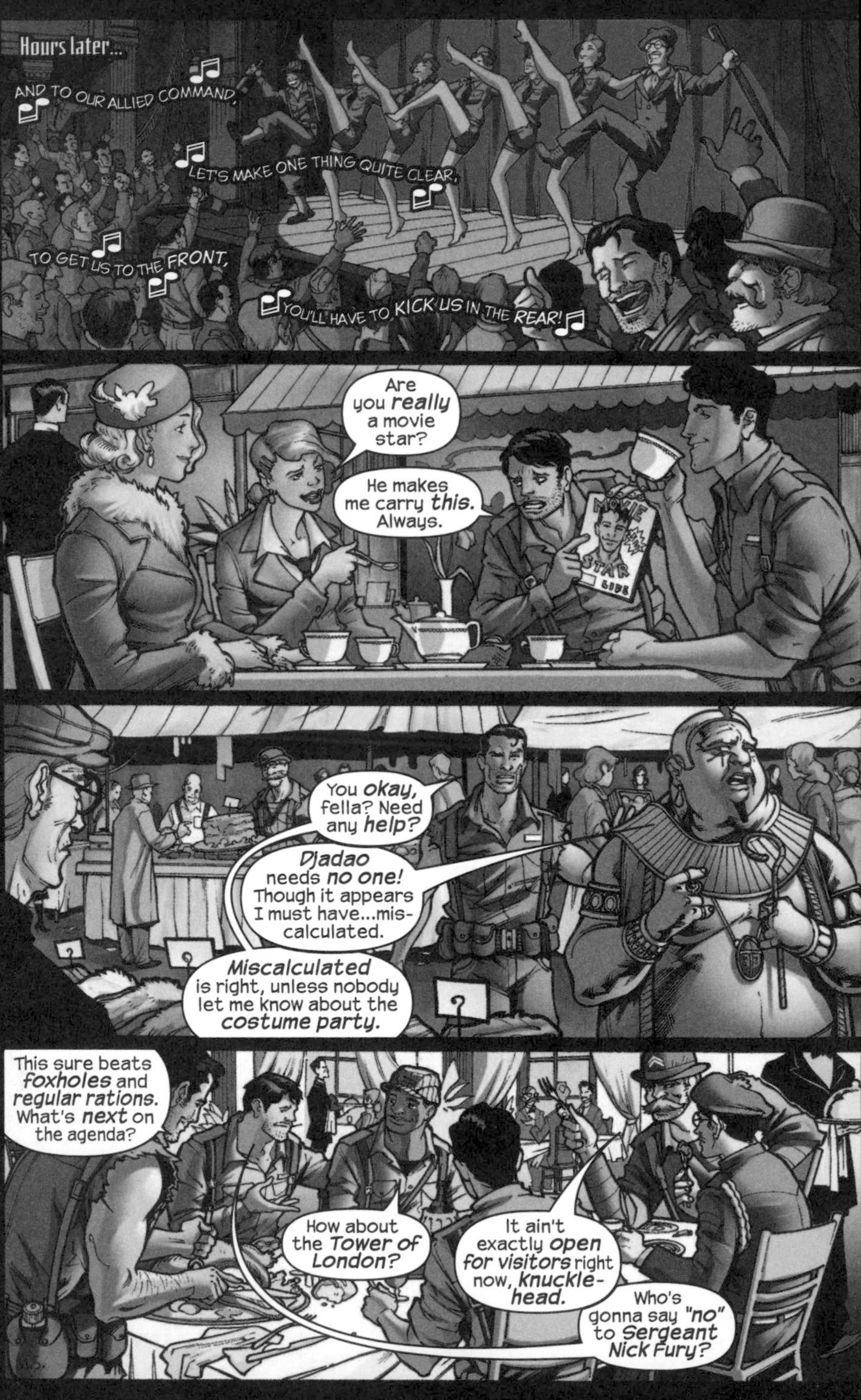

Hours later...
AND TO OUR ALLIED COMMAND,
LET'S MAKE ONE THING QUITE CLEAR,
TO GET US TO THE FRONT,
YOU'LL HAVE TO KICK US IN THE REAR!
Are you really a movie star?
He makes me carry this. Always.
MOVIE STAR
You okay, fella? Need any help?
Djadao needs no one! Though it appears I must have...mis-calculated.
Miscalculated is right, unless nobody let me know about the costume party.
This sure beats foxholes and regular rations. What's next on the agenda?
How about the Tower of London?
It ain't exactly open for visitors right now, knucklehead.
Who's gonna say "no" to Sergeant Nick Fury?

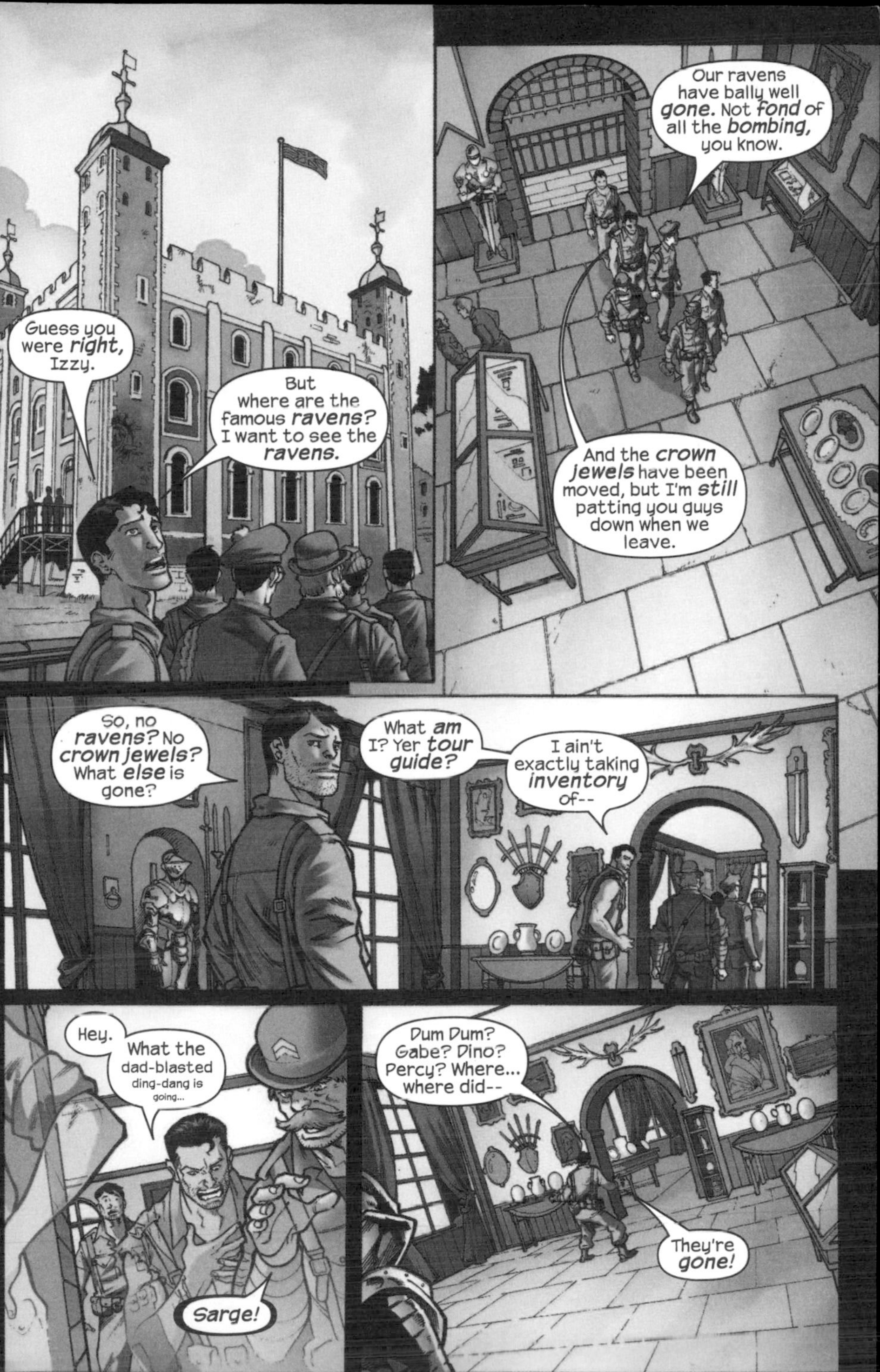

Guess you were right, Izzy.
But where are the famous ravens? I want to see the ravens.
Our ravens have bally well gone. Not fond of all the bombing, you know.
And the crown jewels have been moved, but I'm still patting you guys down when we leave.
So, no ravens? No crown jewels? What else is gone?
What am I? Yer tour guide?
I ain't exactly taking inventory of--
Hey.
What the dad-blasted ding-dang is going...
Sarge!
Dum Dum? Gabe? Dino? Percy? Where... where did--
They're gone!

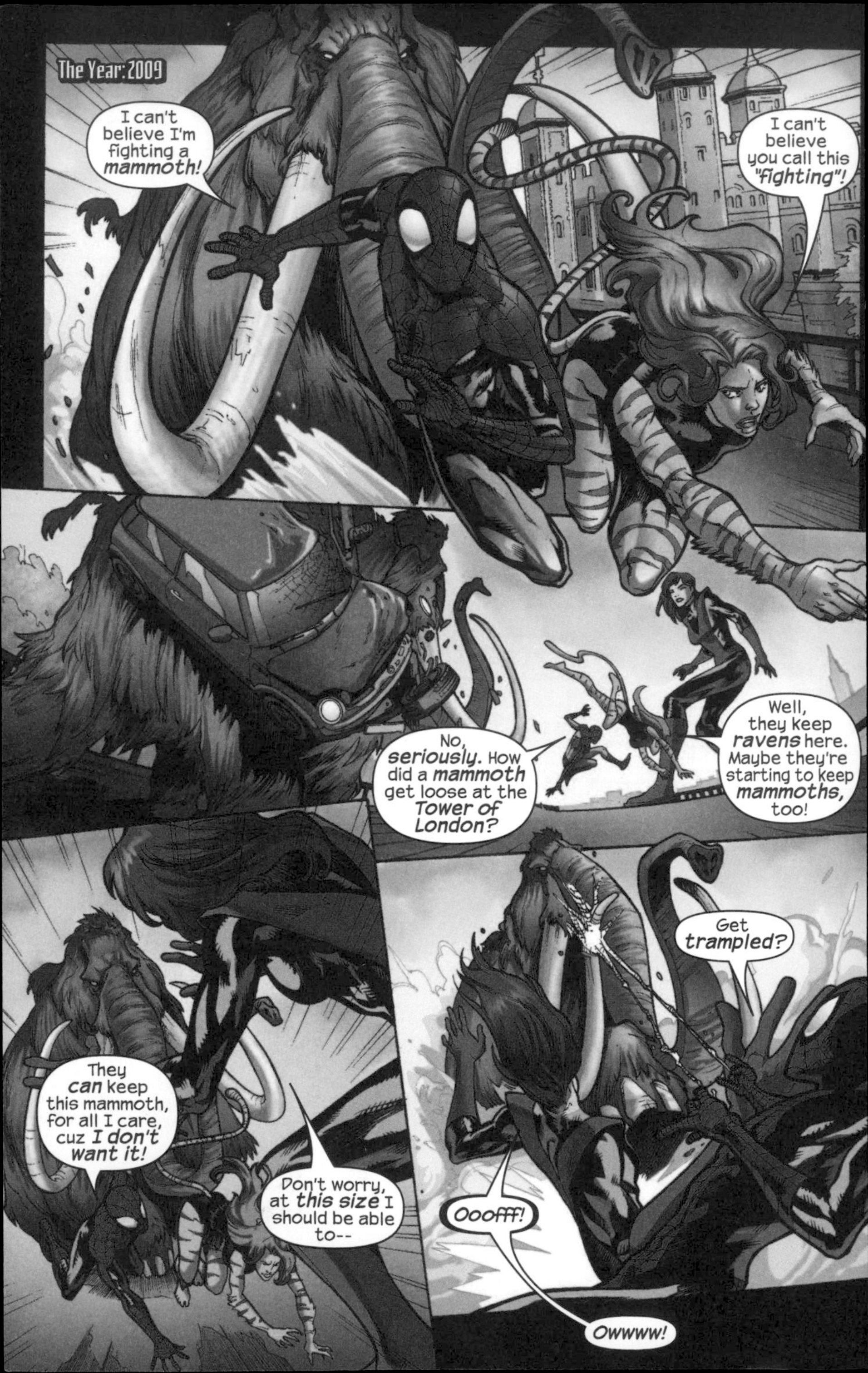
The Year: 2009
I can't believe I'm fighting a *mammoth*!
I can't believe you call this *"fighting"*!
No, *seriously*. How did a *mammoth* get loose at the *Tower of London*?
Well, they keep *ravens* here. Maybe they're starting to keep *mammoths*, too!
They *can* keep this mammoth, for all I care, cuz *I don't want it*!
Don't worry, at *this size* I should be able to--
Get *trampled*?
Ooofff!
Owwww!

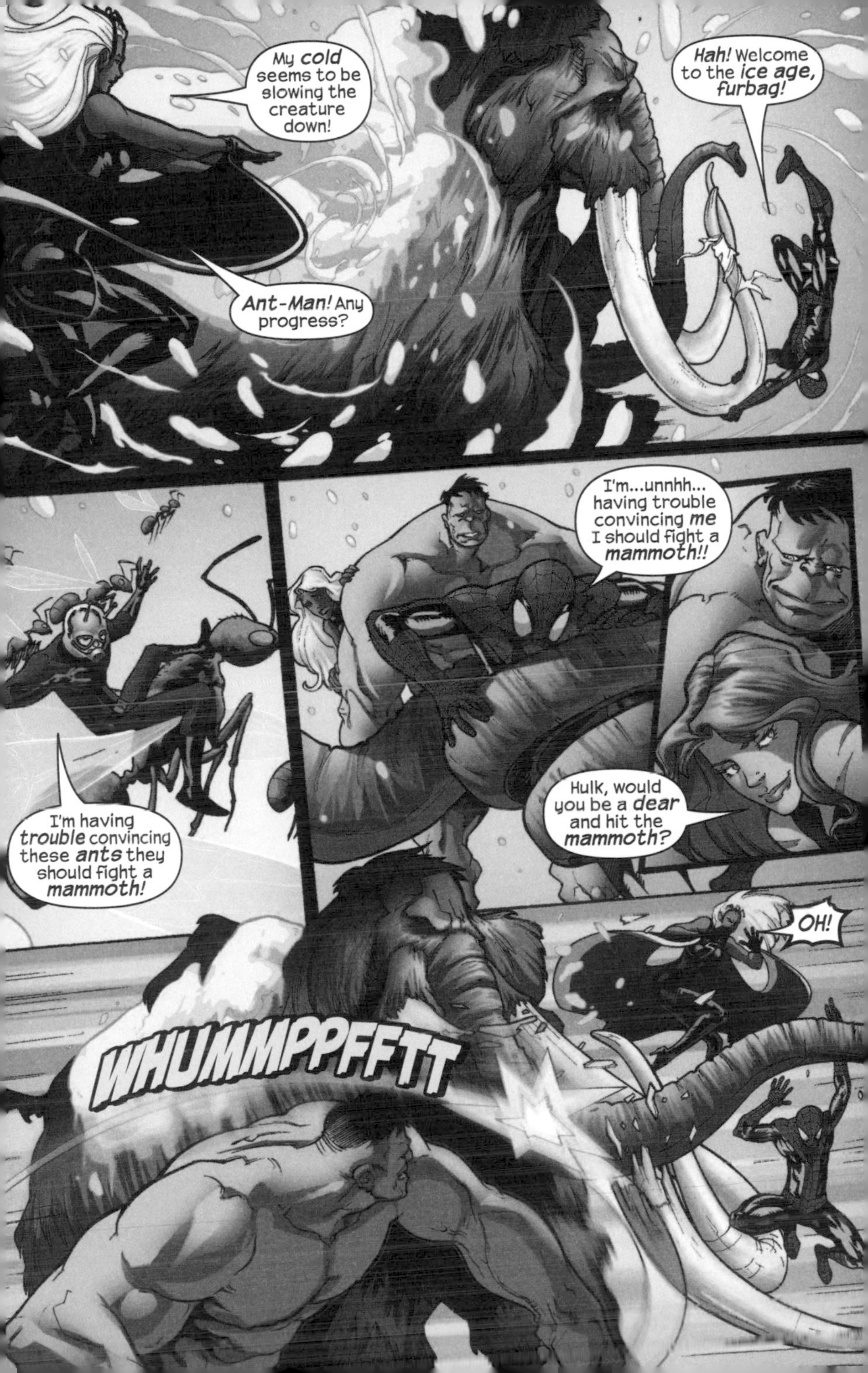
My cold seems to be slowing the creature down!
Hah! Welcome to the ice age, furbag!
Ant-Man! Any progress?
I'm having trouble convincing these ants they should fight a mammoth!
I'm...unnhh... having trouble convincing me I should fight a mammoth!!
Hulk, would you be a dear and hit the mammoth?
OH!
WHUMMPPFFTT

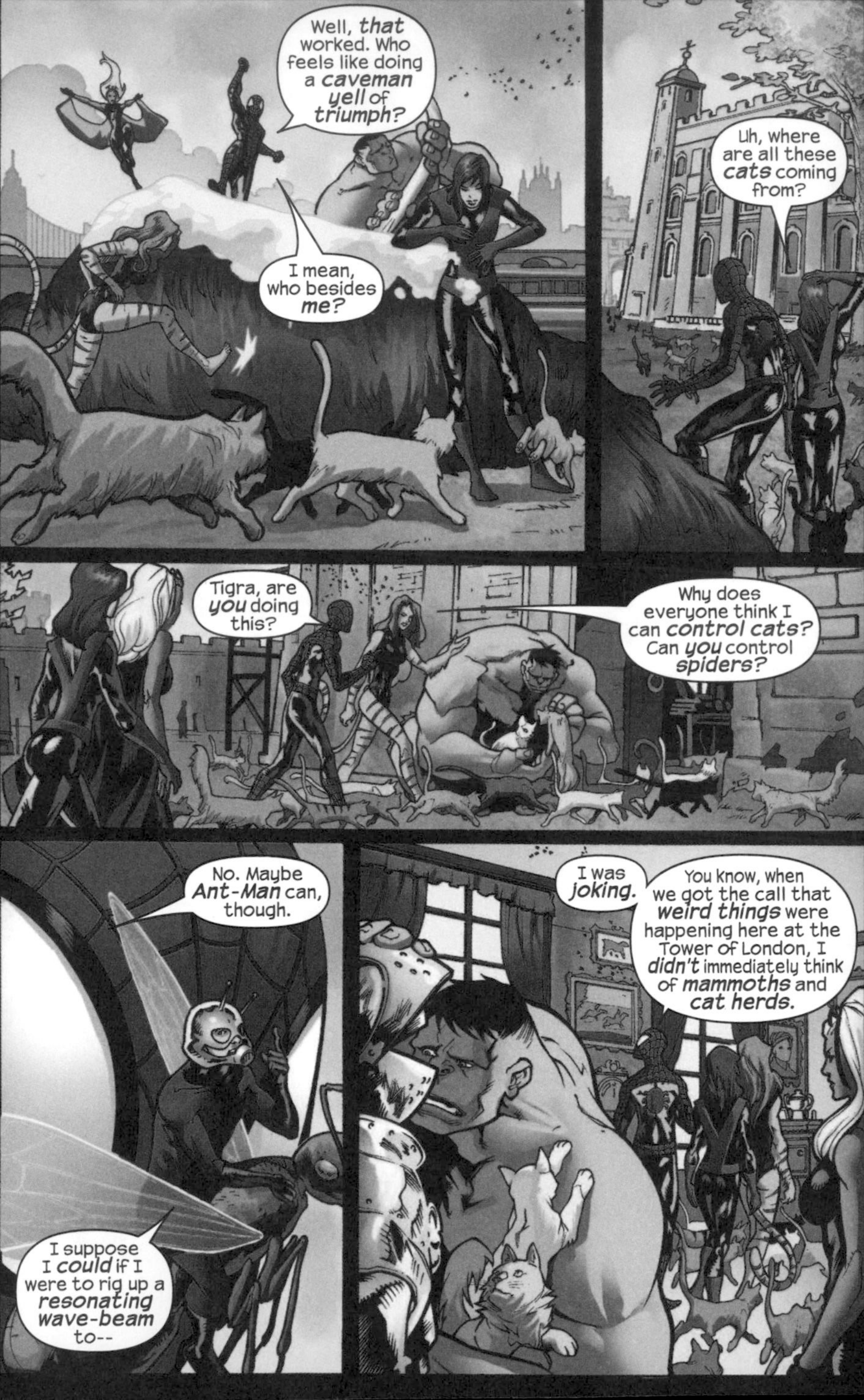
Well, that worked. Who feels like doing a caveman yell of triumph?
I mean, who besides me?
Uh, where are all these cats coming from?
Tigra, are you doing this?
Why does everyone think I can control cats? Can you control spiders?
No. Maybe Ant-Man can, though.
I suppose I could if I were to rig up a resonating wave-beam to--
I was joking.
You know, when we got the call that weird things were happening here at the Tower of London, I didn't immediately think of mammoths and cat herds.

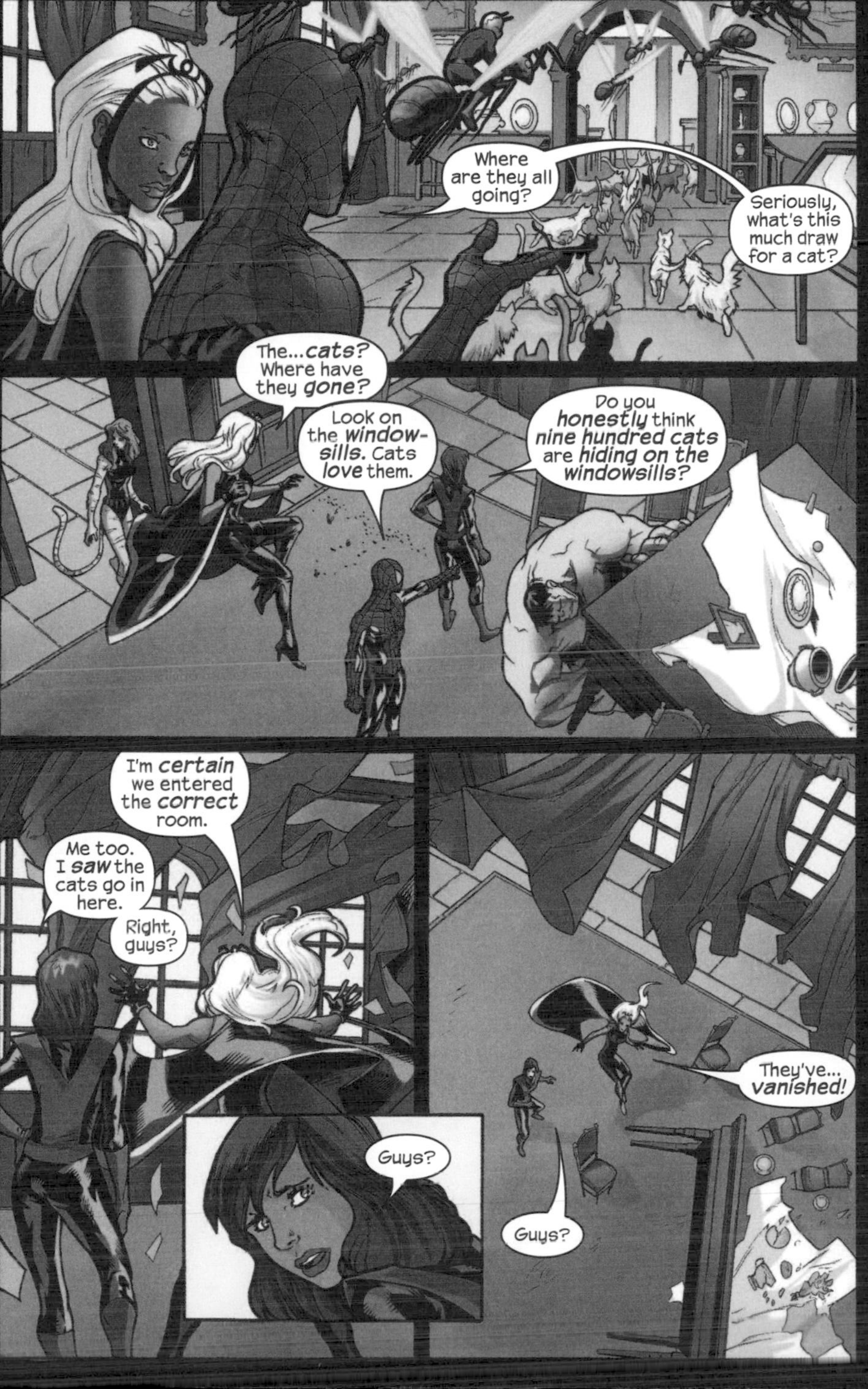
Where are they all going?
Seriously, what's this much draw for a cat?
The...cats? Where have they gone?
Look on the windowsills. Cats love them.
Do you honestly think nine hundred cats are hiding on the windowsills?
I'm certain we entered the correct room.
Me too. I saw the cats go in here.
Right, guys?
They've... vanished!
Guys?
Guys?

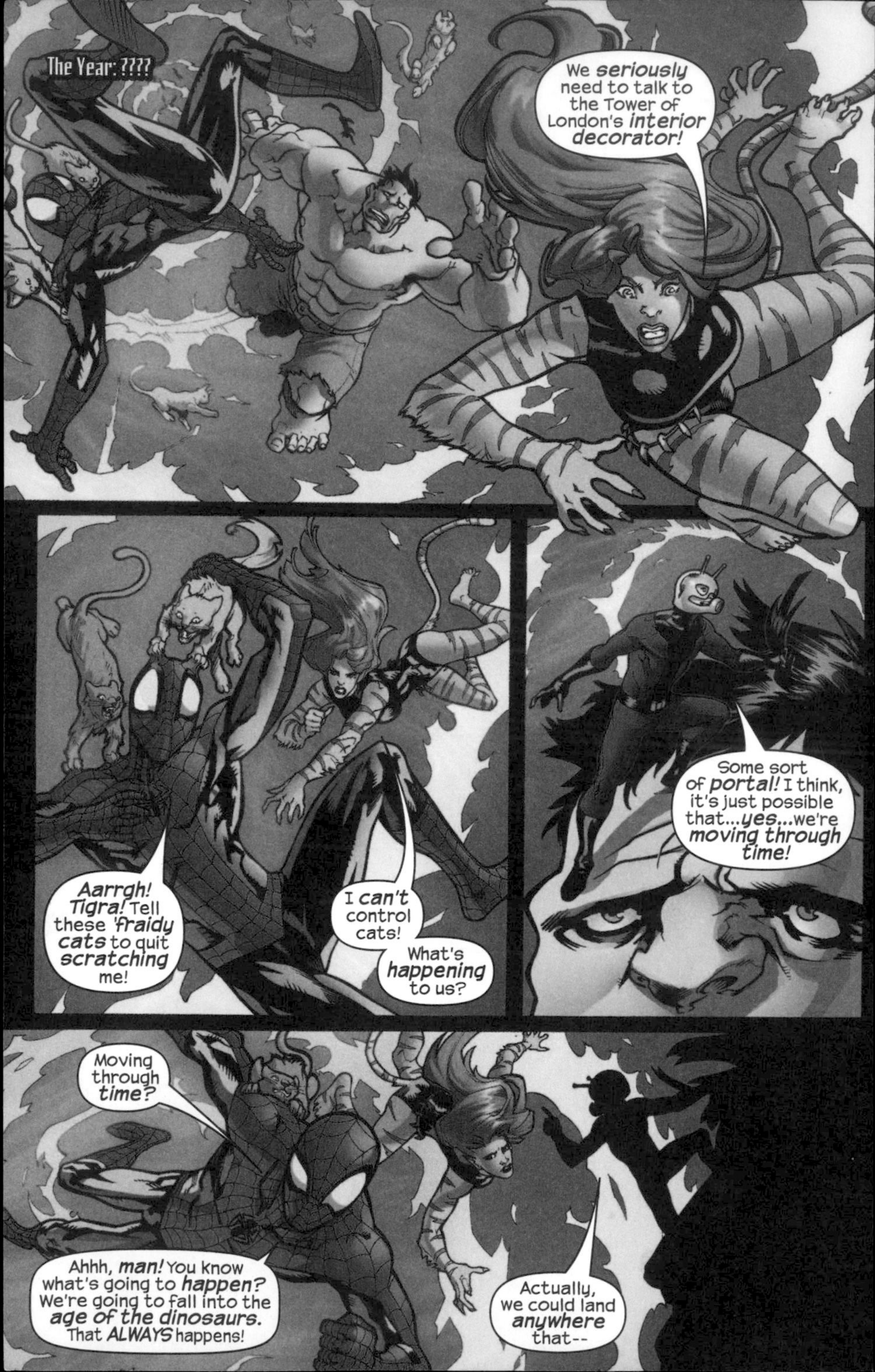
The Year: ????
We seriously need to talk to the Tower of London's interior decorator!
Aarrgh! Tigra! Tell these 'fraidy cats to quit scratching me!
I can't control cats!
What's happening to us?
Some sort of portal! I think, it's just possible that...yes...we're moving through time!
Moving through time?
Ahhh, man! You know what's going to happen? We're going to fall into the age of the dinosaurs. That ALWAYS happens!
Actually, we could land anywhere that--

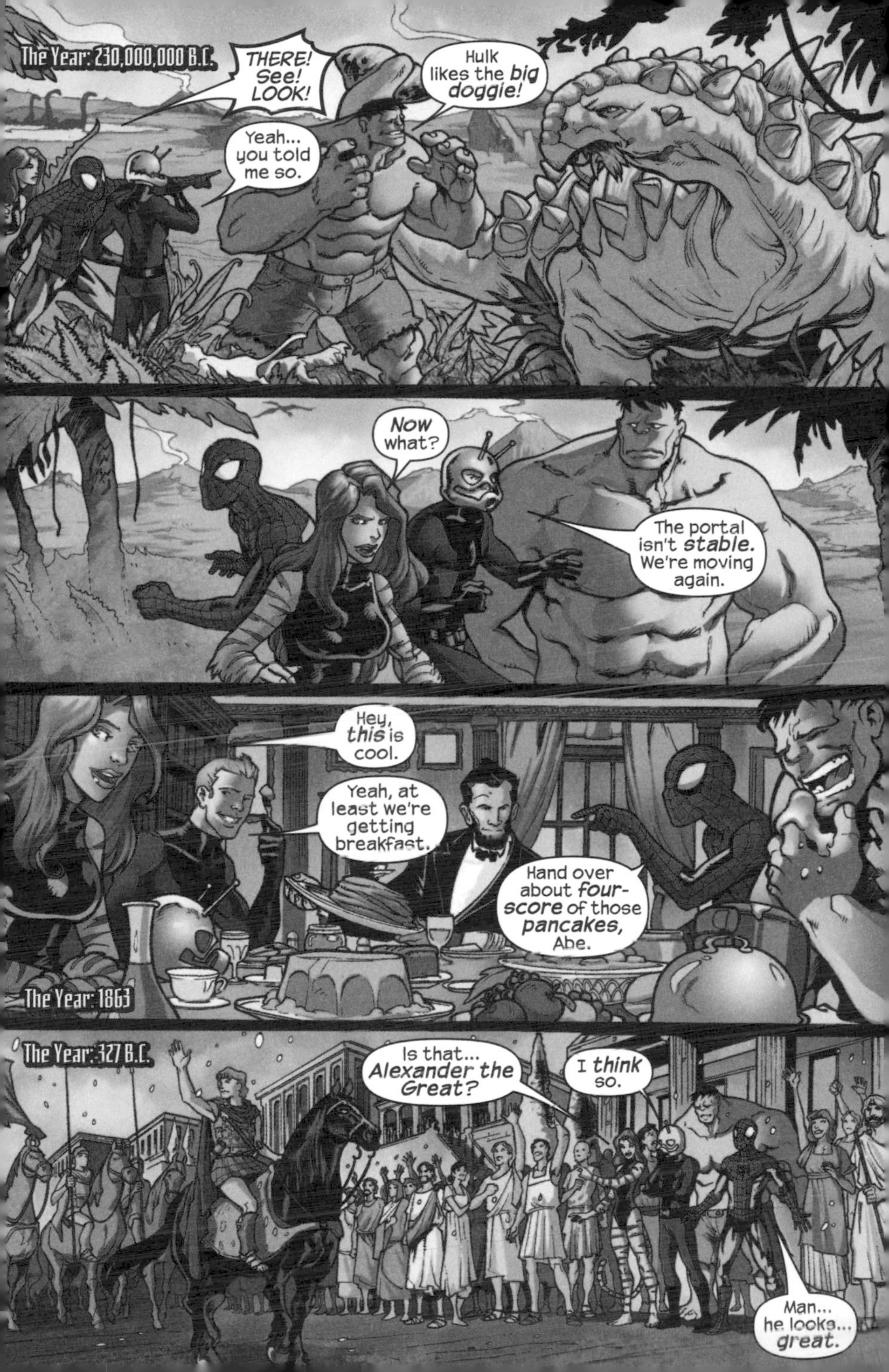
The Year: 230,000,000 B.C.
THERE! See! LOOK!
Hulk likes the big doggie!
Yeah... you told me so.
Now what?
The portal isn't stable. We're moving again.
Hey, this is cool.
Yeah, at least we're getting breakfast.
Hand over about four-score of those pancakes, Abe.
The Year: 1863
The Year: 327 B.C.
Is that... Alexander the Great?
I think so.
Man... he looks... great.

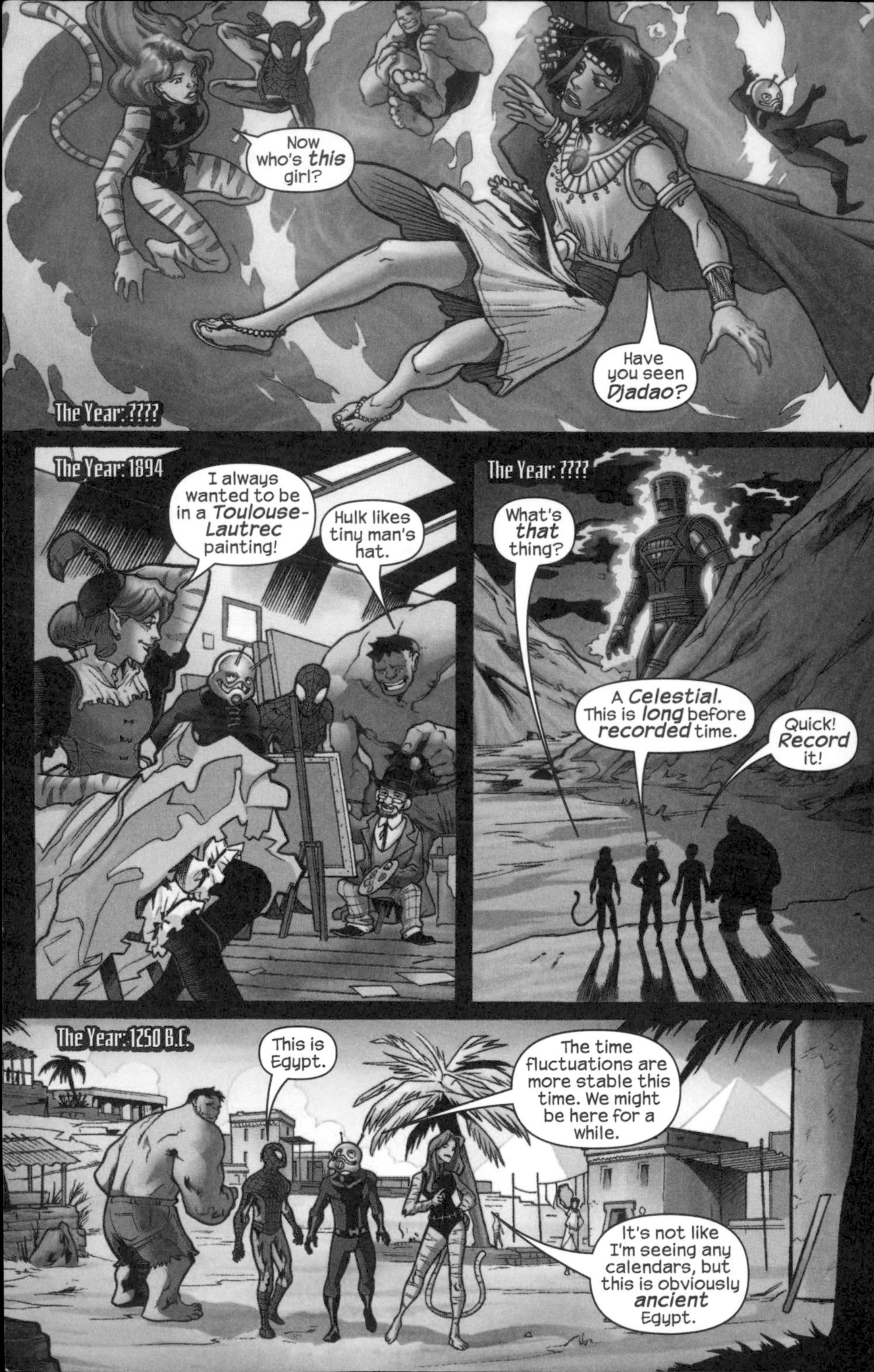
Now who's this girl?
Have you seen Djadao?
The Year: ????
The Year: 1894
I always wanted to be in a Toulouse-Lautrec painting!
Hulk likes tiny man's hat.
The Year: ????
What's that thing?
A Celestial. This is long before recorded time.
Quick! Record it!
The Year: 1250 B.C.
This is Egypt.
The time fluctuations are more stable this time. We might be here for a while.
It's not like I'm seeing any calendars, but this is obviously ancient Egypt.

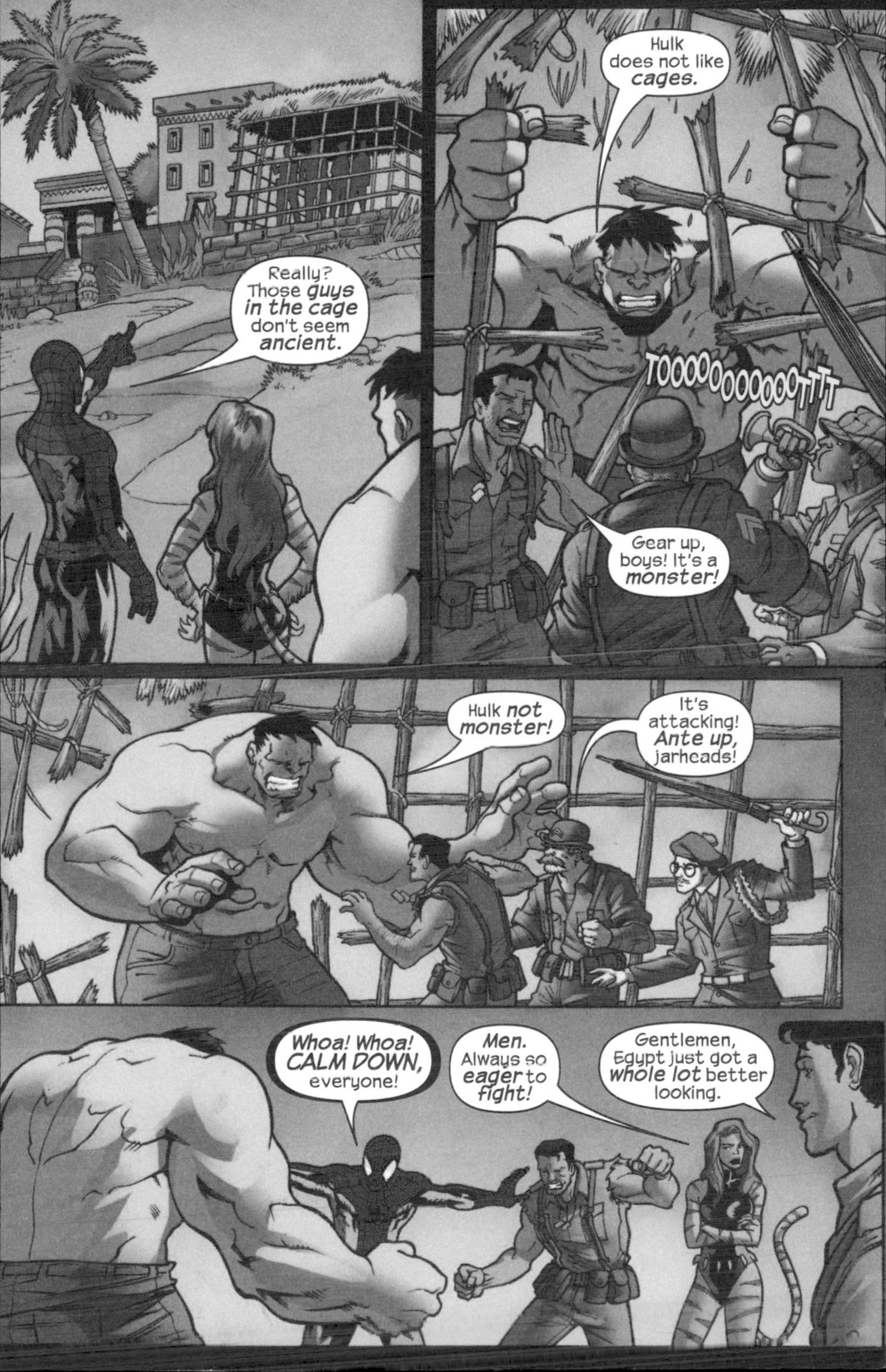
Really? Those guys in the cage don't seem ancient.
Hulk does not like cages.
TOOOOOOOOOOOTTTT
Gear up, boys! It's a monster!
Hulk not monster!
It's attacking! Ante up, jarheads!
Whoa! Whoa! CALM DOWN, everyone!
Men. Always so eager to fight!
Gentlemen, Egypt just got a whole lot better looking.

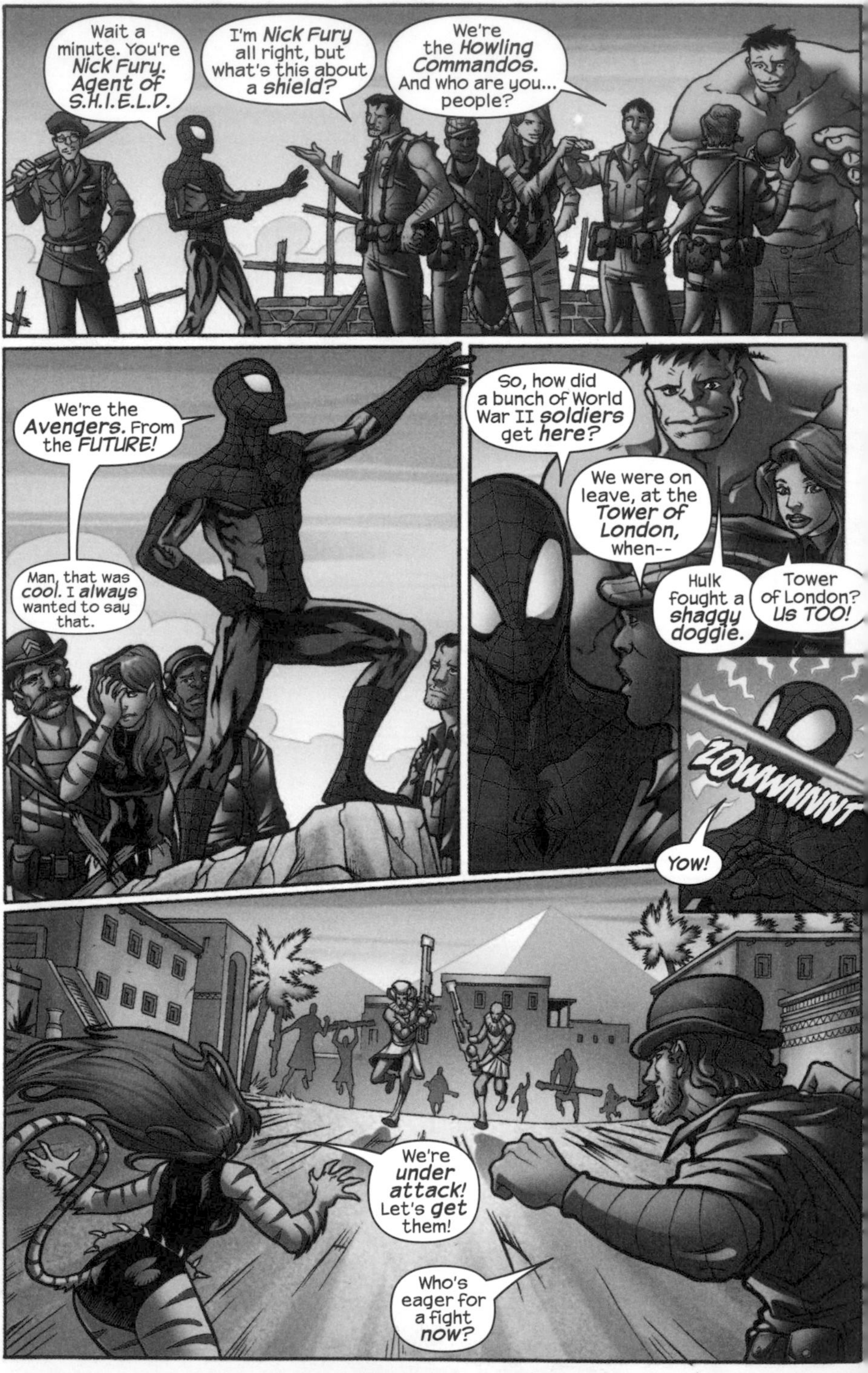

Wait a minute. You're Nick Fury. Agent of S.H.I.E.L.D.
I'm Nick Fury all right, but what's this about a shield?
We're the Howling Commandos. And who are you... people?
We're the Avengers. From the FUTURE!
Man, that was cool. I always wanted to say that.
So, how did a bunch of World War II soldiers get here?
We were on leave, at the Tower of London, when--
Hulk fought a shaggy doggie.
Tower of London? Us TOO!
ZOWWNNNT
YOW!
We're under attack! Let's get them!
Who's eager for a fight now?

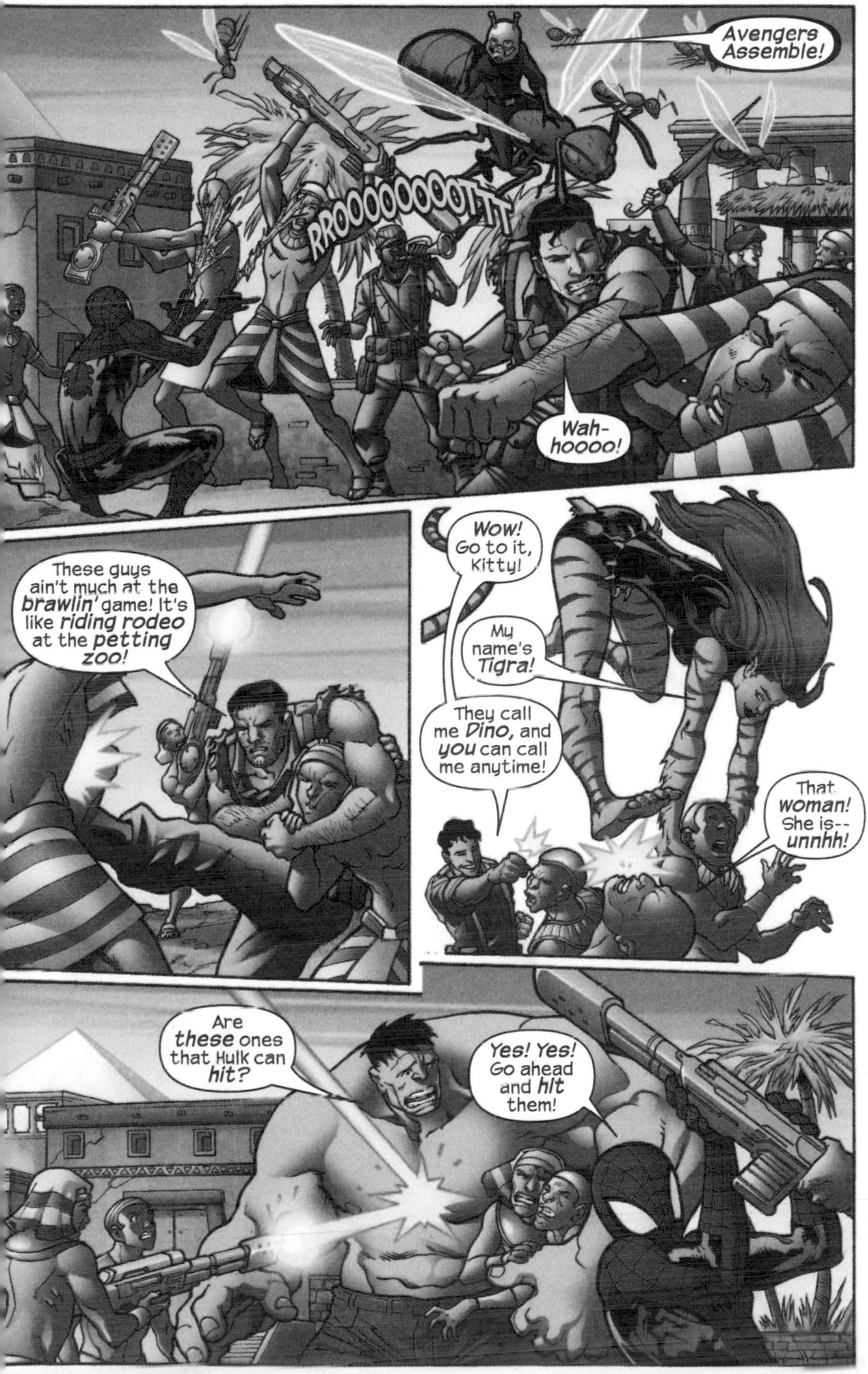
Avengers Assemble!
RROOOOOOOOTTTT
Wah-hoooo!
These guys ain't much at the brawlin' game! It's like riding rodeo at the petting zoo!
Wow! Go to it, Kitty!
My name's Tigra!
They call me Dino, and you can call me anytime!
That woman! She is-- unnhh!
Are these ones that Hulk can hit?
Yes! Yes! Go ahead and hit them!

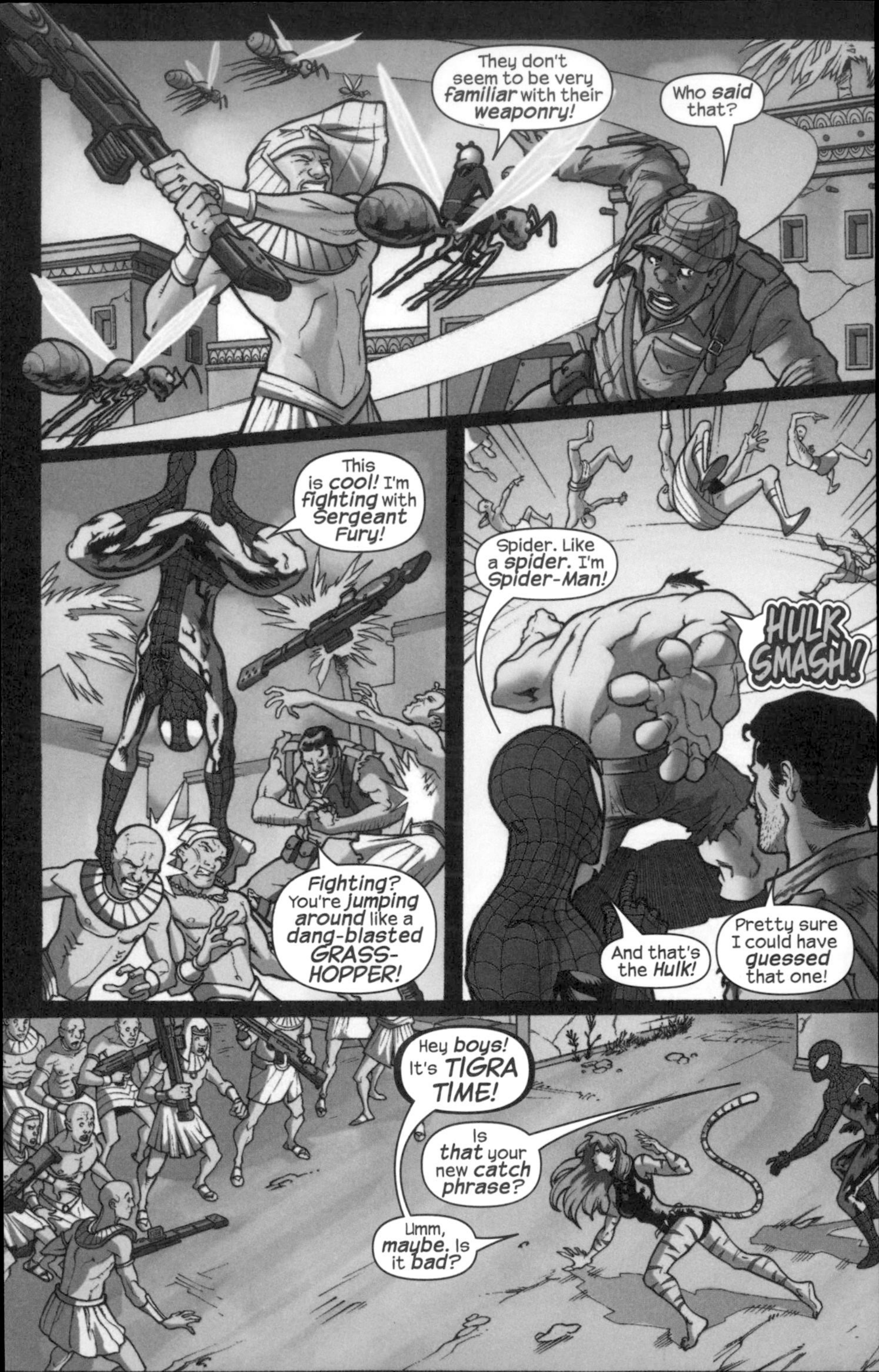
They don't seem to be very familiar with their weaponry!
Who said that?
This is cool! I'm fighting with Sergeant Fury!
Fighting? You're jumping around like a dang-blasted GRASS-HOPPER!
Spider. Like a spider. I'm Spider-Man!
HULK SMASH!
And that's the Hulk!
Pretty sure I could have guessed that one!
Hey boys! It's TIGRA TIME!
Is that your new catch phrase?
Umm, maybe. Is it bad?

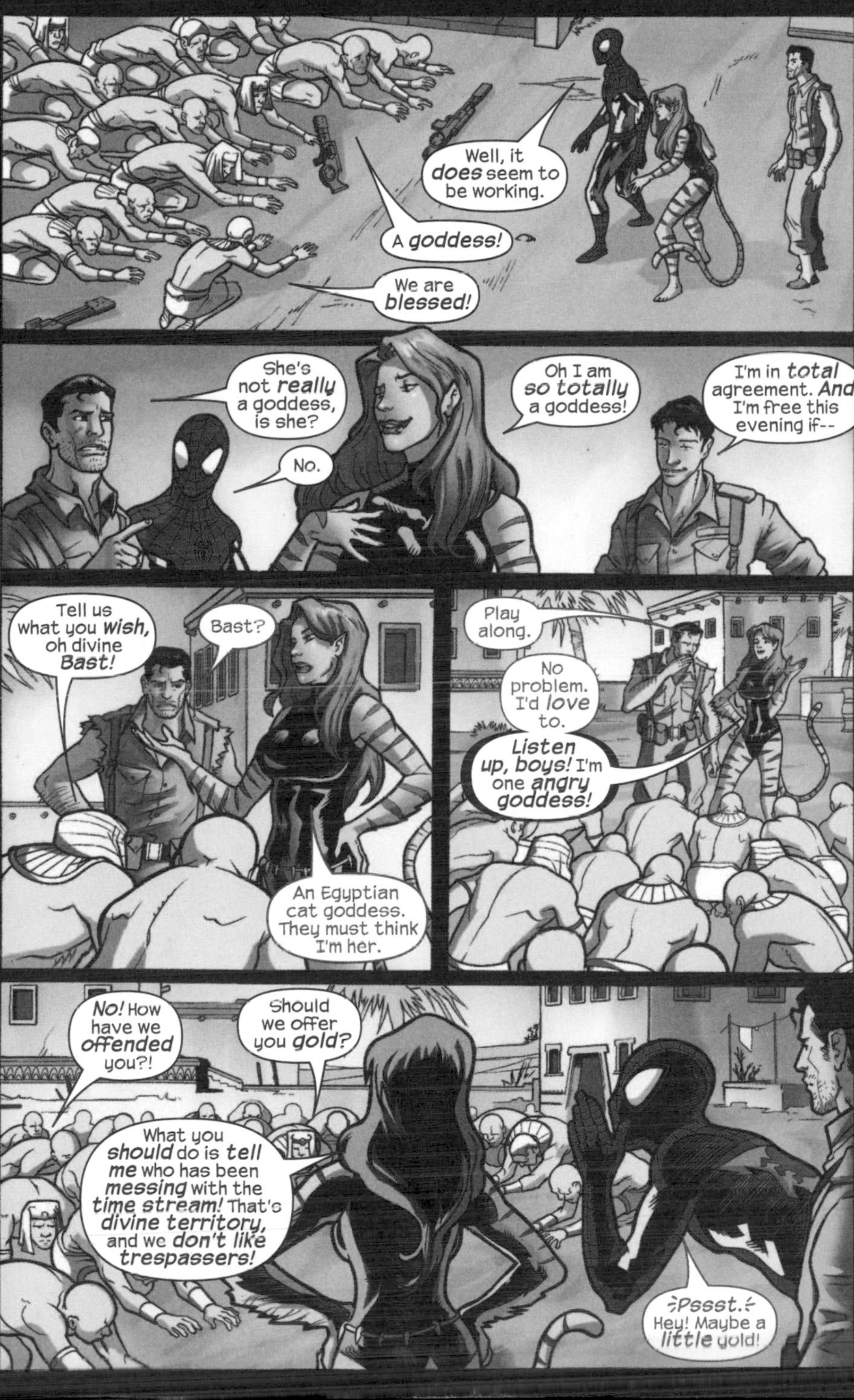

Well, it does seem to be working.
A goddess!
We are blessed!
She's not really a goddess, is she?
No.
Oh I am so totally a goddess!
I'm in total agreement. And I'm free this evening if--
Tell us what you wish, oh divine Bast!
Bast?
An Egyptian cat goddess. They must think I'm her.
Play along.
No problem. I'd love to.
Listen up, boys! I'm one angry goddess!
No! How have we offended you?!
Should we offer you gold?
What you should do is tell me who has been messing with the time stream! That's divine territory, and we don't like trespassers!
Pssst.
Hey! Maybe a little gold!

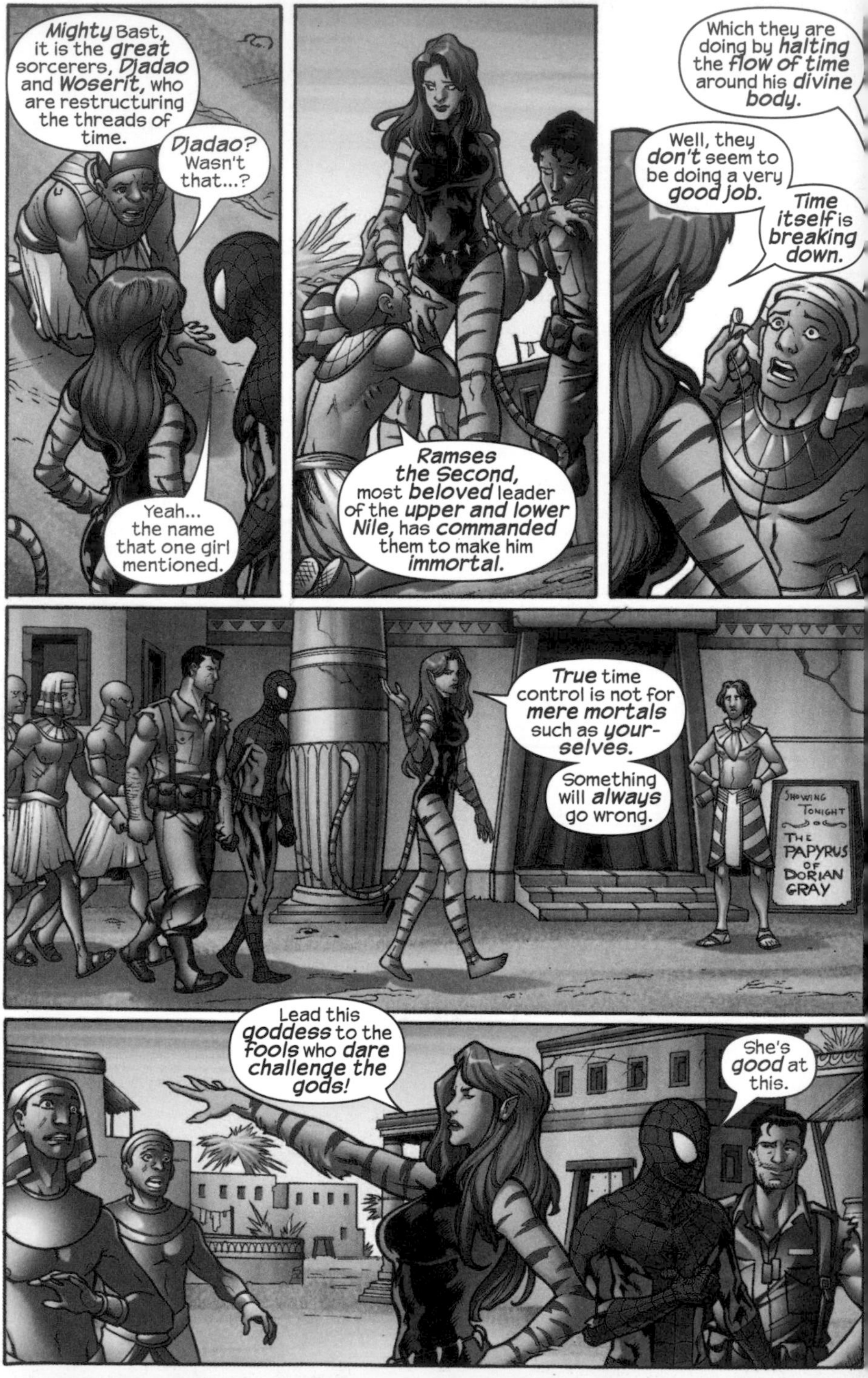

Mighty Bast, it is the great sorcerers, Djadao and Woserit, who are restructuring the threads of time.
Djadao? Wasn't that...?
Yeah... the name that one girl mentioned.
Ramses the Second, most beloved leader of the upper and lower Nile, has commanded them to make him immortal.
Which they are doing by halting the flow of time around his divine body.
Well, they don't seem to be doing a very good job.
Time itself is breaking down.
True time control is not for mere mortals such as your-selves.
Something will always go wrong.
Showing Tonight
The Papyrus of Dorian Gray
Lead this goddess to the fools who dare challenge the gods!
She's good at this.

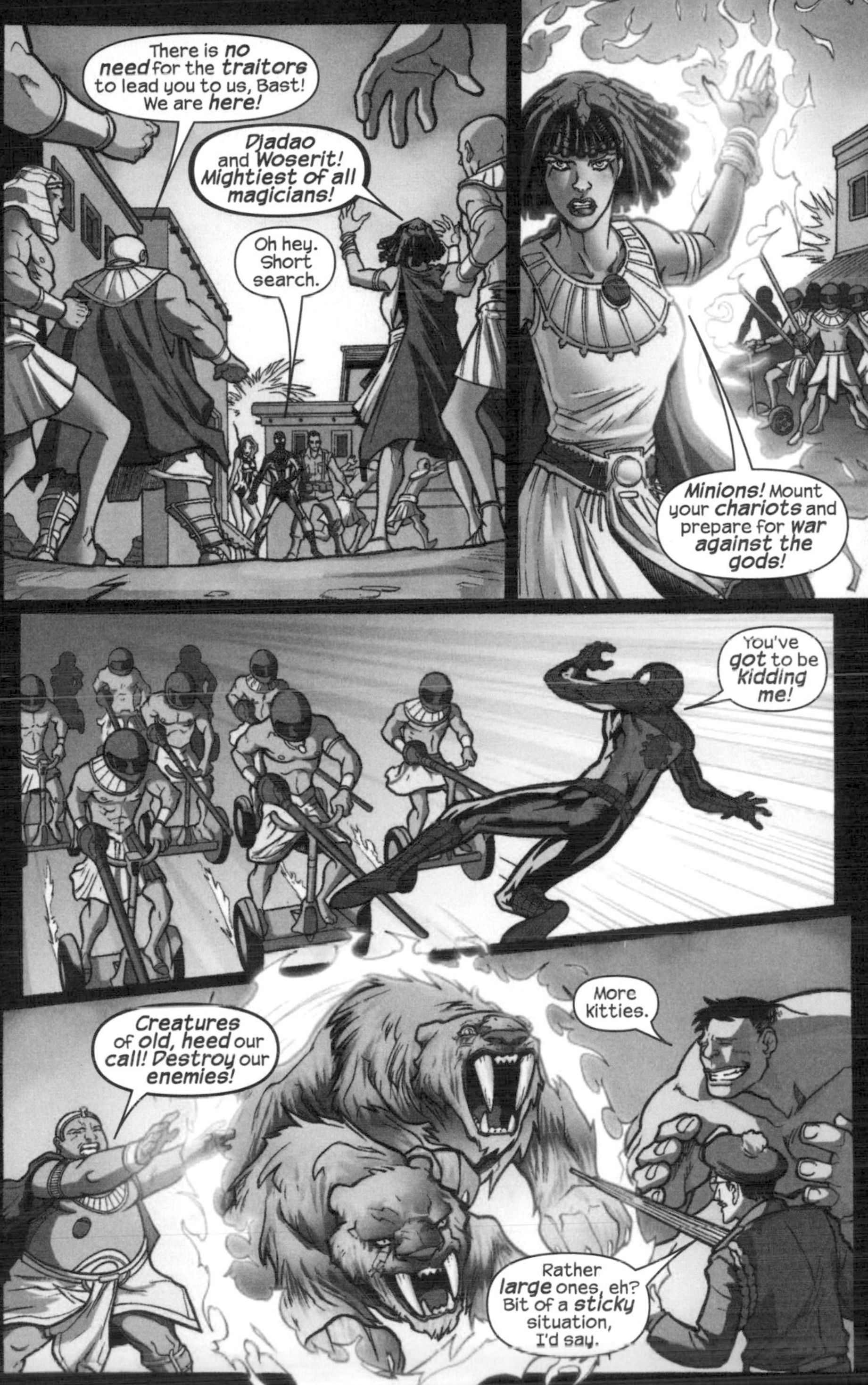
There is no need for the traitors to lead you to us, Bast! We are here!
Djadao and Woserit! Mightiest of all magicians!
Oh hey. Short search.
Minions! Mount your chariots and prepare for war against the gods!
You've got to be kidding me!
Creatures of old, heed our call! Destroy our enemies!
More kitties.
Rather large ones, eh? Bit of a sticky situation, I'd say.

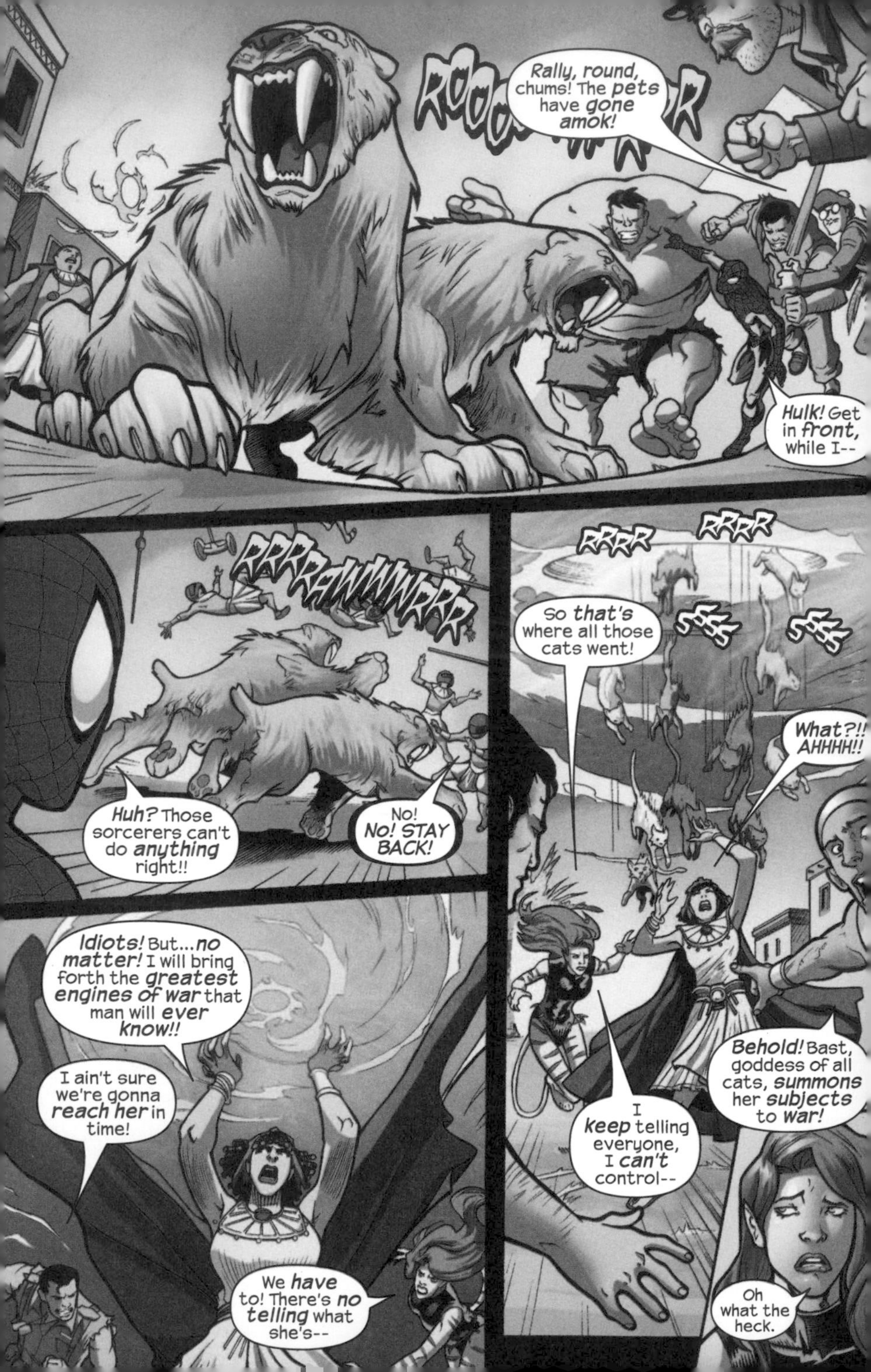

ROOOOWWWWR
Rally, round, chums! The pets have gone amok!
Hulk! Get in front, while I--
RRRRAWWWWRRR
Huh? Those sorcerers can't do anything right!!
No! No! STAY BACK!
RRRR
RRRR
So that's where all those cats went!
SSS
SSS
What?!! AHHHH!!
Idiots! But...no matter! I will bring forth the greatest engines of war that man will ever know!!
I ain't sure we're gonna reach her in time!
We have to! There's no telling what she's--
I keep telling everyone, I can't control--
Behold! Bast, goddess of all cats, summons her subjects to war!
Oh what the heck.

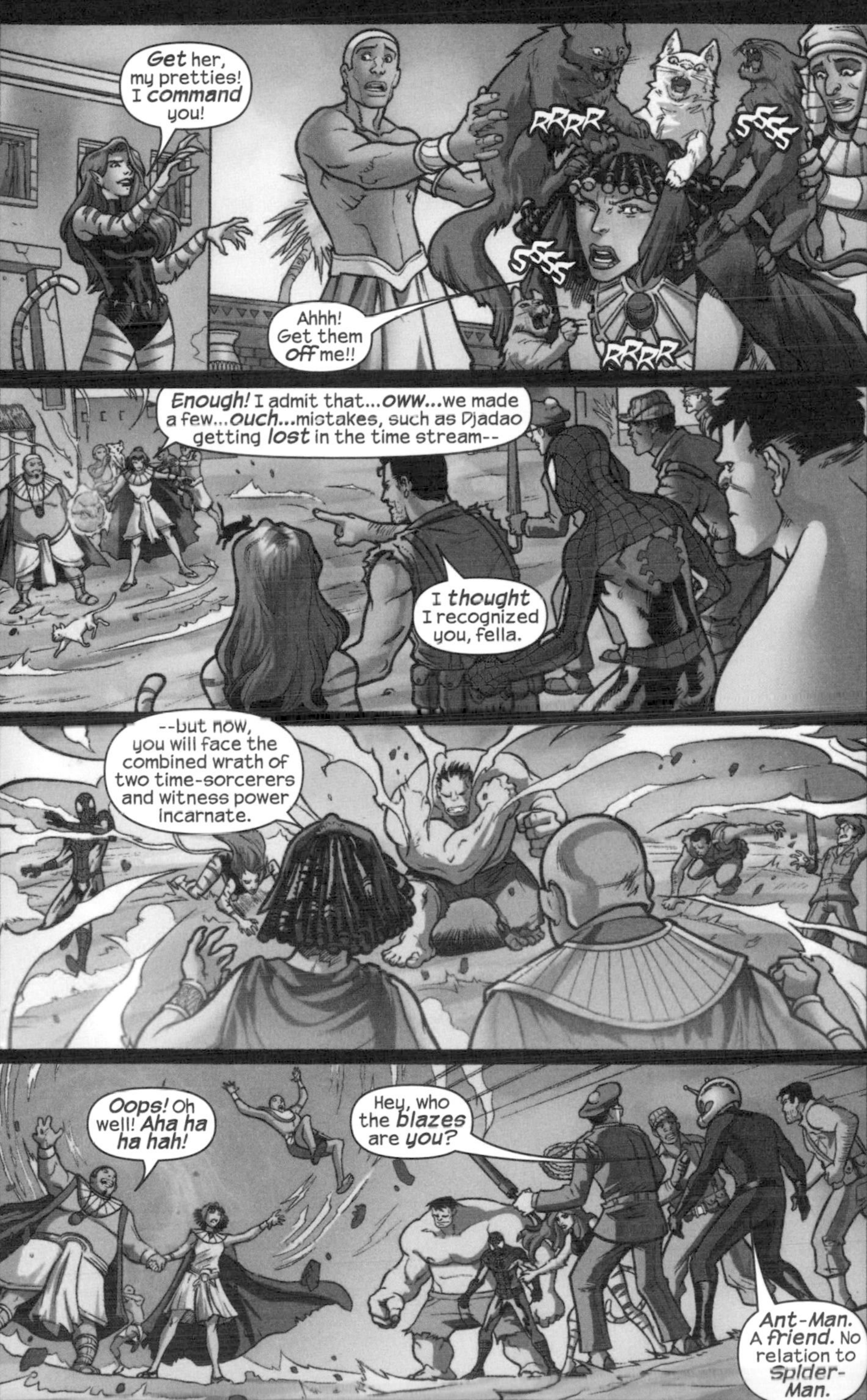
Get her, my pretties! I command you!
RRRR
SSSS
SSSS
Ahhh! Get them off me!!
RRRR
Enough! I admit that...oww...we made a few...ouch...mistakes, such as Djadao getting lost in the time stream--
I thought I recognized you, fella.
--but now, you will face the combined wrath of two time-sorcerers and witness power incarnate.
Oops! Oh well! Aha ha ha hah!
Hey, who the blazes are you?
Ant-Man. A friend. No relation to Spider-Man.

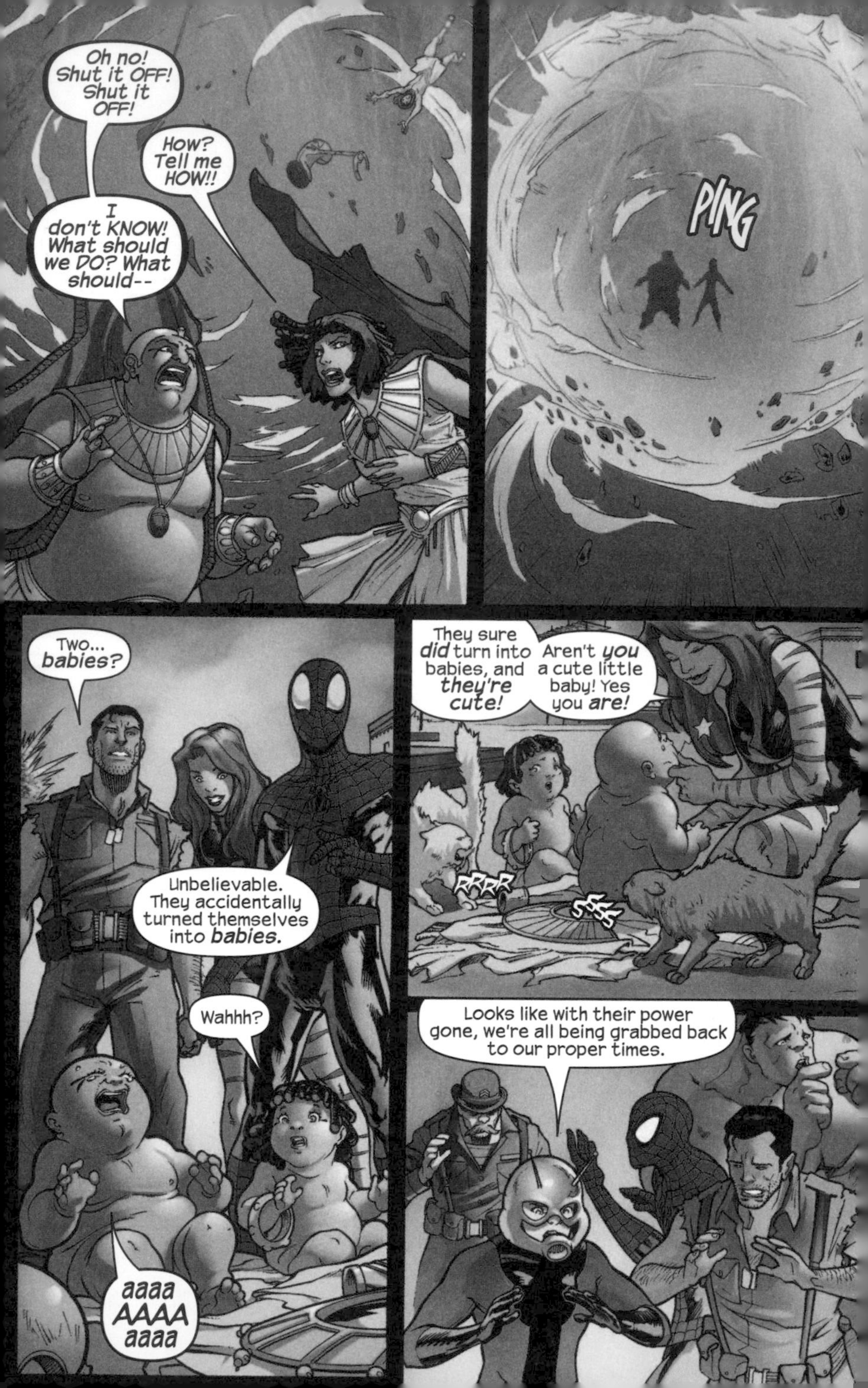
Oh no! Shut it OFF! Shut it OFF!
How? Tell me HOW!!
I don't KNOW! What should we DO? What should--
PING
Two... babies?
Unbelievable. They accidentally turned themselves into babies.
Wahhh?
aaaa AAAA aaaa
They sure did turn into babies, and they're cute!
Aren't you a cute little baby! Yes you are!
RRRR
SSSS
Looks like with their power gone, we're all being grabbed back to our proper times.

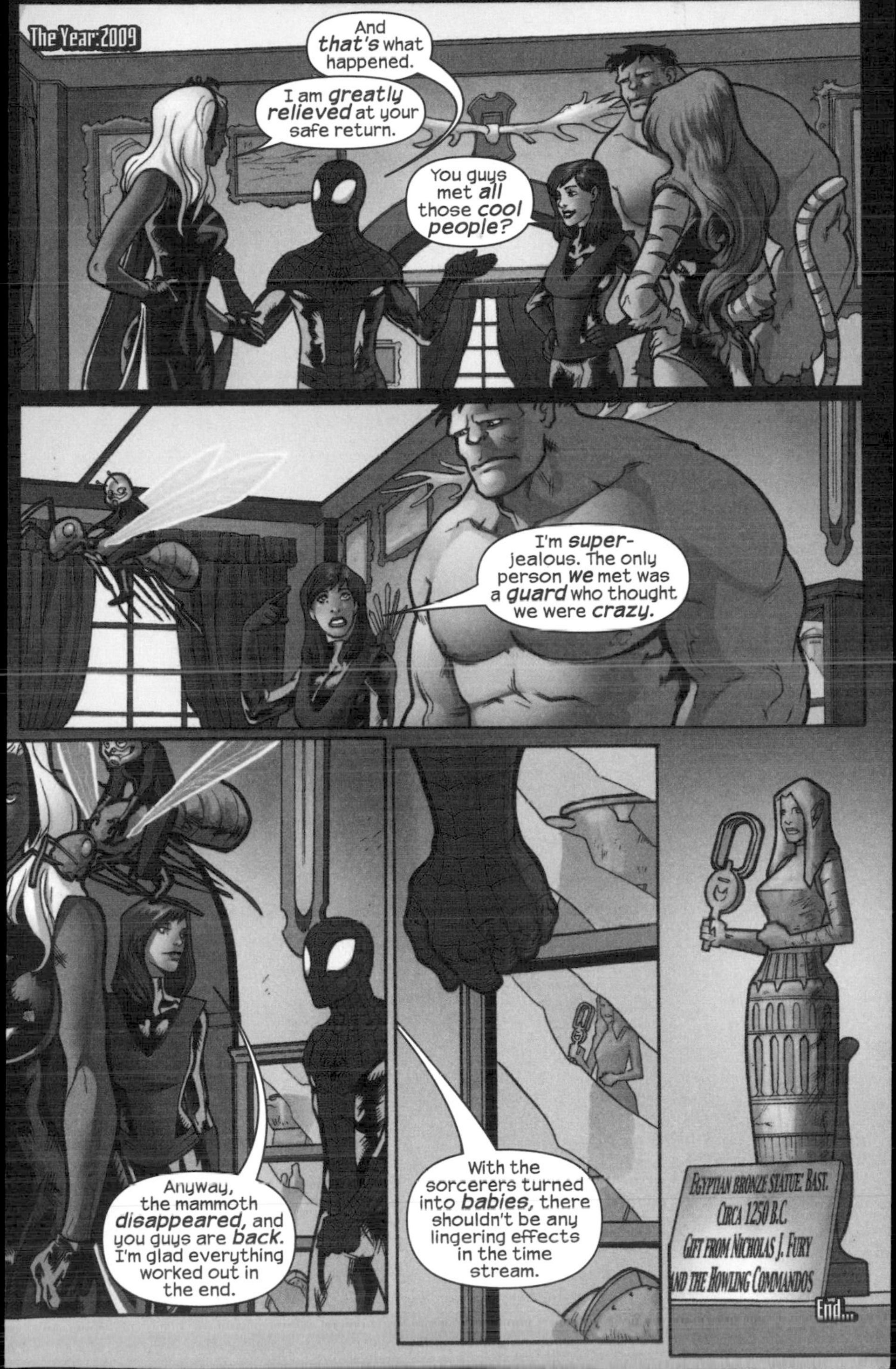
The Year: 2009
And that's what happened.
I am greatly relieved at your safe return.
You guys met all those cool people?
I'm super-jealous. The only person we met was a guard who thought we were crazy.
Anyway, the mammoth disappeared, and you guys are back. I'm glad everything worked out in the end.
With the sorcerers turned into babies, there shouldn't be any lingering effects in the time stream.
Egyptian Bronze Statue: Bast.
Circa 1250 B.C.
Gift from Nicholas J. Fury
and the Howling Commandos
End...

#35

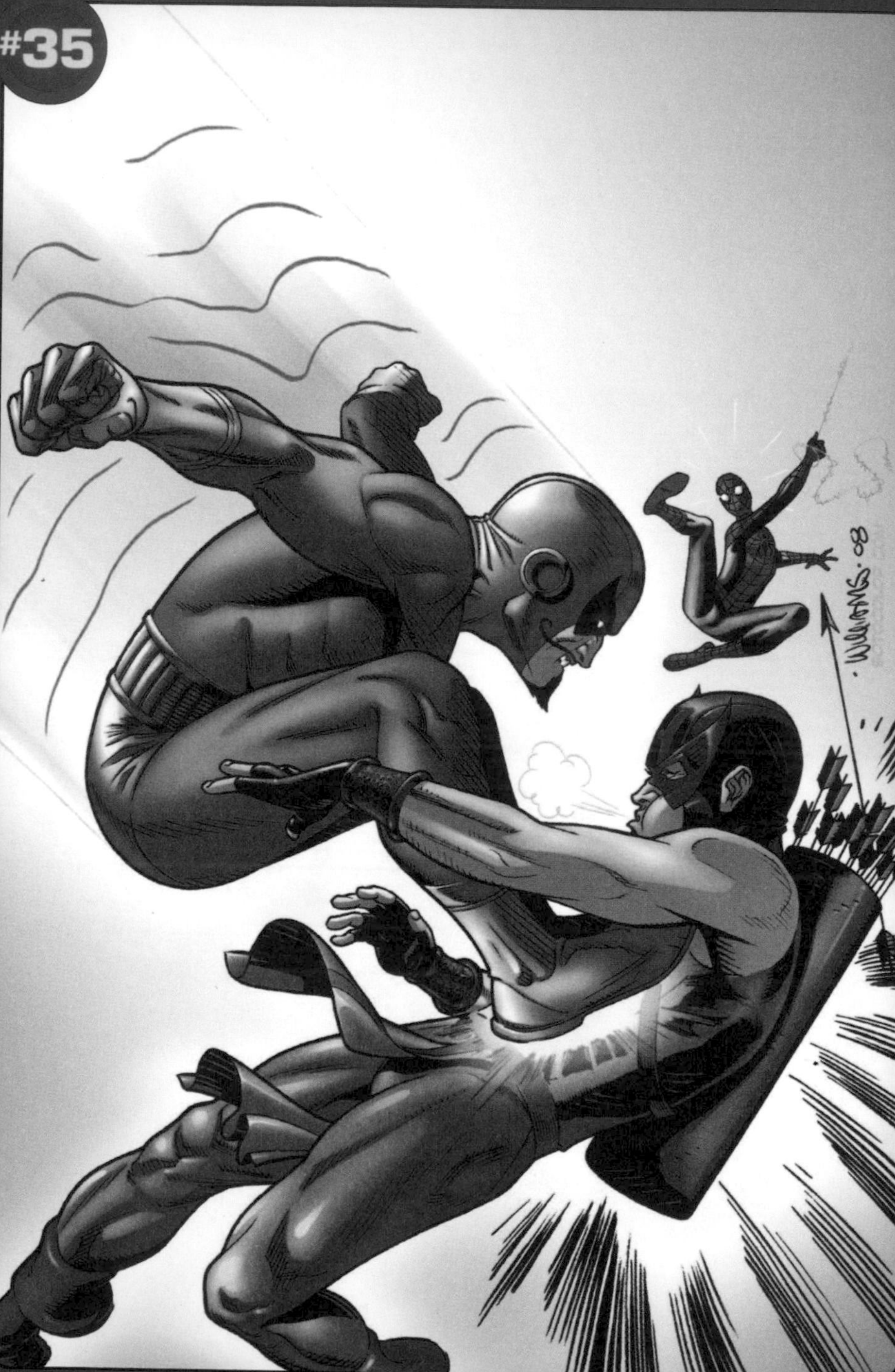

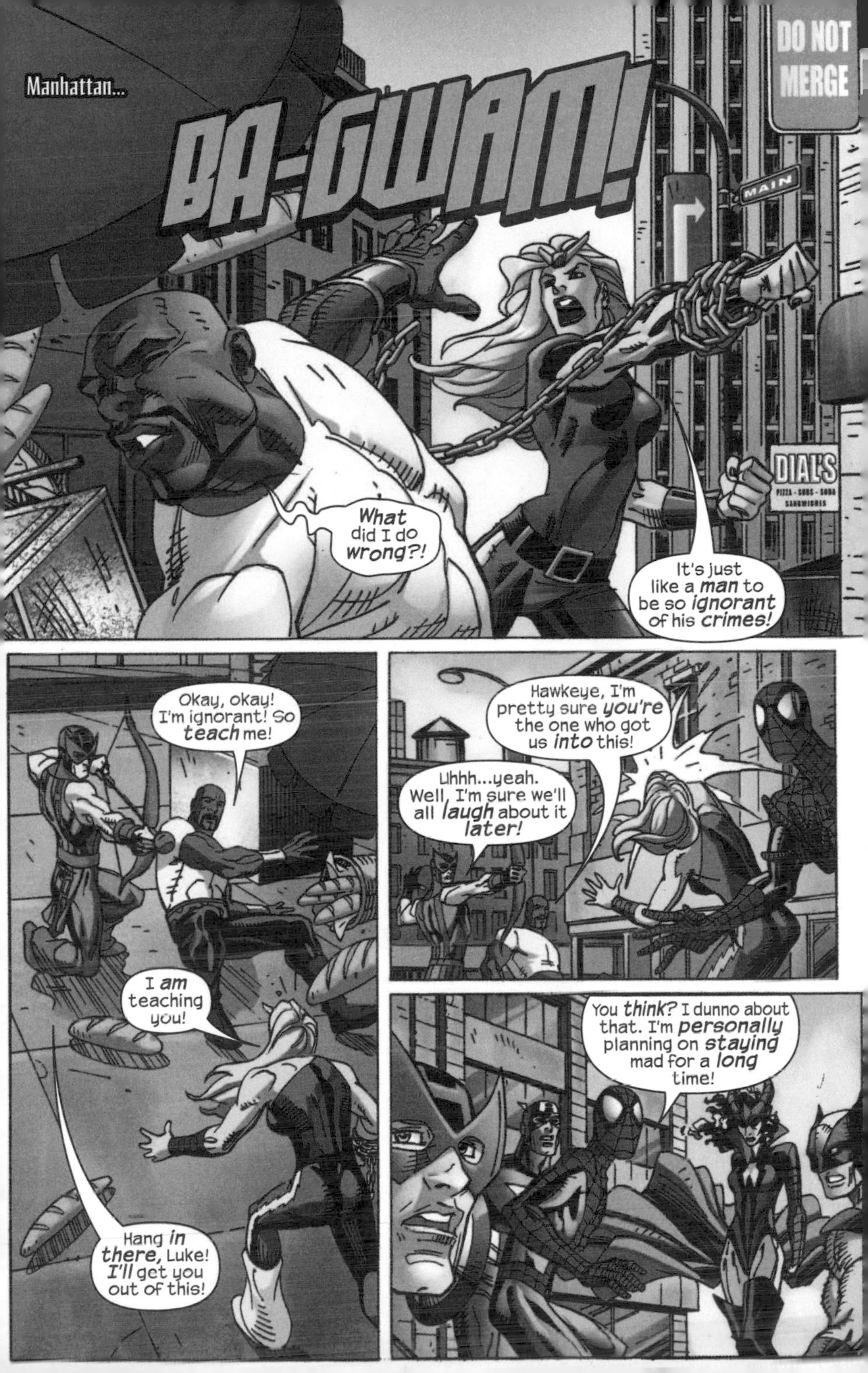
Manhattan...
BA-GWAM!
DO NOT MERGE
MAIN
DIAL'S
PIZZA - SUBS - SODA
SANDWICHES
What did I do wrong?!
It's just like a man to be so ignorant of his crimes!
Okay, okay! I'm ignorant! So teach me!
I am teaching you!
Hang in there, Luke! I'll get you out of this!
Hawkeye, I'm pretty sure you're the one who got us into this!
Uhhh...yeah. Well, I'm sure we'll all laugh about it later!
You think? I dunno about that. I'm personally planning on staying mad for a long time!

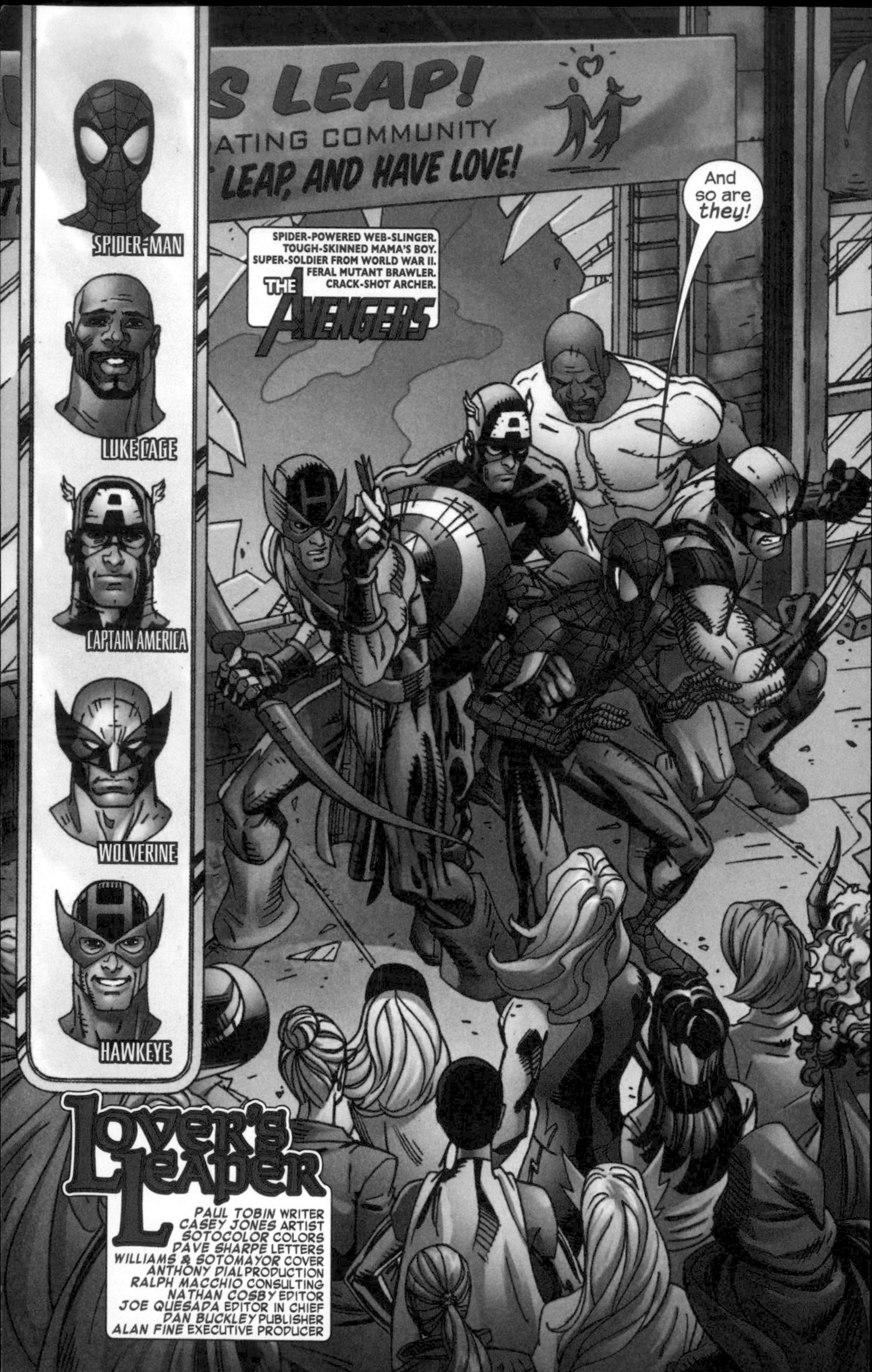
S LEAP!
ATING COMMUNITY
LEAP, AND HAVE LOVE!
And so are they!
SPIDER-POWERED WEB-SLINGER.
TOUGH-SKINNED MAMA'S BOY.
SUPER-SOLDIER FROM WORLD WAR II.
FERAL MUTANT BRAWLER.
CRACK-SHOT ARCHER.
THE AVENGERS
SPIDER-MAN
LUKE CAGE
CAPTAIN AMERICA
WOLVERINE
HAWKEYE
Lover's Leaper
PAUL TOBIN WRITER
CASEY JONES ARTIST
SOTOCOLOR COLORS
DAVE SHARPE LETTERS
WILLIAMS & SOTOMAYOR COVER
ANTHONY DIAL PRODUCTION
RALPH MACCHIO CONSULTING
NATHAN COSBY EDITOR
JOE QUESADA EDITOR IN CHIEF
DAN BUCKLEY PUBLISHER
ALAN FINE EXECUTIVE PRODUCER

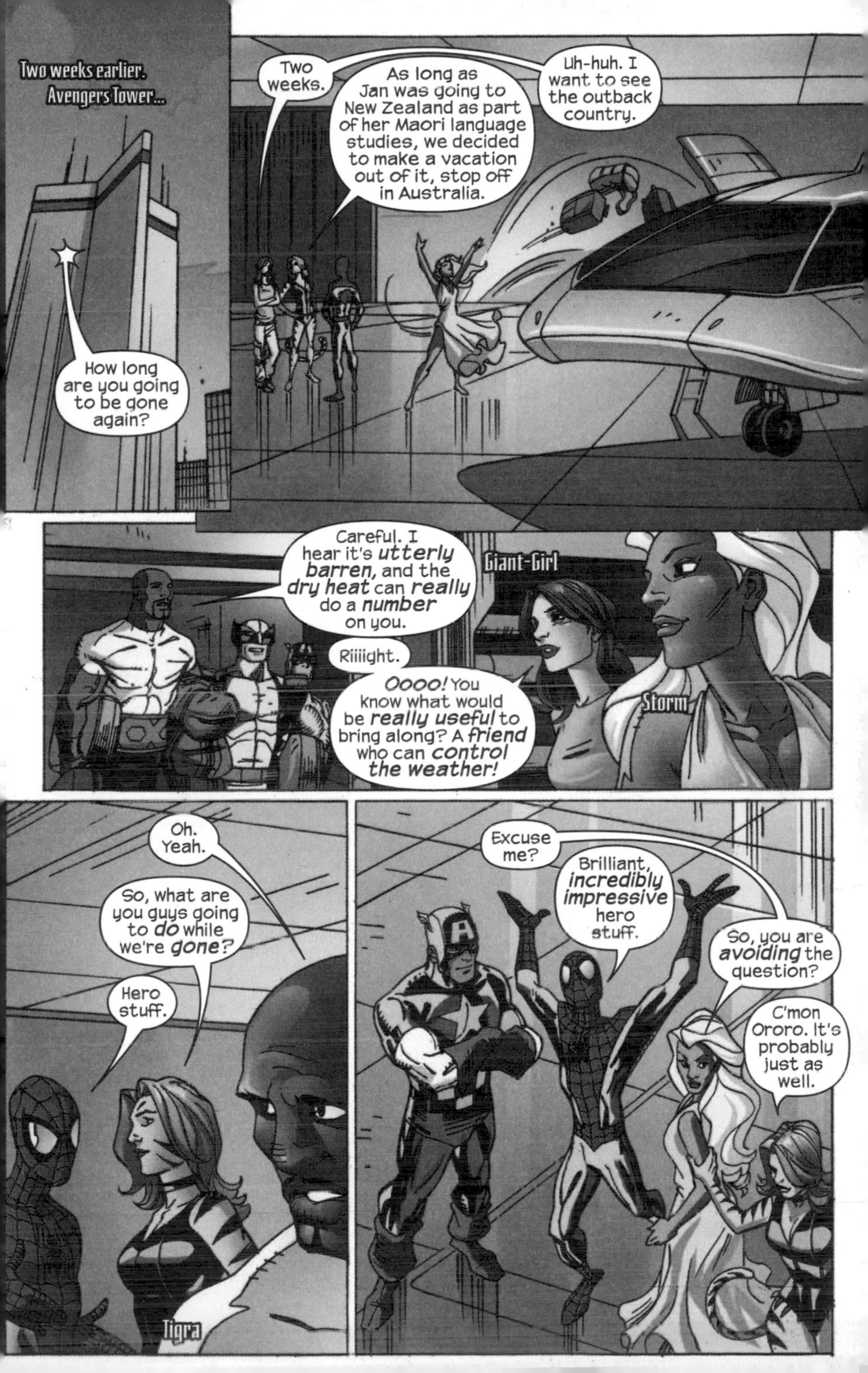

Two weeks earlier.
Avengers Tower...
How long are you going to be gone again?
Two weeks.
As long as Jan was going to New Zealand as part of her Maori language studies, we decided to make a vacation out of it, stop off in Australia.
Uh-huh. I want to see the outback country.
Careful. I hear it's *utterly barren,* and the *dry heat* can *really* do a *number* on you.
Giant-Girl
Riiiight.
Oooo! You know what would be *really useful* to bring along? A *friend* who can *control the weather!*
Storm
Oh. Yeah.
So, what are you guys going to *do* while we're *gone?*
Hero stuff.
Tigra
Excuse me?
Brilliant, *incredibly impressive* hero stuff.
So, you are *avoiding* the question?
C'mon Ororo. It's probably just as well.

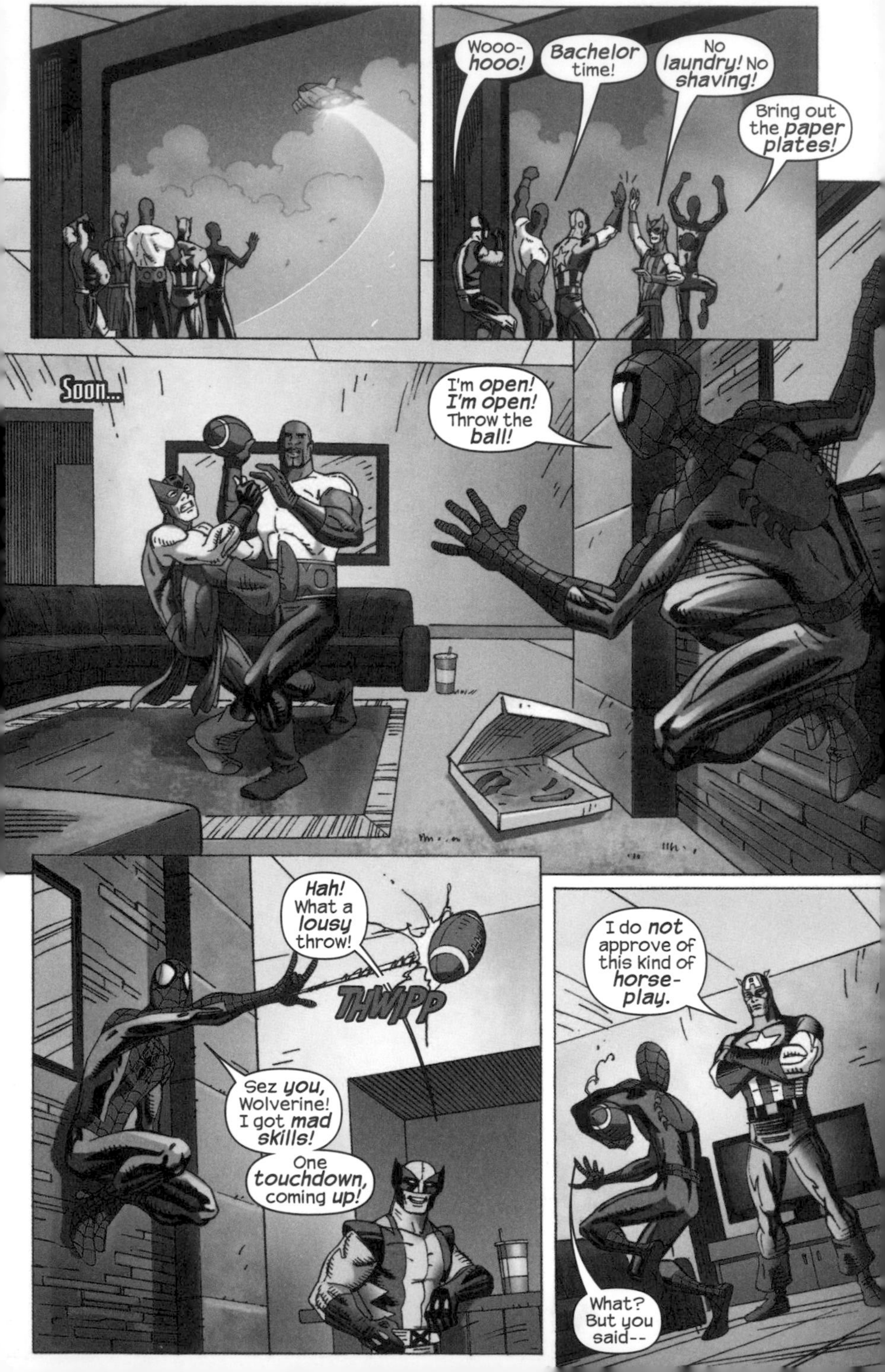
Wooo-hooo!
Bachelor time!
No laundry! No shaving!
Bring out the paper plates!
Soon...
I'm open! I'm open! Throw the ball!
Hah! What a lousy throw!
THWIPP
Sez you, Wolverine! I got mad skills!
One touchdown, coming up!
I do not approve of this kind of horse-play.
What? But you said--

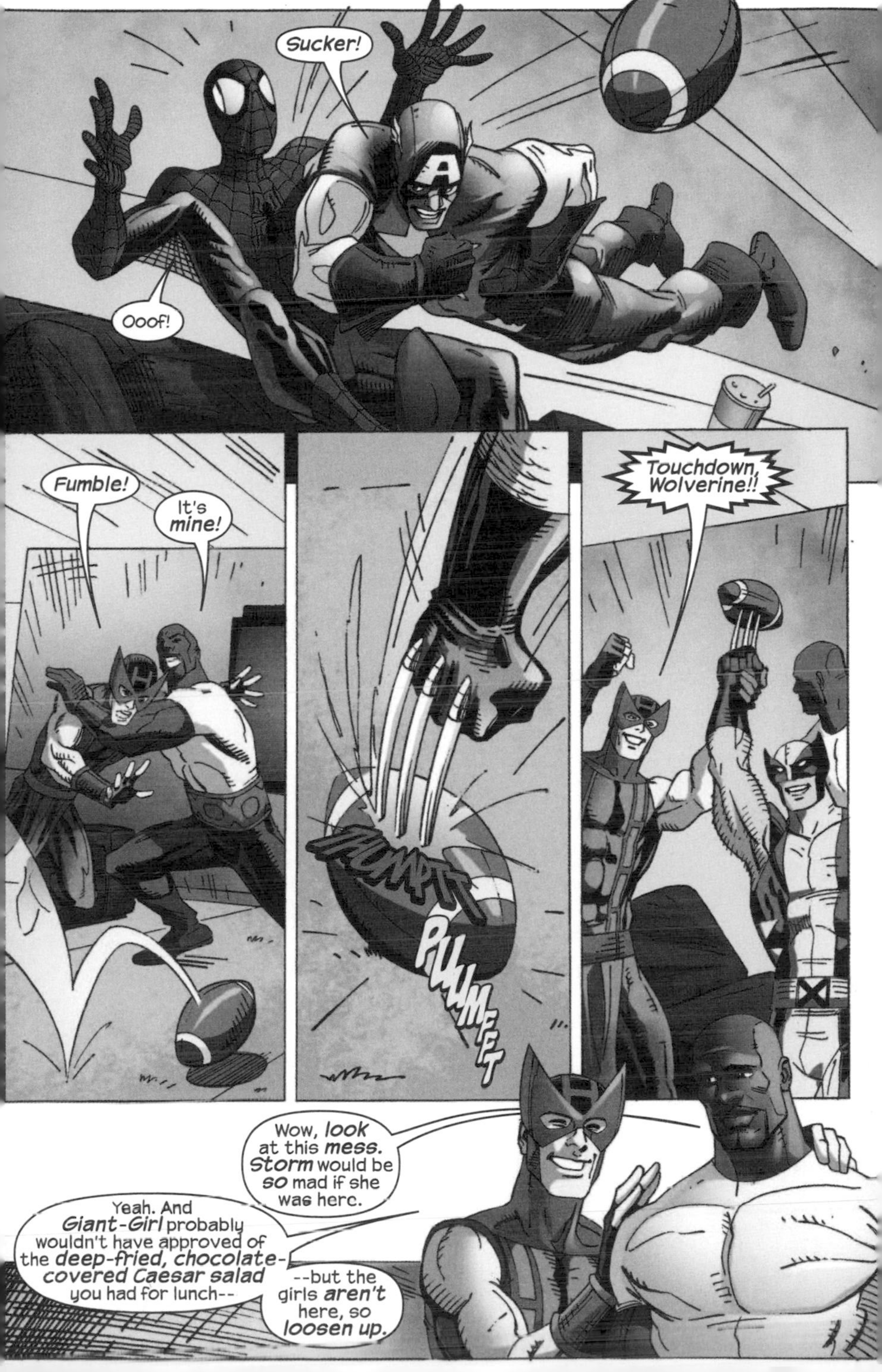
Sucker!
Ooof!
Fumble!
It's mine!
THUMPT
PLUMMFT
Touchdown, Wolverine!!
Wow, look at this mess. Storm would be so mad if she was here.
Yeah. And Giant-Girl probably wouldn't have approved of the deep-fried, chocolate-covered Caesar salad you had for lunch--
--but the girls aren't here, so loosen up.

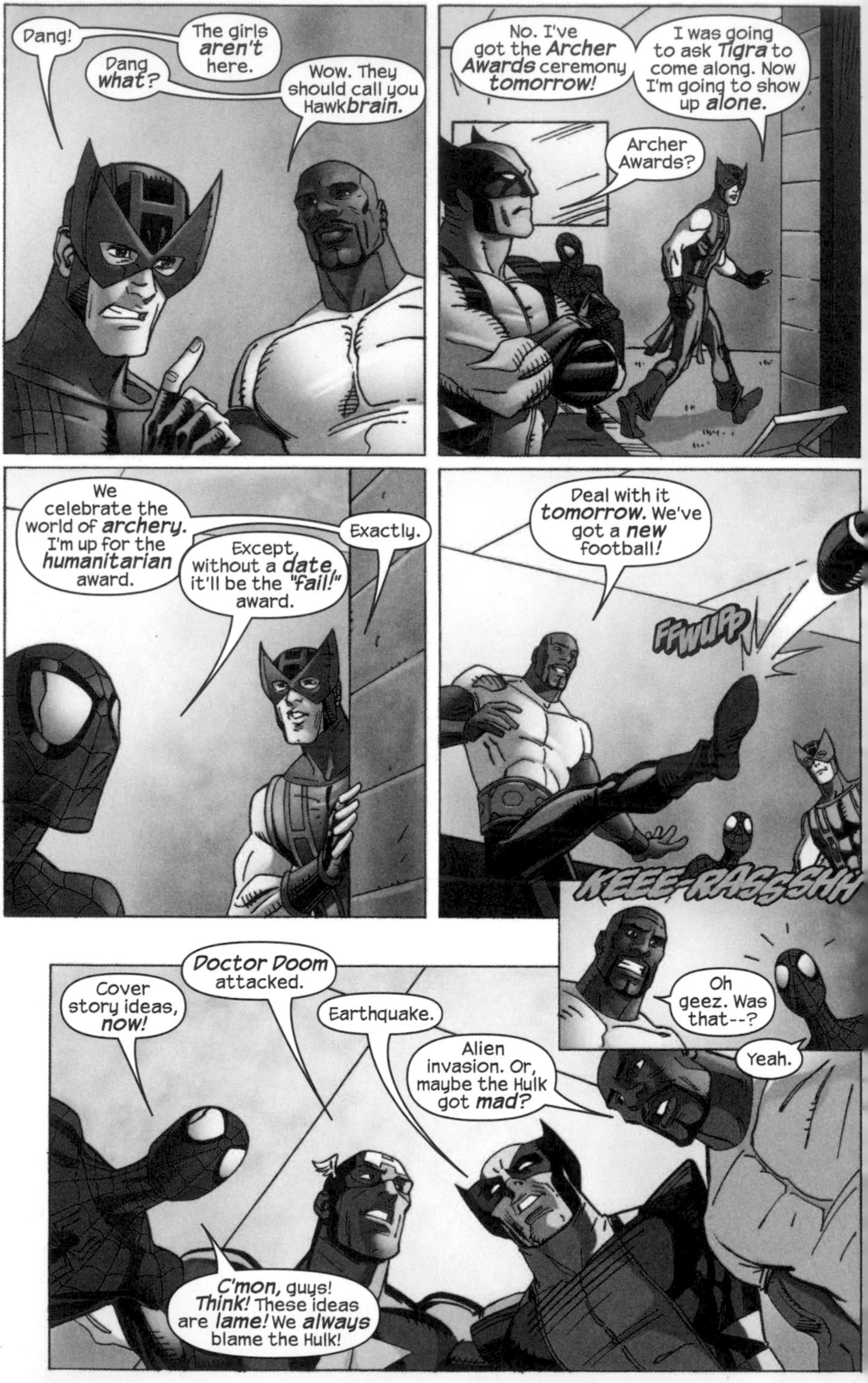

Dang!
The girls aren't here.
Dang what?
Wow. They should call you Hawkbrain.
No. I've got the Archer Awards ceremony tomorrow!
I was going to ask Tigra to come along. Now I'm going to show up alone.
Archer Awards?
We celebrate the world of archery. I'm up for the humanitarian award.
Exactly.
Except, without a date, it'll be the "fail!" award.
Deal with it tomorrow. We've got a new football!
FFWUPP
KEEE-RASSSHH
Oh geez. Was that--?
Yeah.
Cover story ideas, now!
Doctor Doom attacked.
Earthquake.
Alien invasion. Or, maybe the Hulk got mad?
C'mon, guys! Think! These ideas are lame! We always blame the Hulk!

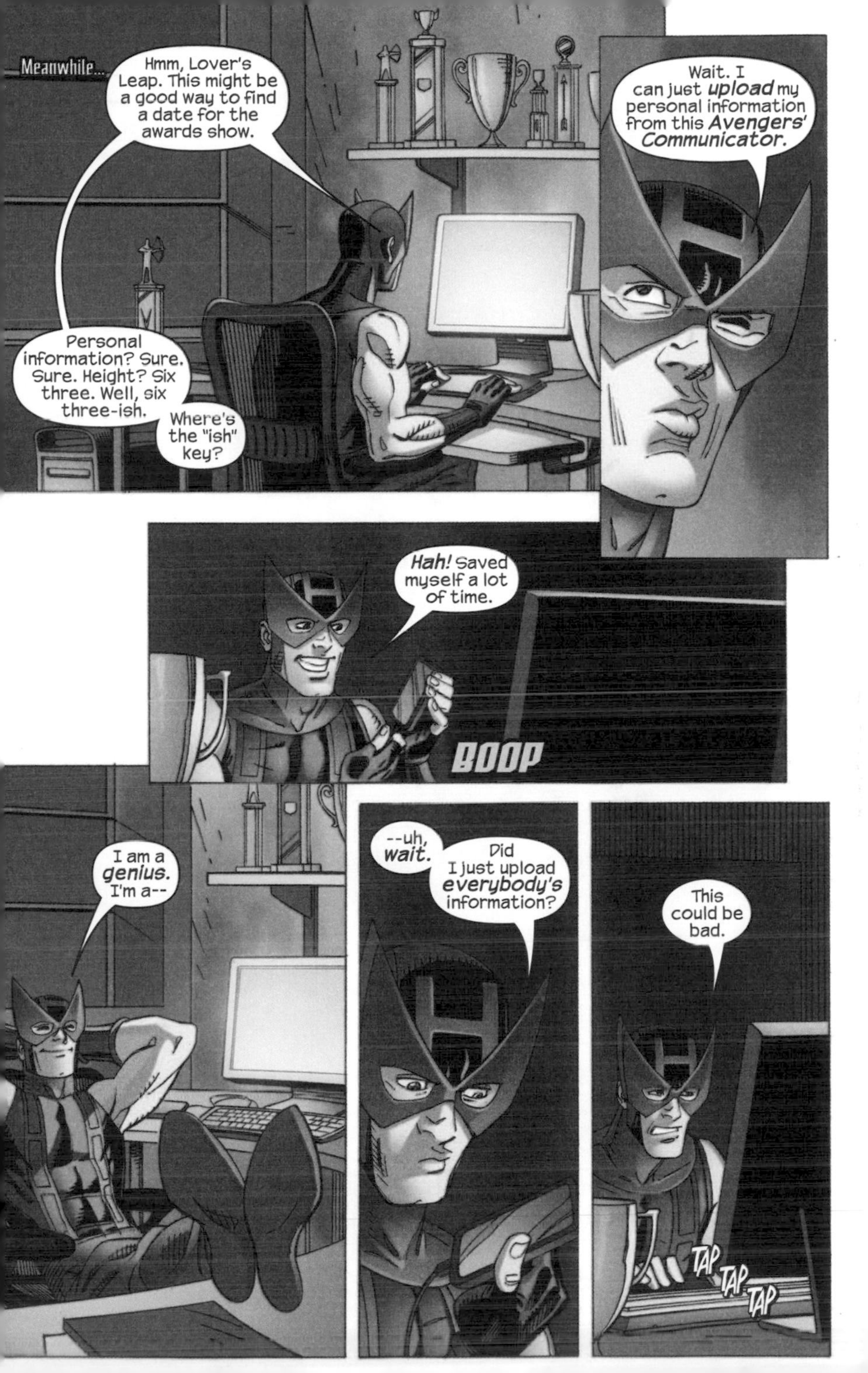
Meanwhile...
Hmm, Lover's Leap. This might be a good way to find a date for the awards show.
Personal information? Sure. Sure. Height? Six three. Well, six three-ish.
Where's the "ish" key?
Wait. I can just upload my personal information from this Avengers' Communicator.
Hah! Saved myself a lot of time.
BOOP
I am a genius. I'm a--
--uh, wait.
Did I just upload everybody's information?
This could be bad.
TAP TAP TAP

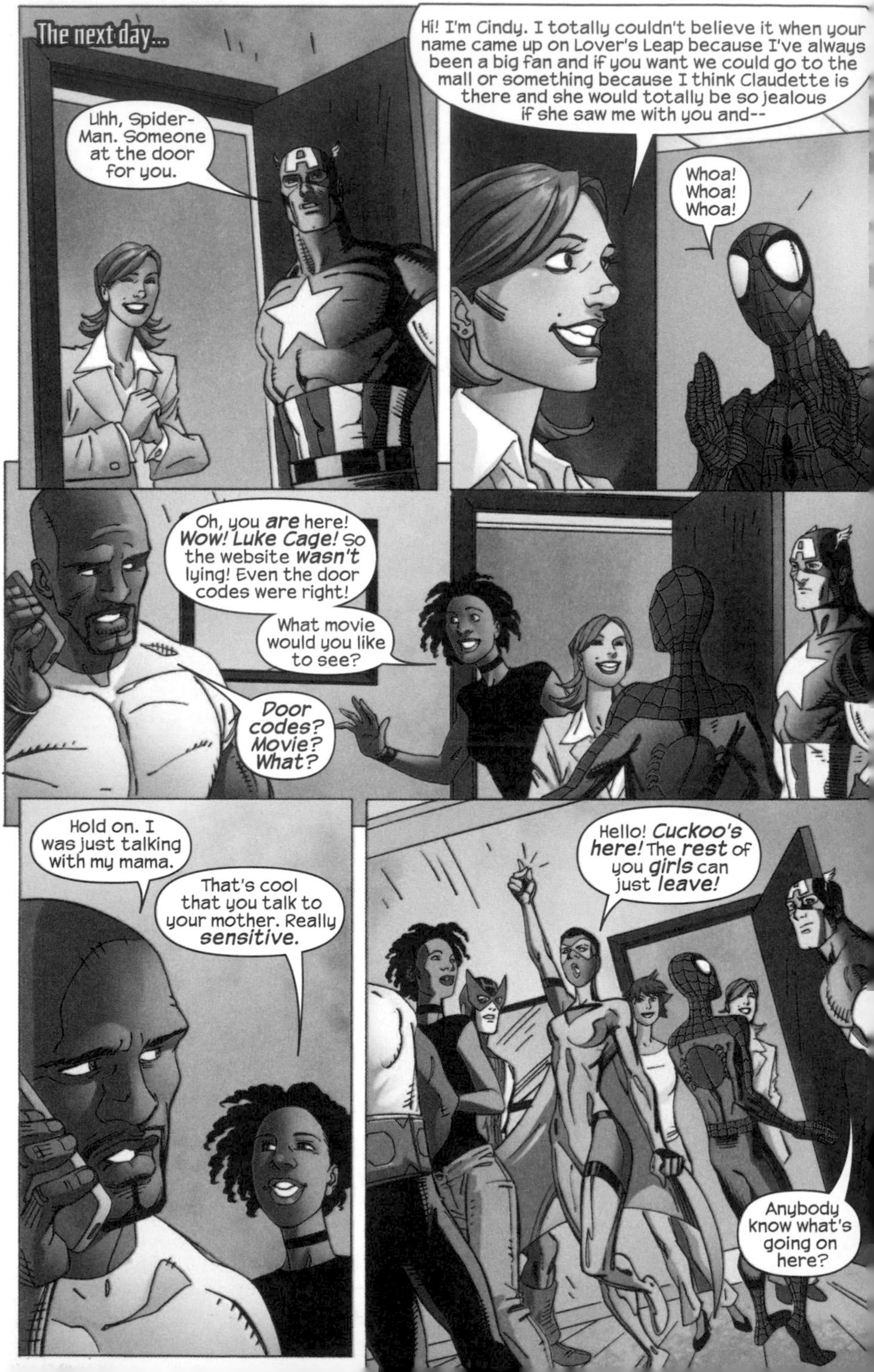
The next day...
Uhh, Spider-Man. Someone at the door for you.
Hi! I'm Cindy. I totally couldn't believe it when your name came up on Lover's Leap because I've always been a big fan and if you want we could go to the mall or something because I think Claudette is there and she would totally be so jealous if she saw me with you and--
Whoa! Whoa! Whoa!
Oh, you are here! Wow! Luke Cage! So the website wasn't lying! Even the door codes were right!
What movie would you like to see?
Door codes? Movie? What?
Hold on. I was just talking with my mama.
That's cool that you talk to your mother. Really sensitive.
Hello! Cuckoo's here! The rest of you girls can just leave!
Anybody know what's going on here?

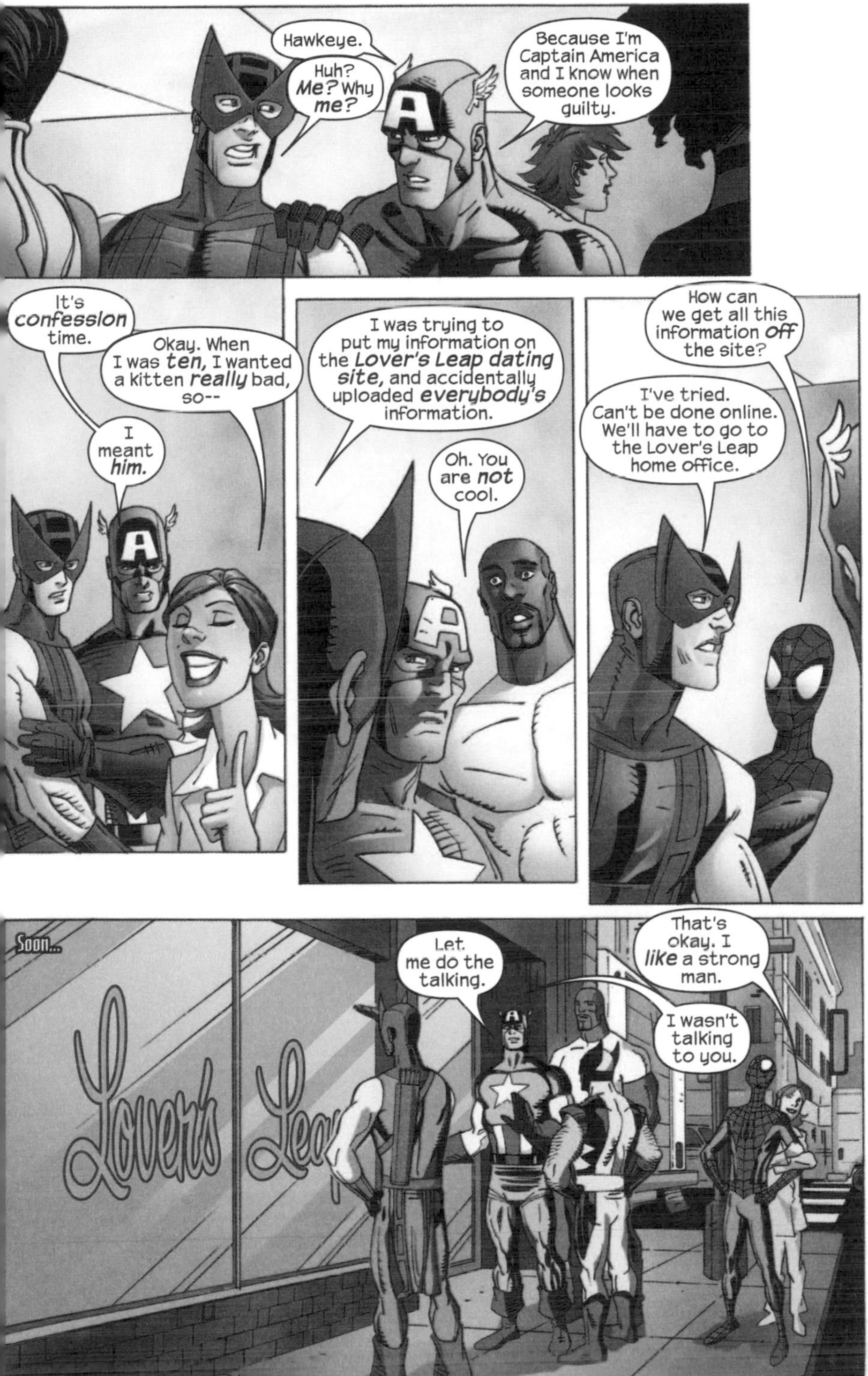
Hawkeye.
Huh? Me? Why me?
Because I'm Captain America and I know when someone looks guilty.
It's confession time.
Okay. When I was ten, I wanted a kitten really bad, so--
I meant him.
I was trying to put my information on the Lover's Leap dating site, and accidentally uploaded everybody's information.
Oh. You are not cool.
How can we get all this information off the site?
I've tried. Can't be done online. We'll have to go to the Lover's Leap home office.
Soon...
Let me do the talking.
That's okay. I like a strong man.
I wasn't talking to you.
Lover's Leap

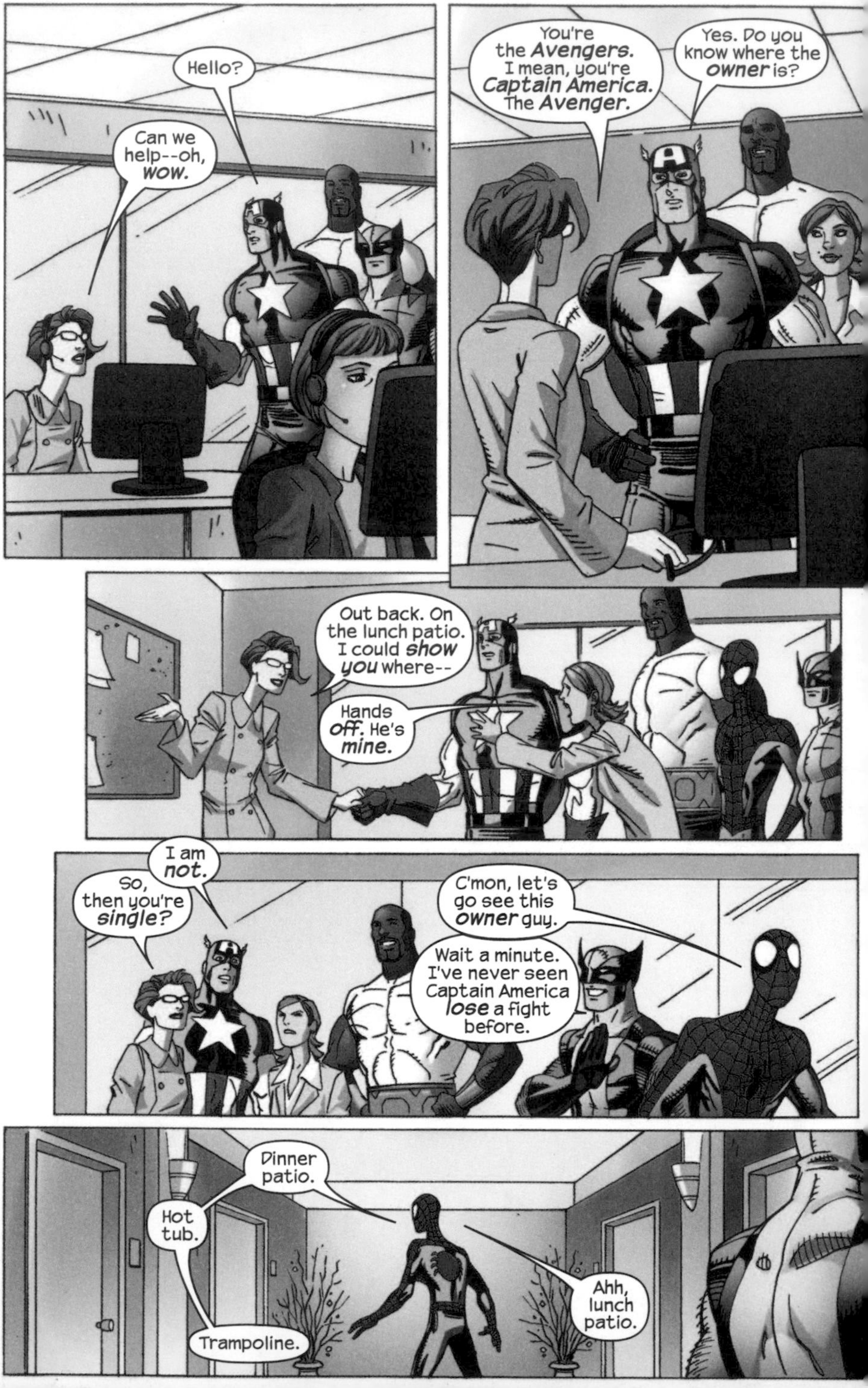
Hello?
Can we help--oh, *wow.*
You're the *Avengers.* I mean, you're *Captain America.* The *Avenger.*
Yes. Do you know where the *owner* is?
Out back. On the lunch patio. I could *show you* where--
Hands *off.* He's *mine.*
So, then you're *single?*
I am *not.*
C'mon, let's go see this *owner* guy.
Wait a minute. I've never seen Captain America *lose* a fight before.
Dinner patio.
Hot tub.
Trampoline.
Ahh, lunch patio.

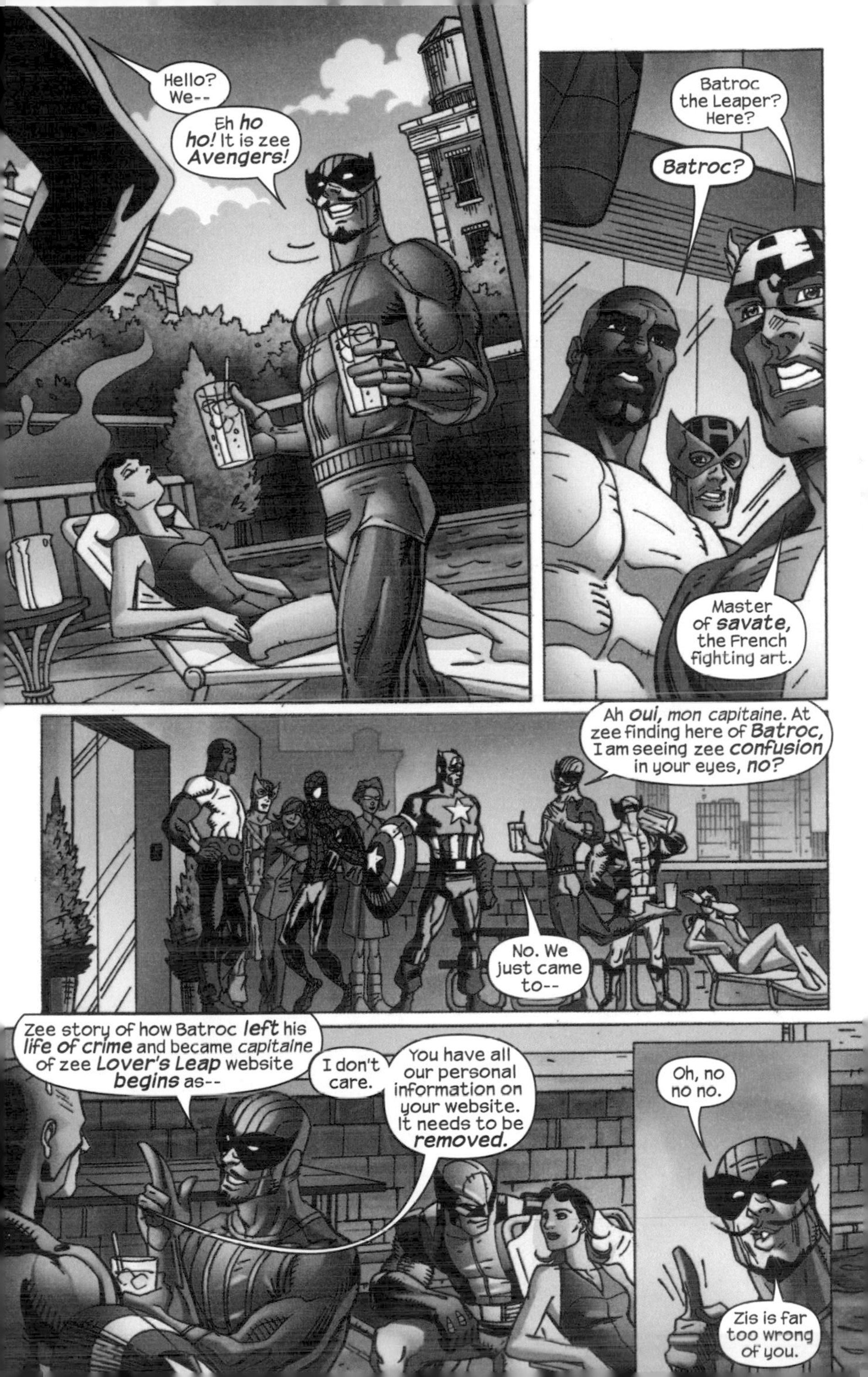
Hello? We--
Eh *ho ho!* It is zee *Avengers!*
Batroc the Leaper? Here?
Batroc?
Master of *savate,* the French fighting art.
Ah *oui, mon capitaine.* At zee finding here of *Batroc,* I am seeing zee *confusion* in your eyes, *no?*
No. We just came to--
Zee story of how Batroc *left* his *life of crime* and became *capitaine* of zee *Lover's Leap* website *begins* as--
I don't care.
You have all our personal information on your website. It needs to be *removed.*
Oh, no no no.
Zis is far too wrong of you.

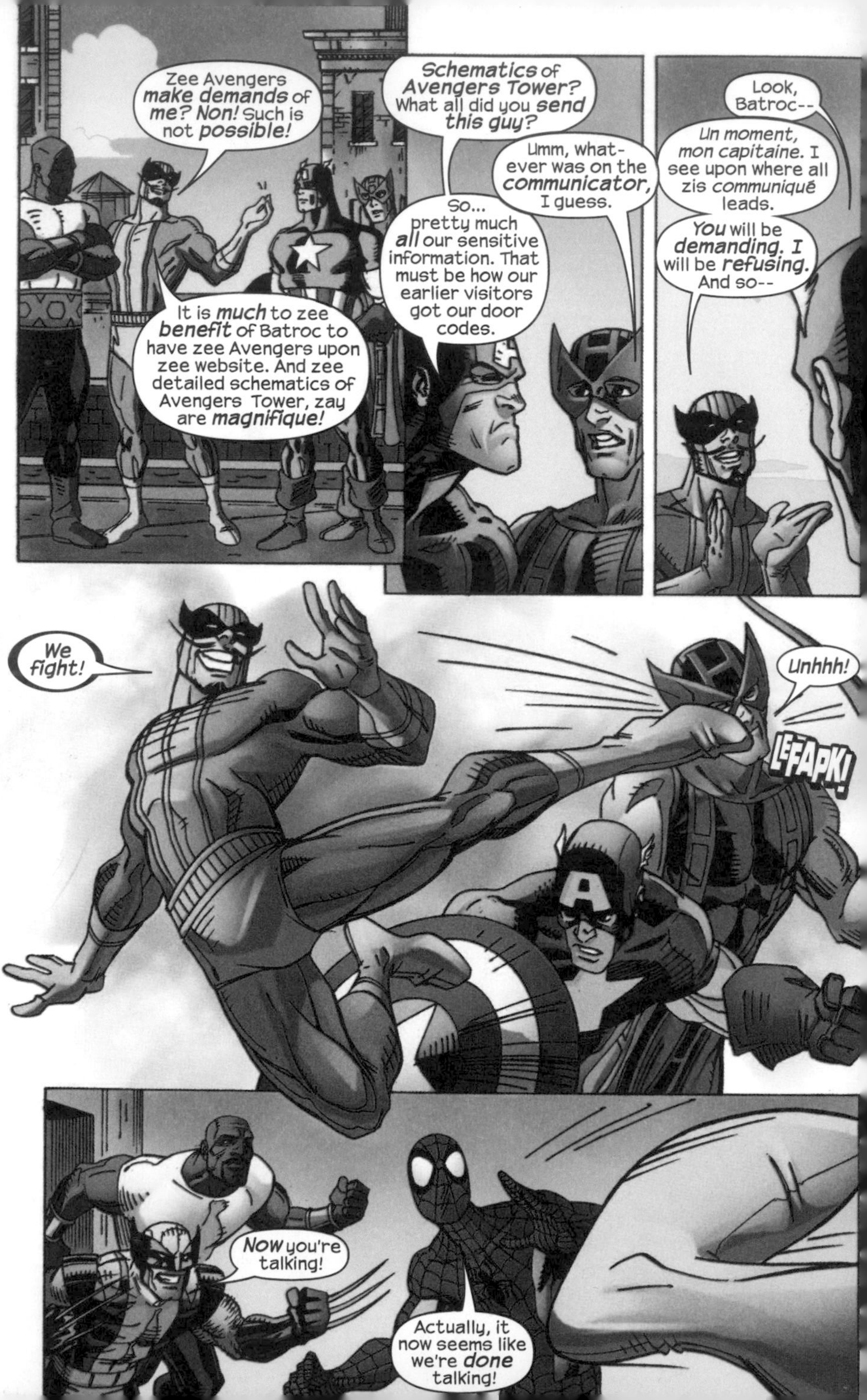
Zee Avengers make demands of me? Non! Such is not possible!
It is much to zee benefit of Batroc to have zee Avengers upon zee website. And zee detailed schematics of Avengers Tower, zay are magnifique!
Schematics of Avengers Tower? What all did you send this guy?
Umm, whatever was on the communicator, I guess.
So... pretty much all our sensitive information. That must be how our earlier visitors got our door codes.
Look, Batroc--
Un moment, mon capitaine. I see upon where all zis communiqué leads.
You will be demanding. I will be refusing. And so--
We fight!
Unhhh!
LEFAPK!
Now you're talking!
Actually, it now seems like we're done talking!

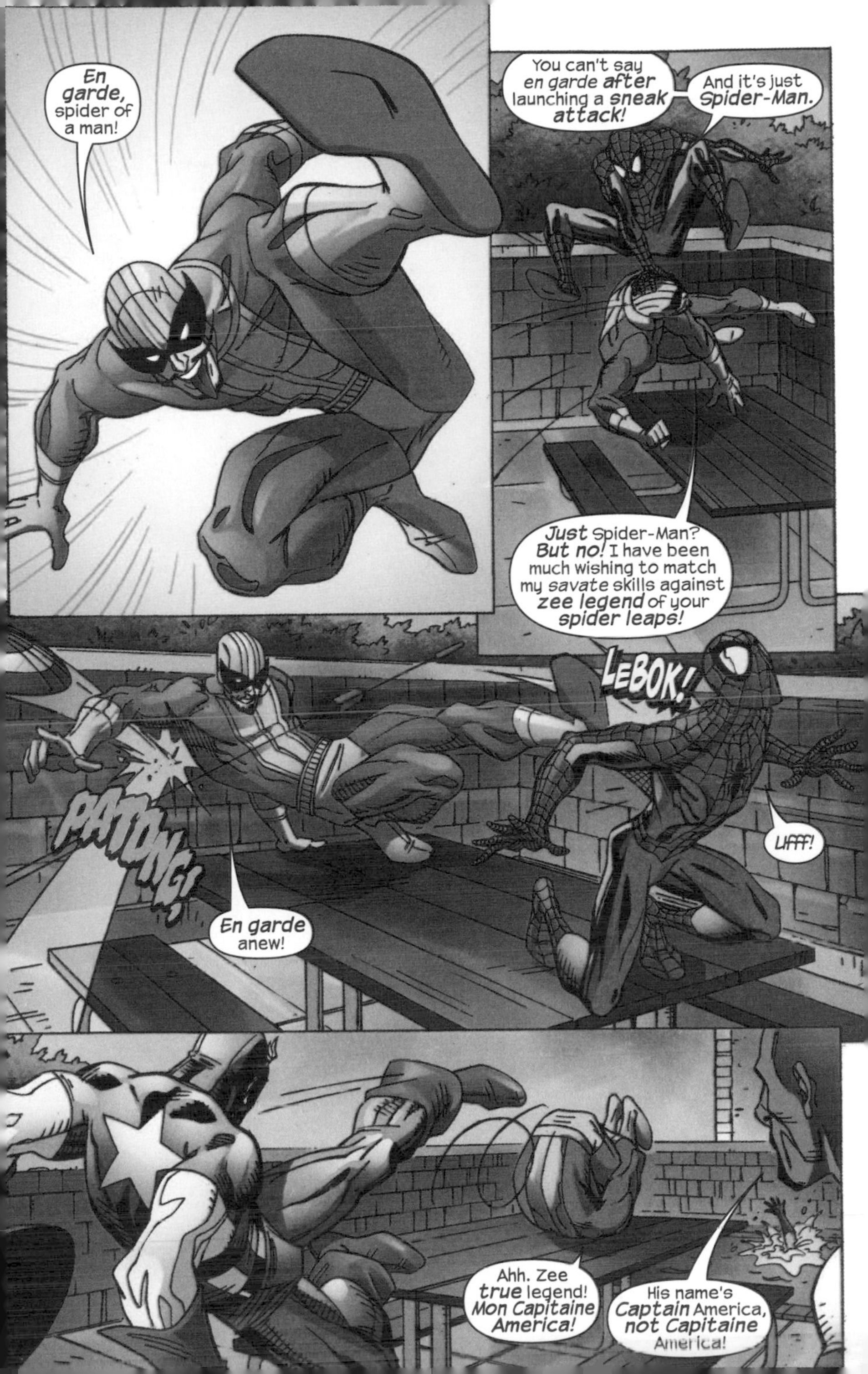
En garde, spider of a man!
You can't say en garde after launching a sneak attack!
And it's just Spider-Man.
Just Spider-Man? But no! I have been much wishing to match my savate skills against zee legend of your spider leaps!
LEBOK!
PATONG!
UFFF!
En garde anew!
Ahh. Zee true legend! Mon Capitaine America!
His name's Captain America, not Capitaine America!

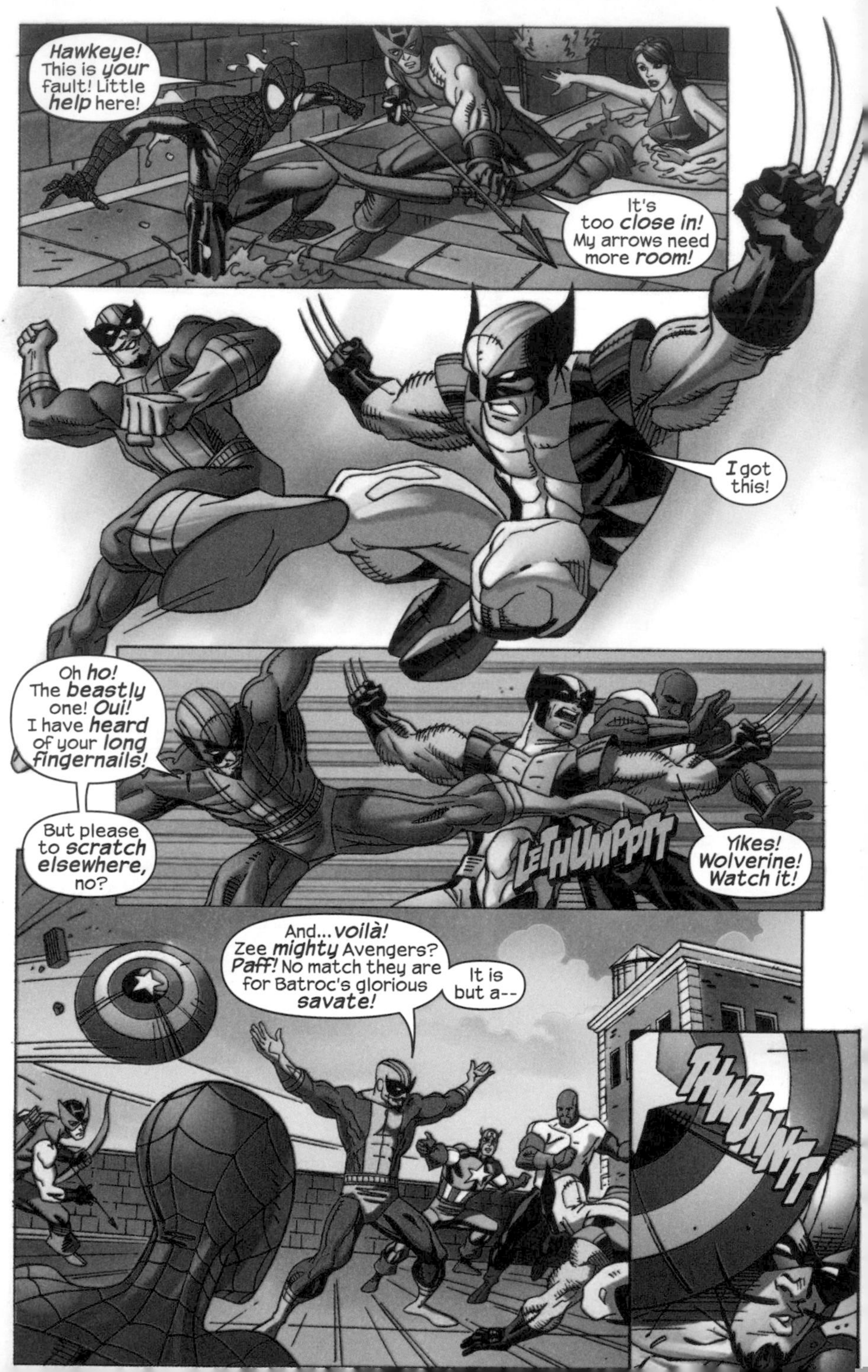
Hawkeye! This is your fault! Little help here!
It's too close in! My arrows need more room!
I got this!
Oh ho! The beastly one! Oui! I have heard of your long fingernails!
But please to scratch elsewhere, no?
LETHUMPPTT
Yikes! Wolverine! Watch it!
And... voilà! Zee mighty Avengers? Paff! No match they are for Batroc's glorious savate!
It is but a--
THWUNNTT

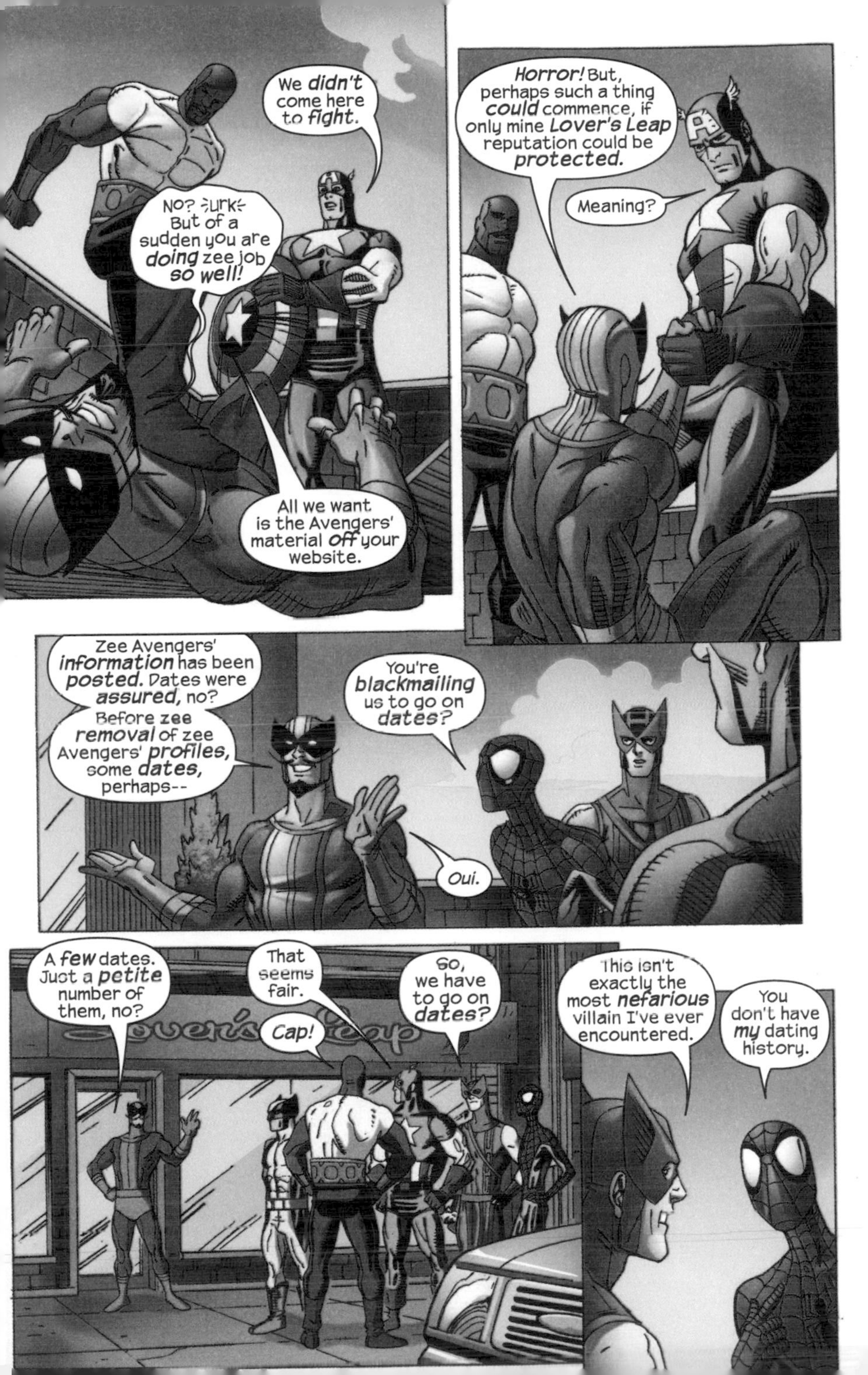
We didn't come here to fight.
No? -Urk- But of a sudden you are doing zee job so well!
All we want is the Avengers' material off your website.
Horror! But, perhaps such a thing could commence, if only mine Lover's Leap reputation could be protected.
Meaning?
Zee Avengers' information has been posted. Dates were assured, no? Before zee removal of zee Avengers' profiles, some dates, perhaps--
You're blackmailing us to go on dates?
Oui.
A few dates. Just a petite number of them, no?
That seems fair.
Cap!
So, we have to go on dates?
This isn't exactly the most nefarious villain I've ever encountered.
You don't have my dating history.

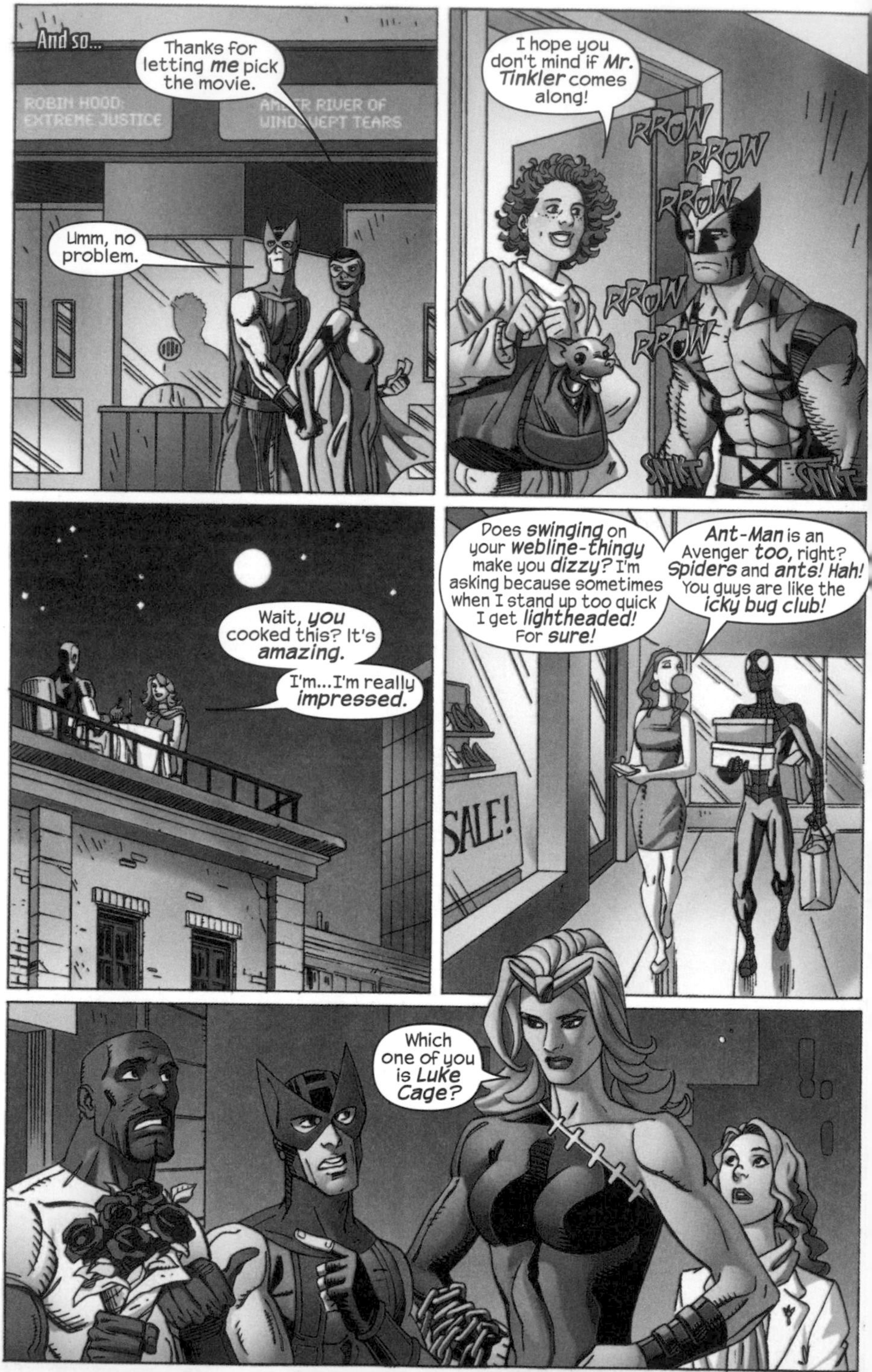
And so...
Thanks for letting me pick the movie.
ROBIN HOOD: EXTREME JUSTICE
Umm, no problem.
I hope you don't mind if Mr. Tinkler comes along!
RROW RROW RROW RROW RROW
SNIKT SNIKT
Wait, you cooked this? It's amazing.
I'm...I'm really impressed.
Does swinging on your webline-thingy make you dizzy? I'm asking because sometimes when I stand up too quick I get lightheaded! For sure!
Ant-Man is an Avenger too, right? Spiders and ants! Hah! You guys are like the icky bug club!
SALE!
Which one of you is Luke Cage?

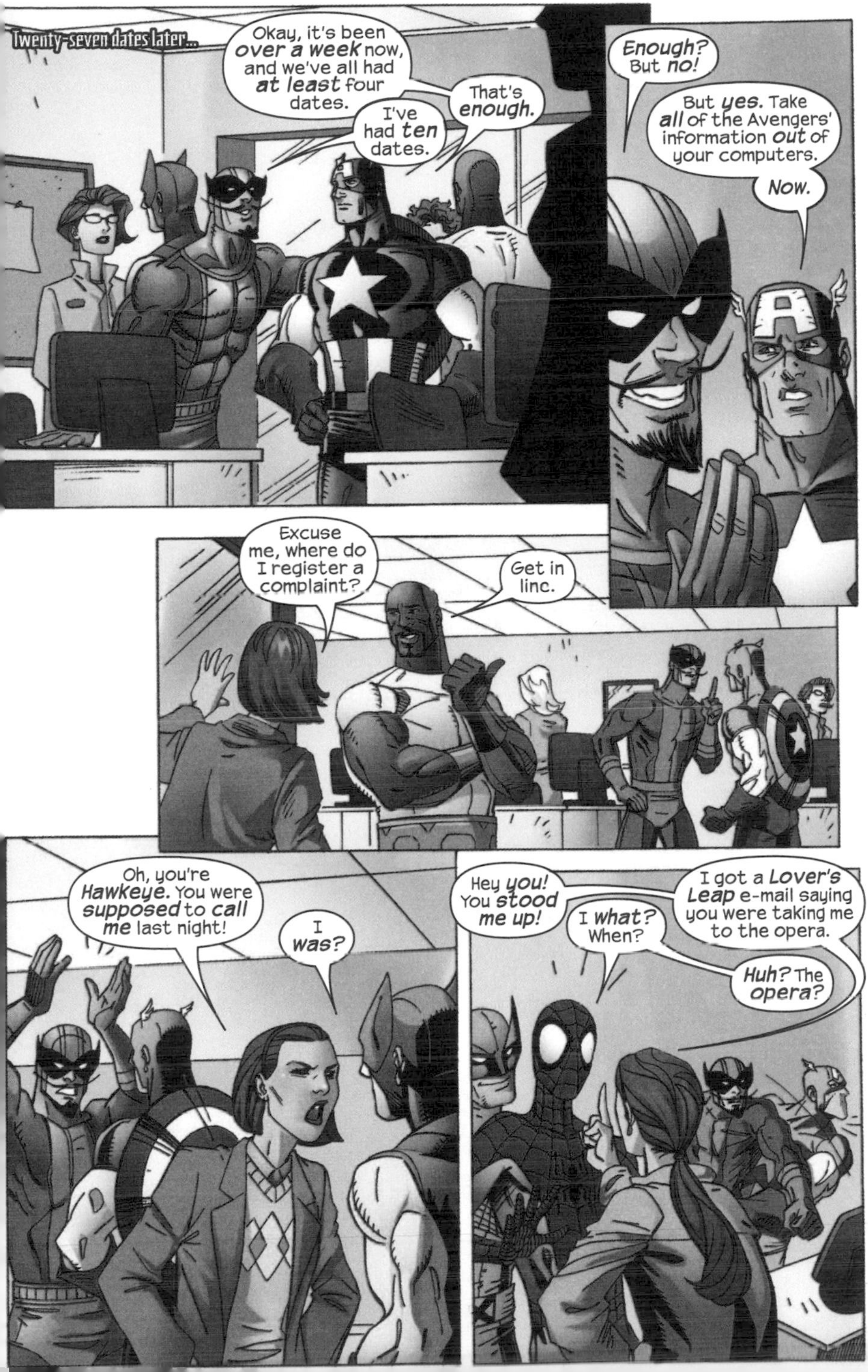

Twenty-seven dates later...
Okay, it's been over a week now, and we've all had at least four dates.
I've had ten dates.
That's enough.
Enough? But no!
But yes. Take all of the Avengers' information out of your computers.
Now.
Excuse me, where do I register a complaint?
Get in linc.
Oh, you're Hawkeye. You were supposed to call me last night!
I was?
Hey you! You stood me up!
I what? When?
I got a Lover's Leap e-mail saying you were taking me to the opera.
Huh? The opera?

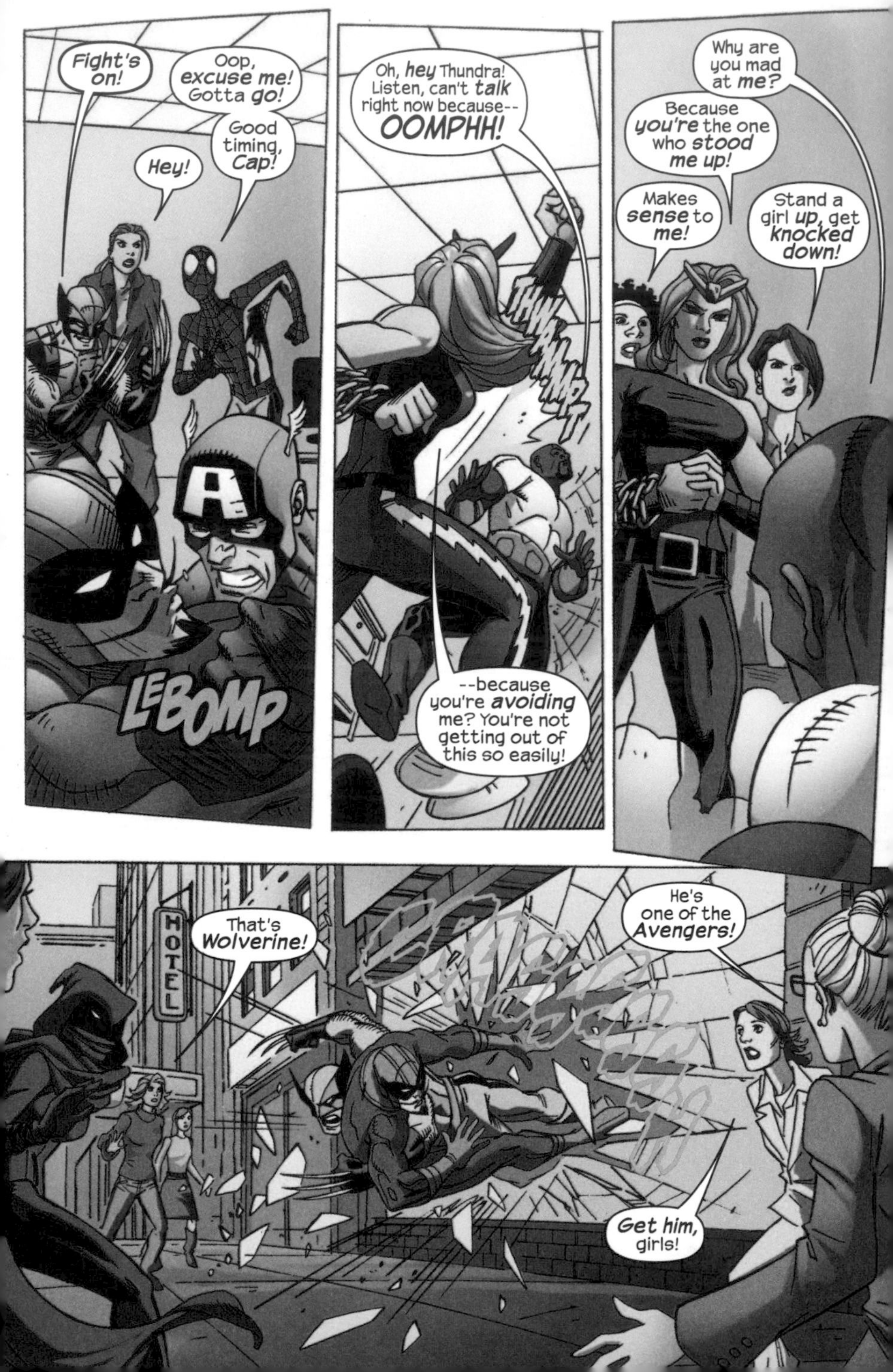

Fight's on!
Oop, excuse me! Gotta go!
Good timing, Cap!
Hey!
LEBOMP
Oh, hey Thundra! Listen, can't talk right now because-- OOMPHH!
--because you're avoiding me? You're not getting out of this so easily!
Why are you mad at me?
Because you're the one who stood me up!
Makes sense to me!
Stand a girl up, get knocked down!
That's Wolverine!
HOTEL
He's one of the Avengers!
Get him, girls!

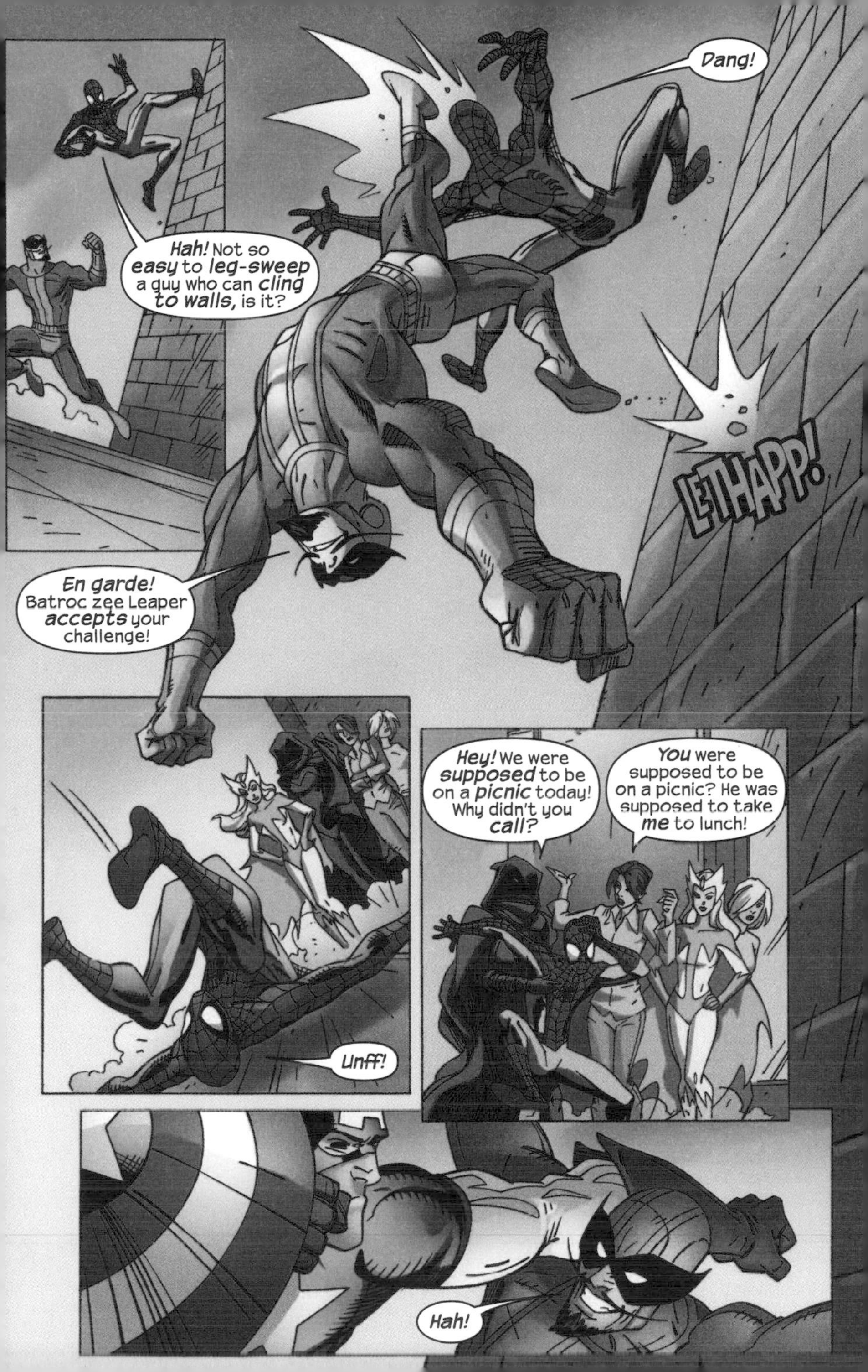
Hah! Not so easy to leg-sweep a guy who can cling to walls, is it?
Dang!
LETHAPP!
En garde! Batroc zee Leaper accepts your challenge!
Unff!
Hey! We were supposed to be on a picnic today! Why didn't you call?
You were supposed to be on a picnic? He was supposed to take me to lunch!
Hah!

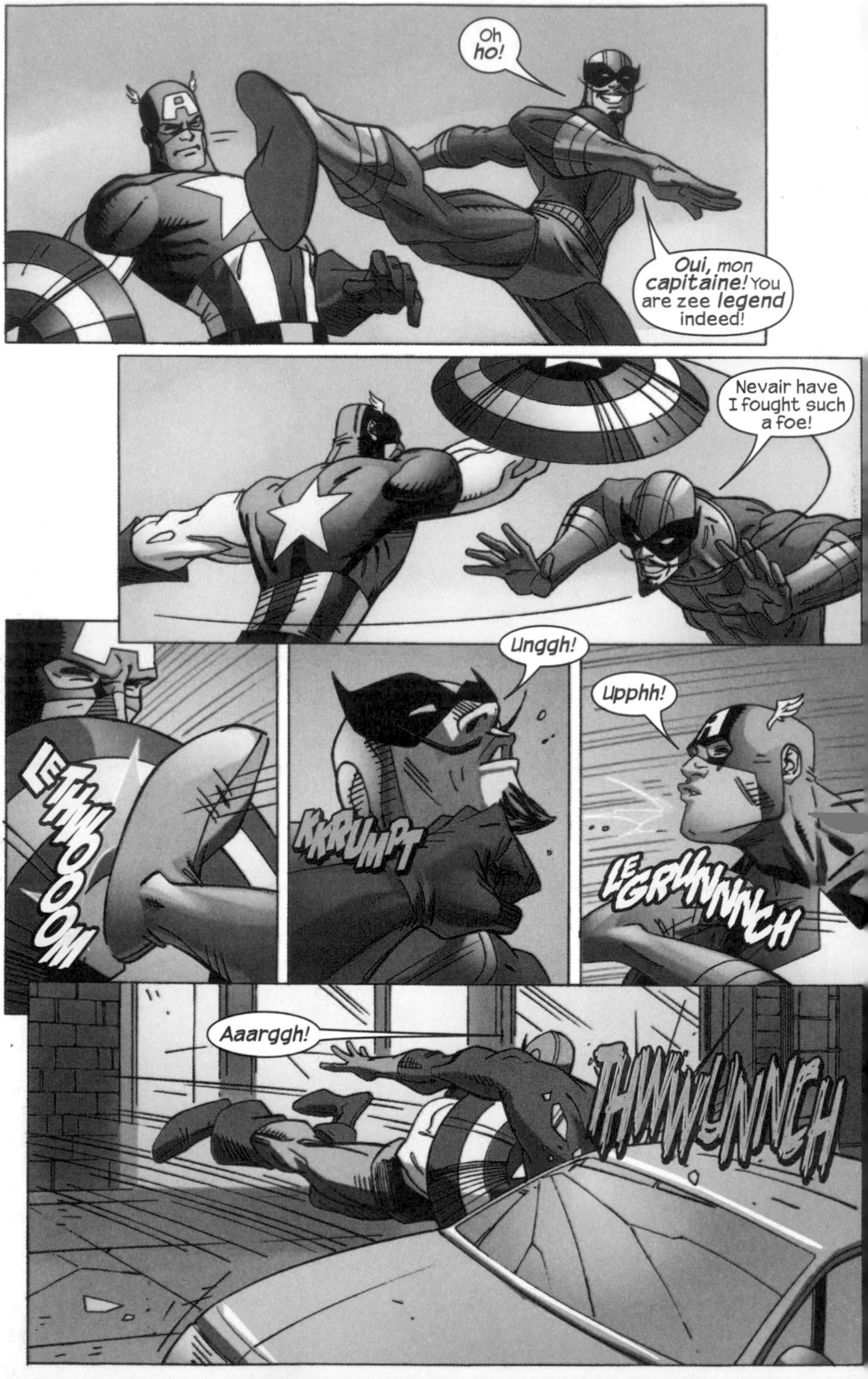
Oh ho!
Oui, mon capitaine! You are zee legend indeed!
Nevair have I fought such a foe!
LE THWOOOOOM
Unggh!
KKRUMPT
Upphh!
LE GRUNNNCH
Aaarggh!
THWUNNCH

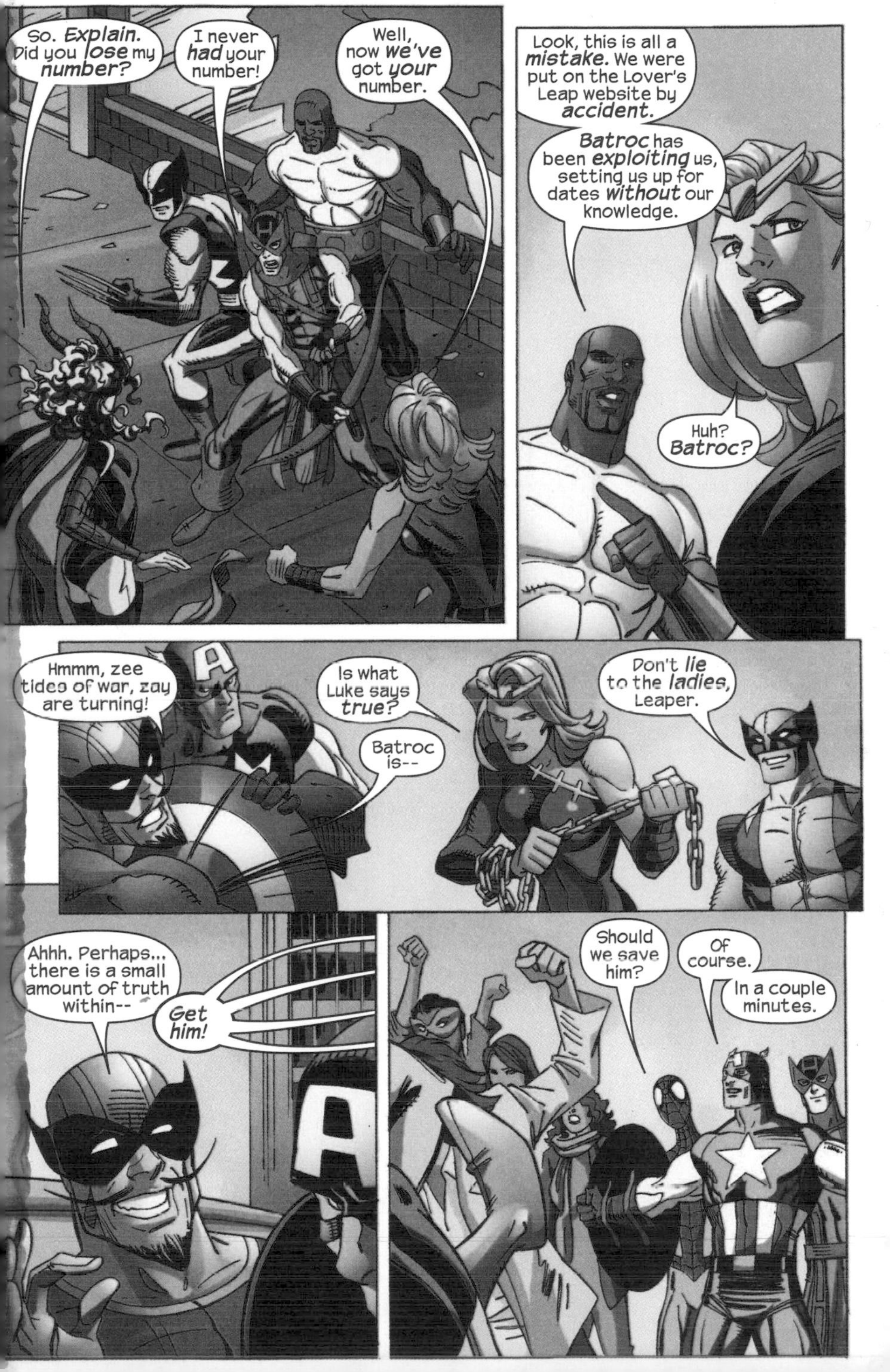
So. Explain. Did you lose my number?
I never had your number!
Well, now we've got your number.
Look, this is all a mistake. We were put on the Lover's Leap website by accident.
Batroc has been exploiting us, setting us up for dates without our knowledge.
Huh? Batroc?
Hmmm, zee tides of war, zay are turning!
Is what Luke says true?
Batroc is--
Don't lie to the ladies, Leaper.
Ahhh. Perhaps... there is a small amount of truth within--
Get him!
Should we save him?
Of course.
In a couple minutes.

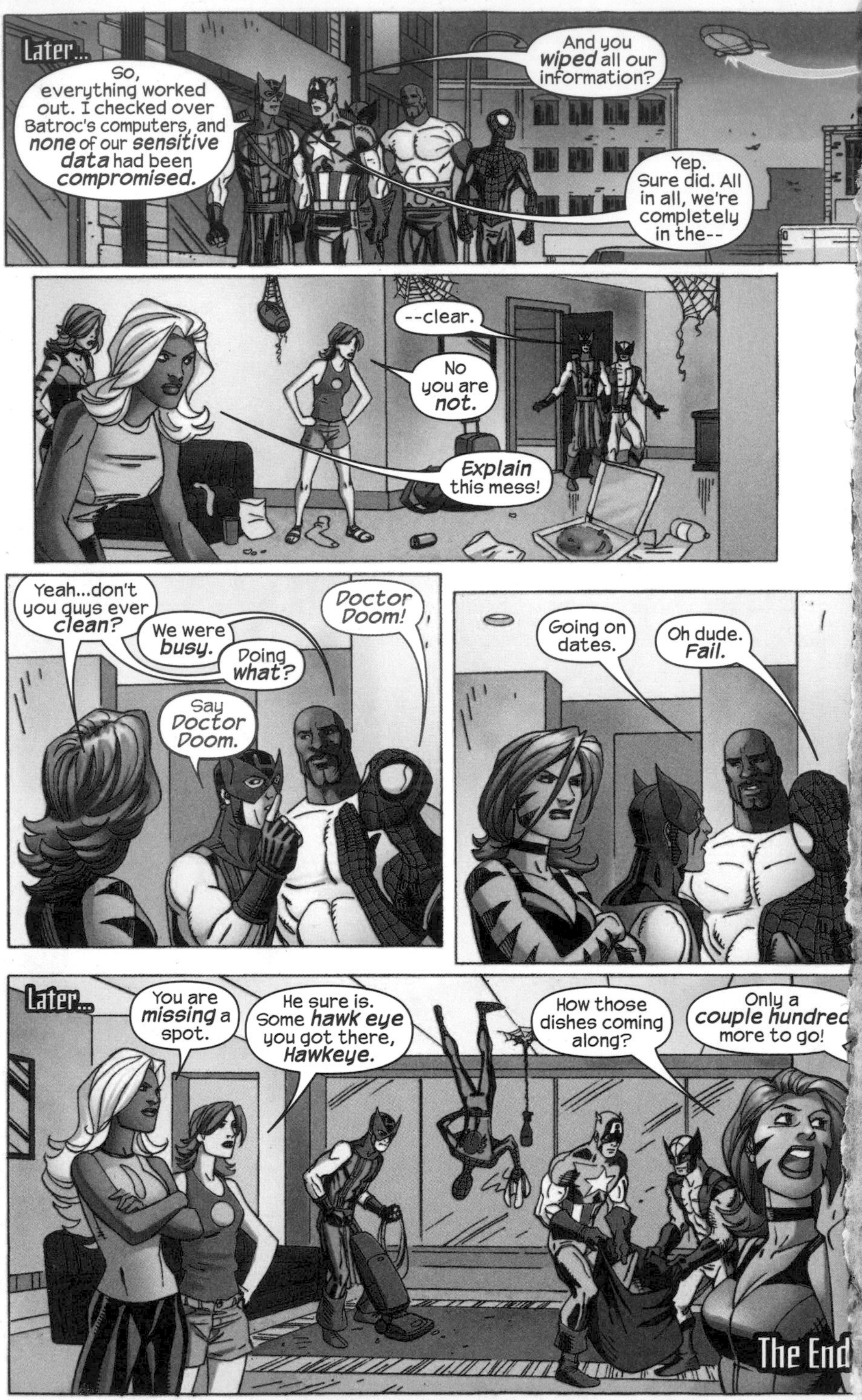

Later...
So, everything worked out. I checked over Batroc's computers, and none of our sensitive data had been compromised.
And you wiped all our information?
Yep. Sure did. All in all, we're completely in the--
--clear.
No you are not.
Explain this mess!
Yeah...don't you guys ever clean?
We were busy.
Doing what?
Doctor Doom!
Say Doctor Doom.
Going on dates.
Oh dude. Fail.
Later...
You are missing a spot.
He sure is. Some hawk eye you got there, Hawkeye.
How those dishes coming along?
Only a couple hundred more to go!
The End